The Vampire Diaries novels

VOL. I: THE AWAKENING
VOL. II: THE STRUGGLE
VOL. III: THE FURY
VOL. IV: DARK REUNION
THE RETURN VOL. 1: NIGHTFALL
THE RETURN VOL. 2: SHADOW SOULS
THE RETURN VOL. 3: MIDNIGHT
THE HUNTERS VOL. 1: PHANTOM
THE HUNTERS VOL. 2: MOONSONG
THE HUNTERS VOL. 3: DESTINY RISING

Stefan's Diaries novels

VOL. 1: ORIGINS
VOL. 2: BLOODLUST
VOL. 3: THE CRAVING
VOL. 4: THE RIPPER
VOL. 5: THE ASYLUM
VOL. 6: THE COMPELLED

The Secret Circle novels

THE INITIATION AND THE CAPTIVE PART I
THE CAPTIVE PART II AND THE POWER
THE DIVIDE
THE HUNT

CREATED BY

L. J. Smith

The Vampire Diaries

THE HUNTERS

VOL. 3

DESTINY RISING

HARPER TEEN

An Imprint of HarperCollins*Publishers*

HarperTeen is an imprint of HarperCollins Publishers.

Produced by Alloy Entertainment
151 West 26th Street, New York, NY 10001

Library of Congress Cataloging-in-Publication Data is available.
ISBN 978-0-06-201773-4 (trade bdg.) — ISBN 978-0-06-221369-3 (int. ed.)

Typography by Jennifer Heuer
12   13   14   15   16   CG/RRDH   10   9   8   7   6   5   4   3   2   1
❖
First Edition

ear Diary,

　　Last night, I had a terrifying dream.

　　Everything was as it had been just a few short hours before. I was back in the Vitale Society's underground chamber, and Ethan was holding me captive, his knife cold and steady at my throat. Stefan and Damon watched us, their faces wary, bodies tensed, waiting for the moment when one of them would be able to dash in and save me. But I knew they would be too late. I knew that, despite their supernatural speed, Ethan would cut my throat and I would die.

　　There was so much pain in Stefan's eyes. It broke my heart to know how much my death would hurt him. I hated the idea of dying without Stefan knowing that I had chosen him, only him—that all my indecision was behind us.

Ethan pulled me even closer, his arm as tight and unyielding as a band of steel across my chest. I felt the cold edge of the knife bite into my flesh.

Then without warning Ethan fell, and Meredith was standing there, her hair streaming behind her, her face as wild and determined as a vengeful goddess's, her stave still raised from the killing blow she'd put through his heart.

It should have been a moment of joy and relief. In real life, it was: the moment when I knew I was going to live, when I was about to find myself safe in Stefan's arms.

But in the dream, Meredith's face was blotted out by a flash of pure white light. I felt myself growing colder and colder, my body freezing, my emotions muffled into a chilly calm. My humanity was slipping away, and something hard and inflexible and . . . other . . . was taking its place.

In the heat of the battle, I had let myself forget what James had told me: that my parents had promised me to the Guardians, that I was fated to become one of them. And now they had come to claim me.

I woke up terrified.

Elena Gilbert paused and lifted the pen from the page of her journal, reluctant to write any more. Putting what she was most afraid of into words would make it feel more real.

She glanced around her dorm room, her new home. Bonnie and Meredith had come and gone while Elena slept. Bonnie's covers were flung back, and her laptop was gone from her desk. Meredith's side of the room, usually painstakingly organized, showed evidence of how exhausted Meredith must have been: the bloodstained clothes she had worn to fight Ethan and his vampire followers had been left on the floor. Her weapons were strewn across the bed, mostly shoved to one side, as if the young vampire hunter had curled up among them to sleep.

Elena sighed. Maybe Meredith would understand how Elena felt. She knew what it was like to have a destiny decided for you, to discover that your own hopes and dreams meant nothing in the end.

But Meredith had embraced her fate. There was nothing more important to her now, or that she loved more, than being a hunter of monsters and keeping the innocent safe.

Elena didn't think she could find the same kind of joy in her new destiny.

I don't want to be a Guardian, she wrote miserably. *The Guardians killed my parents. I don't*

*think I can ever get past that. If it wasn't for
them, my selfless parents would still be alive and
I wouldn't be constantly worrying about the lives
of the people I love. The Guardians only believe in
one thing: Order. Not Justice. Not Love.*

*I never want to be like that. I never want to be
one of them.*

*But do I have a choice? James made it sound
like becoming a Guardian was just something that
would happen to me—something I wouldn't be
able to avoid. Powers would suddenly manifest
themselves, and I would change, ready for whatever horrible thing comes next.*

Elena scrubbed at her face with the back of her hand.
Even after her long sleep, her eyes felt gritty and strained.

I haven't told anyone yet, she wrote. *Meredith
and Damon knew I was upset after I saw James,
but they don't know what he told me. So much
happened last night that I never got a chance to
tell them.*

*I need to talk to Stefan about this. I know that
when I do, everything will start to feel . . . better.*

But I'm scared to tell him.

After Stefan and I broke up, Damon made me

see the choice I needed to make. One path led to the daylight with the possibility of being a normal girl with an almost-normal, almost-human life with Stefan. The second into the night, embracing Power, adventure, and all the exhilaration the darkness can hold, with Damon.

I chose the light, chose Stefan. But if I'm fated to become a Guardian, is the path of darkness and Power unavoidable? Will I become someone who can do the unthinkable—take the lives of people as loving and pure as my parents? What kind of normal girl could I be, as a Guardian?

Elena was jolted from her thoughts by the sound of a key in the door. She closed the velvet-covered journal and shoved it quickly under her mattress.

"Hi," she said as Meredith came into the room.

"Hi yourself," Meredith said, grinning at her. Her dark-haired friend couldn't have gotten more than a few hours of sleep—she'd been out hunting vampires with Stefan and Damon after Elena had gone to bed, and she'd left before Elena had woken up—but she looked refreshed and cheerful, her gray eyes bright and her olive-skinned cheeks slightly flushed.

Purposefully tucking her own anxiety away, Elena smiled at her.

"Been saving the world all day, superhero?" Elena asked, teasing her just a little.

Meredith raised one delicate eyebrow. "As a matter of fact," she said, "I just came from the reading room at the library. Don't *you* have any papers due?"

Elena felt her own eyes widen. With all that had been happening, she hadn't really been thinking about her classes. She'd enjoyed her college courses so far, and she'd been an honor roll student in high school, but lately different parts of her life had taken over. *Did* she have something due?

What does it matter, though? The thought was heavy and dispiriting. *If I have to be a Guardian, college won't make any difference.*

"Hey," Meredith said, clearly misinterpreting Elena's sudden expression of dismay. Meredith reached forward and touched her shoulder with cool, strong fingers. "Don't worry about it. You'll get on top of everything."

Elena swallowed and nodded. "Absolutely," she said, forcing a smile.

"I did a little world-saving last night with Damon and Stefan, though," Meredith said, almost shyly. "We killed four vampires in the woods at the edge of campus." She lifted her vampire-slayer's stave carefully from her bed and wrapped her hand around its smooth center. "It feels really good," she said. "Doing what I've trained for. What I was born for."

Elena winced a little at this: *What was I born for?* But there was something she needed to say to Meredith that she hadn't said last night. "You saved me, too," Elena said simply. "Thank you."

Meredith's eyes warmed. "Anytime," she said lightly. "We need you around—you know that." She flipped open the narrow black case for her stave and put it inside. "I'm going to meet Stefan and Matt back at the library and see if we can get the bodies out of the Vitales' secret room. Bonnie said her concealment spell wouldn't last very long, and now that it's dark we should dispose of them."

Elena felt a twinge of anxiety in her chest. "What if the other vampires have come back?" she asked. "Matt told us he thought there was more than one entrance."

Meredith shrugged. "That's why I'm taking the stave," she said. "There aren't many of Ethan's vampires left, and they're mostly pretty new. Stefan and I can handle them."

"Damon's not coming with you guys?" Elena asked, climbing off the bed.

"I thought you and Stefan were back together," Meredith said. She fixed Elena with a quizzical gaze.

"We are," Elena said, and felt her face getting hot. "At least I think so. I'm trying not to . . . do anything to mess that up now. Damon and I are friends. I hope. I just thought you said Damon was with you earlier, hunting vampires."

Meredith's shoulders relaxed. "Yeah, he was with us,"

she said ruefully. "He enjoyed the fighting, but he got quieter as the night went on. He seemed a little . . ." She hesitated. "I don't know, tired, maybe." Meredith shrugged and her voice lightened. "You know Damon. He's only going to be useful on his own terms."

Reaching for her jacket, Elena said, "I'm coming with you." She wanted to see Stefan, to see him without Damon. If she was going to try to take that day-lit path with Stefan—Guardian or not—then she needed to bring her secrets out into the light, and face Stefan with nothing to hide.

When Elena and Meredith got to the library, Stefan and Matt were already there, waiting in the nearly bare room with the words RESEARCH OFFICE stenciled on its door. Stefan met Elena's eyes with a small, serious smile, and she suddenly felt shy. She'd put him through a lot the last few weeks, and they'd been apart so much lately that it almost felt as if they were starting over.

Next to him, Matt looked terrible. Drawn and pale, his face was set grimly and he clutched a large flashlight in one hand. His eyes were bleak and haunted. While destroying the Vitale vampires had been a victory for the others, those vampires had been Matt's friends. He had admired Ethan, thinking he was human. Elena slipped up beside him and squeezed his arm, trying to silently reassure him. His arm tensed in hers, but he shifted slightly closer to her.

"Down we go, then," Meredith said briskly. She and Stefan rolled back the small rug in the center of the room to reveal the trapdoor beneath, which was still covered with scattered herbs from the locking and protection spells Bonnie had hastily cast the night before. They were able to lift the door easily, though. Apparently, the spell had worn off.

As the four of them trooped down the stairs, Elena looked around curiously. The night before, they'd been in such a panic to save Stefan that she hadn't really observed much of their surroundings. The first flight of stairs was quite plain, wooden and a little rickety, and led to a floor filled with rows and rows of bookcases.

"Library stacks," Meredith muttered. "Camouflage."

The second flight was similar, but when Elena stepped on the first stair, it didn't shake slightly under her feet the way the previous flight had. The banister was smoother beneath her hand, and when they reached the landing, a long empty hallway stretched into darkness in both directions. It was colder here, and as they hesitated for a moment on the landing, Elena shivered. Impulsively, she tucked her hand into Stefan's as they started down the third flight. He didn't look at her, his eyes focused on the stairs ahead of them, but after a moment his fingers tightened around hers reassuringly. Tension flowed out of Elena's body at his touch. *Everything's going to be all right,* she thought.

The third flight of stairs was solid and made of some heavy, polished dark wood that gleamed beneath the dim lights. The banister was twisted with carvings. Elena could see the head of a snake, the elongated body of a swiftly running fox, and other shapes that were harder to make out in passing.

When they reached the bottom of the last flight, they faced the elaborately carved double doors that led to the Vitales' meeting room. The design followed the same motifs as she'd glimpsed on the banister: running animals, twisted snakes, curving mystical symbols. In the center of each door lay a large stylized *V*.

The doors were chained shut, as they had left them. Stefan reached out with the hand that wasn't holding Elena's and easily pulled the chain apart, dropping it to the side of the doors with a heavy clunk. Meredith flung the doors wide open.

The thick, coppery smell of blood came out to meet them. The room stank of death.

Matt held his flashlight steady while Meredith searched for a light switch. Finally, the scene before them was illuminated: the altar from the front of the room lay on its side, the bowl of blood smashed a few feet away. Extinguished torches had left long lines of greasy black smoke smeared on the walls. Vampire bodies lay limply in pools of sticky, half-dried blood, their throats torn by Damon's or Stefan's fangs, or their torsos punctured by Meredith's stave. Elena glanced anxiously at Matt's pale face. He hadn't been down here for the fight; he hadn't seen the massacre. And he had *known* these people, known this room when it was decorated for a celebration.

Eyes scanning the room, Matt swallowed visibly. After a moment, he frowned and spoke, his voice thin. "Where's Ethan?" he asked.

Elena's eyes flew to the spot before the altar where Ethan, leader of the Vitale vampires, had held a knife to her throat. The place where Meredith had killed him with her stave. Meredith made a soft sound of denial.

The floor was dark with Ethan's blood, but his body was nowhere to be found.

2

Warm blood, sweet with desire, filled Damon's mouth and inflamed his senses. He stroked the girl's soft, golden hair with one hand as he pressed his mouth more firmly to her creamy neck. Beneath her skin, he could feel her blood throbbing with the steady beat of her heart. He drew her essence into himself with great, thirst-quenching gulps.

Why had he ever stopped doing this?

He knew why, of course: Elena. Always, for the last year, Elena.

Of course he had still occasionally used his Power to coax victims into willingness. But he'd done it with the uncomfortable awareness that Elena would disapprove, chastened by the image of her blue eyes, serious and knowing, sizing him up and finding him wanting. Not good enough, not in comparison to his squirrel-chewing baby brother.

And when it seemed like Stefan and Elena might be done for good, that he might be the one to end up with his golden princess after all, he had stopped drinking fresh blood. Instead he'd drunk cold, insipid-tasting old blood from hospital donors. He'd even tried the revolting animal blood his brother lived on. Damon's stomach turned at the memory, and he took a deep, refreshing swallow of the girl's glorious blood.

This was what it meant to be a vampire: you had to take in life, human life, to keep your own supernatural life going. Anything else—the dead blood in stored bags or the blood of animals—kept you only a shadow of yourself, your Powers ebbing.

Damon wouldn't forget that again. He had lost himself, but now he was found.

The girl stirred in his arms, making a small questioning noise, and he sent a soothing dose of Power to her, making her pliable and quiescent once more. What was her name? Tonya? Tabby? Tally? He wasn't going to hurt her, anyway. Not permanently. He hadn't *hurt* anyone he'd fed from—not much, not when he was in his right mind—for a long while. No, the girl would leave the woods and go back to her sorority house with nothing worse than a slight spell of dizziness and a vague memory of spending the evening talking with a fascinating man whose face she couldn't quite recall.

She would be fine.

And if he'd chosen her because her long golden hair, blue eyes, and creamy skin reminded him of Elena? Well, that was no one's business but Damon's own.

At last he released her, gently steadying her on her feet when she tottered. She was delicious—*nothing like Elena's blood, though, nowhere near as rich and heady*—but taking any more blood tonight would be unwise.

She was a pretty girl, certainly. He arranged her hair carefully over her shoulders, hiding the marks on her neck, and she blinked at him with dazed, wide eyes.

Those eyes were *wrong*, damn it. They should be darker, a clear lapis lazuli, and fringed with heavy lashes. And the hair was, now that he looked at it closely, obviously dyed.

The girl smiled at him hesitantly, unsure.

"You'd better go back to your room," Damon said. He sent a current of commanding Power into her, and continued. "You won't remember later that you met me. You won't know what happened."

"I'd better get back," she echoed, her voice wrong, the wrong timbre, the wrong tone, not right at all. Her face brightened. "My boyfriend's waiting for me," she added.

Damon felt something inside him snap. In a fraction of

a second, he had pulled the girl roughly back to him. With no care or finesse, he ripped back into her throat, gulping her rich, hot blood furiously. He was punishing her, he realized, and taking pleasure in it.

Now that she was no longer under his thrall, she screamed and struggled, beating against his back with her fists. Damon pinned her with one arm and expertly worked his fangs in and out of her neck to widen the bite, drinking more blood, faster. Her blows grew weaker and she swayed in his arms.

When she went limp, he dropped her, and she landed on the forest floor with a heavy thud.

For a moment, he stared into the dark woods around him, listening to the steady chirp of the crickets. The girl lay unmoving at his feet. Although he had not *needed* to breathe for more than five hundred years, he was gasping, almost dizzy.

He touched his own lips and brought his hand back red and dripping. It had been a long time since he'd lost control of himself like that. Hundreds of years, probably. He stared down at the crumpled body at his feet. The girl looked so small now, her face serene and empty, lashes dark against her pale cheeks.

Damon wasn't sure if she was dead or alive. He realized he didn't want to find out.

He backed away a few steps from the girl, feeling

oddly uncertain, and then turned and ran, swift and silent through the darkness of the woods, listening only to the pounding of his own heart.

Damon had always done what he wanted. Feeling bad about what was *natural* for a vampire, that was for someone like Stefan. But, as he ran, an uncharacteristic sensation in the pit of his stomach nagged at him, something that felt more than a little bit like guilt.

"But you *said* Ethan was dead," Bonnie said. She felt Meredith flinch beside her and bit her tongue. Of course Meredith would be sensitive about Ethan's possible survival; she'd killed him, or had thought she had. Meredith's face was hard and guarded now, revealing nothing.

"I should have cut off his head to make sure," Meredith said, sweeping her flashlight from side to side to illuminate the stone walls of the tunnel. Bonnie nodded to herself, realizing something she should have guessed: Meredith was *angry*.

Meredith's call alerting Bonnie to Ethan's disappearance had come while Bonnie and Zander were having a late dinner at the student union. It had been a sweet, easy date: burgers and Cokes and Zander gently trapping her foot between his two bigger ones under the table as he sneakily stole her fries.

And now, here she and Zander were, looking for

vampires in the secret underground tunnels beneath the campus with Meredith and Matt. Elena and Stefan were doing the same thing in the woods around the campus overhead. *Not the most romantic we-just-got-back-together date*, Bonnie thought with a resigned shrug. *But they do say couples should share their hobbies.*

Matt, striding along on Meredith's other side, seemed grimly determined, his jaw clenched and his eyes fixed straight ahead down the long, dark tunnel. Bonnie felt sorry for him. All the strain the rest of them felt had to be a hundred times worse for Matt right now.

"You with us, Matt?" Meredith asked, apparently reading Bonnie's mind.

Matt sighed and kneaded at the back of his neck with one hand as if his muscles were strained and stiff. "Yeah, I'm with you." He paused and took a breath. "Except . . ." He trailed off and then started again. "Except maybe some of them we can help, right? Stefan could teach them how to be vampires who don't hurt people. Even Damon changed, didn't he? And Chloe . . ." His cheeks were flushed with emotion. "None of them deserved this. They didn't know what they were getting into."

"No," Meredith answered, touching Matt's elbow lightly with one hand. "They didn't."

Bonnie'd known that Matt was friends with the sweet-faced junior Chloe, but she was beginning to understand that he'd felt much more than that. How terrible to know that Meredith might have to thrust a stave through the chest of someone he was falling in love with, and how much worse to know that it was the right thing to do.

Zander had a soft expression in his eyes, and Bonnie realized he was thinking the same thing. He took her hand, his long strong fingers wrapping around hers, and Bonnie snuggled a little closer to him.

But as they rounded a dark bend in the tunnel, Zander suddenly let go of Bonnie and stepped protectively in front of her as Meredith raised her stave. Bonnie, a beat behind the others, didn't see the two figures entwined against the wall until they were already breaking apart. No, not entwined like lovers, she realized, but a vampire clinging to its victim. Matt stiffened, staring at them, and let out a soft involuntary sound of surprise. There was a sudden snarl and a flash of white teeth in the darkness as the vampire, a girl no taller than Bonnie herself, pushed her victim violently away. He fell to the ground at her feet.

Bonnie stepped around Zander, keeping a careful eye on the vampire, who was now huddled against the wall. She flinched involuntarily at the vampire's stare, the feral, fierce look in the dark eyes fixing on her, but kept going until she could kneel down next to the victim and reach to check his pulse. It was steady, but he was bleeding pretty badly, and she took off her jacket and pressed it against his throat to staunch the blood. Her hands were shaking and she concentrated on stilling them, on doing what needed to be done. Beneath the young man's eyelids, she could see his eyes moving rapidly back and forth, as if he was caught in a bad dream, but he stayed unconscious.

The girl—the *vampire*, Bonnie reminded herself—was watching Meredith now, her body tensed to fight or run away. She cringed back as Meredith stepped closer, blocking her in. Meredith raised her stave higher, aiming it at the middle of the girl's chest.

"Wait," the girl said hoarsely, holding out her hands. She looked past Meredith and seemed to see Matt for the first time. "Matt," she said. "Help me. Please." She was staring hard at him, visibly concentrating, and Bonnie realized with a start that the vampire was trying to use Power to make Matt do what she wanted. It wasn't working, though—she must not be strong enough yet—and after a moment her eyes rolled back and she sagged against the wall.

"Beth, we want to give you a chance," Matt said to the vampire. "Do you know what happened to Ethan?"

The girl shook her head emphatically, her long hair flying around her. Her eyes were flicking back and forth between Meredith and the tunnel behind her, and she edged sideways. Meredith followed her, moving closer, the stave pressed against the vampire's chest.

"We can't just kill her," Matt said to Meredith, a slightly

desperate note in his voice. "Not if there's another option."
Meredith snorted in disbelief and angled even closer to the
vampire—Beth, Matt had called her—who bared her teeth
in a silent snarl.

"Hang on a second," Zander said, and stepped over
Beth's victim's unconscious body, brushing past Bonnie.
Before Bonnie really understood what was happening,
Zander had pulled Beth away from Meredith and pressed
her against the wall of the tunnel.

"Hey!" Meredith said indignantly, and then frowned
in confusion. Zander was gazing intently into Beth's eyes,
his face serious and calm. She was staring back at him, her
restless eyes still now, her breathing hard.

"Do you know where Ethan is?" Zander asked in a
low, calm voice, and it felt to Bonnie as if something, some
invisible blast of Power, flew between them.

In a second, Beth's wary face emptied of all expression.
"He's hiding in the safe house at the end of the tunnels,"
she said. Her voice sounded half-asleep, disconnected
from her thoughts.

"Are there other vampires with him?" Zander asked,
his eyes steady on hers.

"Yes," Beth said. "Everyone's staying there until the
equinox, when all Ethan's hopes will be fulfilled."

Two days, Bonnie thought. The others had told her that
Ethan had planned to resurrect Klaus, the Original vampire.

She shivered at the thought. Klaus had been *scary*, one of the scariest things she'd ever seen. But could they really do it? Ethan hadn't gotten Stefan's and Damon's blood, and he couldn't do the resurrection spell without it. Could he?

"Ask her what their defenses are like," Meredith said, getting with the program.

"Is he well defended?" Zander asked.

Beth's head jerked into a stiff nod, as if an invisible puppeteer had pulled her strings. "No one can get to him," she said in that same sleepy monotone. "He's hidden, and every one of us would give our lives to protect him."

Meredith nodded, clearly weighing the words of her next question, but Matt broke in. "Can we save her?" he asked, and the pain in his voice made Bonnie flinch. "Maybe if she wasn't so hungry . . ."

Zander focused in even more strongly on Beth, and Bonnie again felt a wave of Power emanating from him. "Do you want to hurt people, Beth?" he asked quietly.

Beth chuckled, a rich, dark sound, although her face stayed blandly expressionless. That laugh was the first emotion she had shown since Zander had somehow charmed her into blankness and truth. "I don't want to hurt—I want to kill," she said, with a hard amusement in her tone. "I've never felt so alive."

Zander stepped back with a quick animal grace. At the same moment Meredith smoothly shot forward, shoving her stave through Beth's heart.

After the tearing noise of wood through flesh, Beth fell without a sound. Matt's gasp broke the silence, a startled, pained little noise. At Bonnie's knees, Beth's victim stirred, his head turning from one side to the other. Bonnie automatically patted him soothingly with the hand that wasn't keeping pressure on his neck wounds. "It's okay," she said quietly.

Meredith turned to Matt defiantly. "I had to," she said.

Matt bowed his head, his shoulders sagging. "I know," he answered. "Believe me, I know. It's just . . ." He shifted from one foot to the other. "She was a nice girl, before this happened to her."

"I'm sorry," Meredith said quietly, and Matt nodded, still looking at the ground. Then Meredith turned to Zander. "What was that?" she asked. "How did you get her to talk?"

Zander blushed a little. "Um. Well," he said, and shrugged one shoulder self-consciously. "There's this thing some of us Original werewolves can do, if we've practiced. We can make people tell the truth. It doesn't work on everyone, but I thought it was worth a try."

Bonnie stared up at him quizzically. "You didn't tell me that," she said.

Zander lowered himself down onto his knees and faced her across Beth's unconscious victim. His eyes were wide and sincere. "I'm sorry," he said. "I honestly didn't think about it. It's just one of the weird little things we can do."

The unconscious guy's bleeding seemed to have slowed, and Bonnie sat back on her heels. Zander raised his eyebrows at her, looking hopeful, and she smiled back at him. She'd have to find out what these other "little things" were, she guessed.

"Seems like that's something that could be pretty useful," she said, and watched Zander's face relax into a sunny, joyful grin.

Meredith cleared her throat. She was still watching Matt, her eyes full of sympathy, but her voice was dry. "We should get everyone together as soon as possible. If Ethan's still trying to resurrect Klaus, we need to come up with a plan *now*."

Klaus. The stone of the tunnel floor beneath Bonnie's knees was suddenly freezing. Klaus was darkness, violence, and fear. They had only defeated him back in Fell's Church by an extraordinary intervention, by Fell's Church's ghosts rising against him. That wasn't something they'd be able to recreate. What could they do now? Bonnie closed her eyes for a second, dizzy. She could picture, vividly, darkness rising up from below them, thick and choking, eager to consume them. Something evil was coming.

3

Elena laced her fingers through Stefan's, thrilling at even this little touch. It felt like it had been so long since they had been alone together, so long since she'd even been close enough to Stefan to touch him. All this evening she'd found herself leaning against his side, brushing her thumb over his knuckles, wrapping her arm around his waist, tracing her finger along his collarbone: any little touch she could have. Anything to feel the simple, satisfying reality of Stefan, here with her at last.

It was a pleasantly warm night, and there was soft moss underfoot. A breeze rustled the leaves of the forest trees all around them, and through the trees' branches she could glimpse a sky full of stars. It had all the elements of a romantic stroll through the woods, except for the fact that they were searching for bloodthirsty vampires.

"I don't sense anything," Stefan said. His hand was reassuringly tight around hers, but his dark green eyes held a faraway look, and Elena knew he was using his Power to scan the forest. "No vampires and no one in pain or afraid, as far as I can tell. I don't think there's anyone around."

"We'll keep looking, though. Just in case," Elena urged. Stefan nodded. There were limits to Stefan's searching Power: someone much stronger than he was could hide from it; someone much weaker might not catch his attention. And some creatures, like werewolves, he couldn't sense at all.

"I know I shouldn't be thinking about this with everything that's going on, but all I want is to be alone with you," Elena confessed quietly. "Things are happening so fast. If Ethan brings Klaus back . . . it feels like we might not have much time."

Stefan let go of Elena's hand and touched her face lightly, his fingers brushing over her cheeks and the curve of her eyebrow, a thumb ghosting across her lips. His eyes darkened with passion, and he smiled. Then he kissed her, softly at first.

Oh, Elena thought, and then, *yes*.

As if he'd been waiting for her confirmation, Stefan's kisses became more passionate. His hand fisted gently in her hair, and they moved backward until she was pressed against a tree. The bark was rough against her bare shoulders, but Elena didn't care; she just kissed Stefan fiercely, hungrily.

This is right, Elena thought. *This is like coming home,* and she felt Stefan's agreement and the strength of his love. *Yes,* he thought, and *more.*

Their minds entwined and Elena relaxed into the slow familiar spiral of Stefan's thoughts and emotions. There was love there—solid, constant love—and there was a steady bruiselike ache of regret at the time they'd lost. Strongest of all, there was a sense of joyous relief. *I didn't know how I was going to live without you,* Stefan thought to her. *I couldn't live forever, knowing you weren't mine.*

At the thought of *forever,* a thrum of anxiety shot through Elena. Barring a death by violence, *forever* was a given for Stefan. He would go on, unaging and beautiful, always eighteen. And Elena? Would she grow old and die with Stefan eternally young by her side? She didn't doubt that he would stay with her, no matter what.

There were other possibilities. She'd been a vampire once, and she'd suffered, being separated from her human friends and family, divided from the living world. She knew Stefan wouldn't wish that life on her. But it was an option, although they never talked about it.

Her mind touched on a certain bottle tucked in the back of her closet at home, and shied away again. She'd stolen a single bottle of the water of eternal life from the

Guardians when she and her friends had traveled in the Dark Dimension. Its existence, and the choice it offered her, was always at the edges of her mind. But she wasn't ready to make that decision, to end her mortal life. Not yet.

She was still growing, still changing. Was the person Elena was now really the person she wanted to be for the rest of her life? She was so flawed, so unfinished. Drinking the water of eternal life, or becoming a vampire, would close doors Elena wasn't ready to shut yet. She wanted to stay *human*. She ached inside at that: Would she be human now? *Could* she be human, if she had to become a Guardian?

All of this she considered in a private corner of her mind while most of her was focusing on the sweet sensations of Stefan's lips and body against hers and the steady thread of love passing between them. Enough of her emotions must have broken through to Stefan, though, that he responded. *Whatever you want, Elena*, he thought to her, gentle and reassuring. *I'll be with you. Forever. However long that might be for you.*

She knew that meant Stefan would understand even if she decided to live a natural life, to grow old and die. And there would be reasons to do that. Stefan and Damon had both lost something by never aging, never changing. They sensed that part of their humanity was gone.

But how could she face someday abandoning Stefan?

She couldn't imagine dying again, dying and leaving him behind. Elena pressed her back more firmly against the rough bark of the tree and kissed Stefan harder, feeling more fiercely alive with the almost-painful contrast of sensations.

Then she pulled back. She'd kept so much from Stefan since she'd come to Dalcrest. She wasn't going to go down that path again, wasn't going to love him while locking him out of parts of her life.

"There's something I have to tell you," she said. "You need to know everything. I can't—I can't hide things from you, not now." Stefan frowned questioningly, and she dropped her gaze to her hand against his shirt as she twisted the fabric nervously. "James told me something yesterday, before the fight," she blurted. "I'm not who I thought I was, not exactly. The Guardians chose my parents—they *made* me—and my parents were supposed to hand me over when I was twelve to become a Guardian. My parents refused and that was why they died. It wasn't just a random accident. The Guardians killed them. And now after learning this, I'm supposed to become one of them?"

Stefan looked flabbergasted for a moment, and then his face filled with sympathy. "Oh, Elena," he said, and pulled her close again, trying now to comfort her.

Elena let herself relax against his chest. Thank God

Stefan understood that the idea of becoming one of the Guardians, those cold regulators of order, was nothing to celebrate, even if it would bring her Power.

"I'll help you," Stefan said. "If you want to try to bargain your way out of it, or fight this, or go through with it. Whatever you want."

"I know," Elena said, her voice muffled as she pressed her face into his shoulder.

Suddenly, she felt Stefan's body tense against hers and realized he was looking around. "Stefan?" she asked.

He was looking off into the distance over her head, his mouth tight and eyes alert. "I'm sorry, Elena," he said as Elena pulled away and met his gaze. "We'll have to talk about this later. I just felt something. Someone in pain. And now that the wind has changed, I think I smell blood."

Elena tamped down her emotions, forcing herself back into calm rationality. All of this, all her own problems and questions, could wait. They had a job to do. "Where?" she asked.

Stefan took Elena's hand and led her farther into the undergrowth. The trees blocked out more of the stars here, and she stumbled over roots and stones in the darkness. Stefan steadied her, guiding their way.

A moment later, they burst into another clearing. It took Elena's eyes a second to adjust, to see the dark shape Stefan was already moving toward cautiously. Huddled on the ground lay the body of a human.

They dropped to their knees beside it, and Stefan reached out and carefully, gently turned the person over. The body flopped heavily onto its back. *A girl,* Elena realized. A girl about her own age, her face pale and empty. Golden hair shone in the starlight. There was blood on her throat.

"Is she dead?" she asked in a whisper. The girl was so still.

Stefan touched the girl's cheek, then carefully ran his fingers across her neck, below the trickle of blood, not touching the thick red fluid. "Not dead," he said, and Elena let out a sigh of relief. "But she's lost a lot of blood."

"We'd better get her back to campus," Elena said. "And we'll tell the others the vampires are hunting in the woods. We can come back and find who did this."

Stefan was staring down at the girl's wounds, his mouth oddly twisted in an unreadable expression. "Elena, I—I don't think this was Ethan's vampires," he said hesitantly.

"What do you mean?" Elena asked, puzzled. A root was digging into her knees, and she shifted to get more comfortable, pressing one hand against the cold ground. "What else would have done this?"

Stefan frowned and gently touched the girl's neck again, still careful not to come into contact with the blood. "Look at the marks," he said. "The vampire who did this was angry and careless, but he was experienced. The bite is clean and in the perfect place to get the maximum amount of blood without killing the victim." He smoothed the girl's hair carefully, as if to comfort her. He looked like he was in pain, his teeth clenched, his eyes narrow. "Elena, Damon did this," he said.

Everything in Elena tightened and she shook her head, her hair whipping around her. "No," she said. "He wouldn't just leave someone in the woods to die."

Stefan had a far-off look on his face and she instinctively reached out to touch his arm, trying to comfort him. He closed his eyes for a second and leaned into her. "After five hundred years, I can recognize Damon's bite," he said sadly. "Sometimes it seems like he's changed, but Damon doesn't change." The weight of Stefan's words seemed to hit him just as strongly as they hit Elena, and he hunched his shoulders.

For a moment, Elena couldn't breathe, and she gulped, feeling dizzy and sick. *Damon?* Images flashed in her mind's eye: Damon's fathomless, dark eyes hot with fury, sharp with bitterness. And softer, warmer sometimes, when he looked at her or at Stefan. A hard kernel of denial formed in her chest.

"No," she said, and looking at Stefan, she repeated it more firmly. "*No.* Damon's hurting, because of us— because of me." Stefan nodded almost imperceptibly.

"We're not going to give up on him. He has changed, he's done so much for us, for all of us. He *cares*, Stefan, and we can pull him back from this. He didn't kill her. It's not too late."

Stefan was listening to her carefully and after a moment he drew his hand wearily across his face, his features firming with resolve. "We have to keep this a secret," he said. "Meredith and the others can't know what Damon's done."

Elena remembered Meredith's expression as she wielded her stave, and swallowed hard. The hunter in Meredith wouldn't hesitate to kill Damon if she thought he was a real danger to innocent humans. "You're right," she said thinly. "We can't tell anyone."

Reaching across the body of unconscious girl, Stefan took Elena's hand in his again. She clasped his hand tightly, her eyes meeting his in a silent pledge. They would work together; they *would* save Damon. It was going to be all right.

lena didn't tell anyone about the girl they'd found in the woods. Elena and Stefan had shaken the girl and poured cool water on her face, trying to wake her up without having to take her to the hospital. Blood had pooled through the bandages they'd put on the girl's wounds—Damon had bitten too deeply, Stefan said—and finally Stefan had fed her blood from his own wrist, grimacing, to help her heal. He didn't feel right doing that, Elena knew: the exchange of blood was too intimate, meant *love* to Stefan, but what else could they do? They couldn't let her die.

When the girl finally regained consciousness, Stefan Influenced her to forget what had happened, and he and Elena helped her back to her sorority house. By the time they'd left her, near dawn, she'd been flushed and giggling, sure that she'd just been out too late drinking on a fabulous night.

Back in her dorm room, Elena had tried to sleep, but she'd been too worked up. She tossed and turned under her clean cotton sheets, remembering the frustration in Stefan's eyes as he told her, *Damon did this*, and the suppressed flash of panic she'd seen when he said, *We have to keep this a secret.*

She'd known Damon still fed off humans, although she usually managed not to think about it. But he hadn't done any real harm, not for a long time. Now he used his Power to convince pretty girls to give him their blood willingly, and then left them with nothing but a vague memory of an evening spent with a charming and mysterious man with an Italian accent. If that. Sometimes they just had a hole in their memory.

And, sure, it was wrong. Elena knew that, even if Damon didn't. The girls weren't in their right minds. He fed on them, and they never really understood. Elena was sure that if it happened to her, or Bonnie, or anyone she cared about, she would have been outraged and disgusted. But she'd been able to ignore the facts when the end result—Damon satisfied, his victims seemingly unscathed—appeared to be so benign.

But this time he clearly hadn't bothered to be careful with the girl, or to make it easy on her. She'd been bleeding alone in the woods, and when she'd finally woken, she had been *screaming*. Elena shuddered at the memory, sick with guilt.

Was this the reality she'd been ignoring? Maybe Damon had been attacking people all this time and hiding it from her, and the idea of the woozy, unaware, and happy victim was a lie. Or maybe there had been a change, and it was Elena's fault. Had Damon done this in a rage, because Elena had chosen Stefan?

Elena tried once more to reach Damon, but when it rang through to voice mail, she pushed the "end call" button on her phone. She'd been calling Damon on and off all morning and had left a couple of messages already, but he hadn't picked up or called her back.

"Was that Stefan?" Bonnie asked, coming out of the bathroom toweling off her hair. Red strands curled wildly over her face in all directions. "Is he on his way?"

"Everybody should be here any minute," Elena answered, not correcting Bonnie's assumption. They had decided to meet today to start planning their defense against the Vitale vampires, and to try to figure out how to stop them before they could resurrect Klaus.

And soon, everyone (except Damon) was there: Meredith sitting on her bed, gray eyes alert as she carefully sharpened a hunting knife; Matt, still looking pale, hunched over in Elena's desk chair; Bonnie and Zander cuddled together on Bonnie's bed, adorably happy with the flush of new love despite the seriousness of the situation. As Elena looked over at them, Zander murmured something in Bonnie's ear and she blushed.

Stefan joined Elena on her bed, taking her hand in his. Still, after a year, Elena felt a jolt of excitement move from her fingertips straight to her heart. Elena stared at him for a moment, looking for some indication of how upset he'd been the night before, a clue about whether he'd managed to talk to Damon yet, but there was nothing.

"Okay, everybody," Meredith said, running her thumb along the sharpened blade of her knife. "We know that Ethan is hiding—"

"Wait," Elena said. "There's something I need to tell all of you." Stefan's eyes snapped to hers, hard and bright, and she realized she had been wrong about him being calm. The secret about Damon had him tightly strung.

"Um," she said, feeling uncharacteristically nervous. She remembered how they had all felt about the cold, didactic Guardians they had met in the Dark Dimensions, the ones who had stripped her of her Powers (painfully— she couldn't forget how much it had *hurt* when they cut her Wings) and who had refused to bring Damon back from death. But she pushed her jaw out proudly, stubbornly, and kept going.

"I just found out that I'm a Guardian," she said flatly.

There was a blank silence.

Finally, Zander broke it. "A guardian of what?" he asked tentatively, glancing to Bonnie for clarification.

Bonnie, frowning, waved one hand in the air in a grand, encompassing gesture. "Of everything, really," she said vaguely. "If Elena means a *Guardian* Guardian." She looked at Elena for confirmation, and Elena nodded. "They're these awful women—at least they look like women—who are meant to keep things running in the universe the way they're supposed to. I don't really understand how Elena could be one, though. They don't live here. It's an alternate-dimension kind of thing. They're not really people, I don't think." She turned to Elena, her face open and confused. "What *do* you mean, Elena?" she asked.

Elena looked away from her, staring at the wall. The skin on her face felt like it was too tight, and her eyes were burning. "James—my history professor—knew my parents when they were in college. He was really close to them," she told her friends, forcing herself to keep it together. "He told me that they agreed to have a child who would be a Guardian on Earth. He said I was supposed to be trained by the Guardians when I was twelve, but my parents didn't want to hand me over." Her voice shook a little, and she stared very hard at the Matisse print she had hung above her bed. Pressing her shoulder against Stefan's, she took comfort in the solidity of his body next to hers, and didn't look at anyone.

Then Meredith was next to her, and her narrow hand took hold of Elena's. In a moment, Bonnie had squeezed herself onto the bed as well and was gazing at Elena with wide, sympathetic brown eyes.

"We're on your side, you know that, Elena," Meredith said calmly, and Bonnie nodded.

"Velociraptor sisterhood, right?" she said, and Elena cracked a tiny smile at their old private joke. "If the Guardians take on one of us, they take on all of us. Even though they're pretty scary. We'll fend them off."

Elena gave a short, half-hysterical laugh. "Thanks," she said. "Really. But I don't think there's any way to get out of this. I don't even know what it means exactly, being a Guardian on Earth."

"Then that's the first thing to find out," Meredith said sensibly. "Alaric's coming up to visit this weekend. He might know something, or at least be able to discover what the story is on Earthly Guardians." Meredith's more-or-less fiancé, Alaric, was working on a doctorate in paranormal studies, and the various contacts he had often came in handy.

"We *will* figure something out, Elena," Bonnie promised.

Elena blinked back tears. Bonnie and Meredith had

drawn closer to her, shutting everyone out for a moment, even though Stefan was still strong beside her. She could always rely on the three of them coming together when one of them was threatened. They'd been watching out for one another since the worst thing they had to worry about was elementary school bullies and mean teachers.

Stefan pulled her closer against him. From their seats, Matt and Zander were watching her with almost identical expressions of sympathy and concern. Meredith was right: Elena wasn't alone. She let out a breath, and her shoulders loosened, releasing some of the misery she'd been holding since James had told her the secret of her birth.

"I'm glad Alaric's coming. And it's a good idea to ask him what he can find out. Maybe James can tell us more, too," Elena said. She tucked a lock of hair behind her ear, thinking. "Actually, he'd *better* be able to tell us something. He's known about this since before I was born. He's had about twenty years to find out something useful." Then she clapped her hands once, and tried to push all her fears aside. "For now, though, we need to focus on Ethan and the vampires." Elena felt her old self coming back to the surface, forceful and energetic and ready to make plans.

Stefan squeezed Elena's knee as he climbed off the bed. "Tonight is our last chance to stop Ethan," he said, standing in the middle of the room and looking at them all seriously. His face was shadowed and intense, his normally leaf-green eyes dark. "Tomorrow is the equinox, when the separation between the realms of the living and the dead is at its weakest. That's when they'll try and resurrect Klaus. Meredith, what's our weapons situation?"

Meredith rose, too, and opened her closet, pulling out her various bags of weapons: her special hunter's stave with its spikes of materials from silver to ash to tiny hypodermic needles, made to affect all the different creatures a hunter might fight; an assortment of knives of various sizes, from a long silver dagger to a thin, practical boot knife, all razor-sharp; staffs and throwing stars and machetes and maces and a number of things Elena couldn't even begin to guess at the names for.

"Wow," said Zander, who had rolled onto his stomach on Bonnie's bed to watch her. He looked at Meredith with new respect and a bit of trepidation. "You're like a one-woman army."

Meredith flushed slightly. "It might be overkill," she said, "but I like to be prepared." She pulled out a wooden trunk from her closet. "And I have this. Alaric helped me gather it all before school started." She opened the box with a half-apologetic glance at Stefan, who flinched and stepped backward, away from the trunk. Elena craned to see. It looked like some kind of plant in there, filling the box to the brim.

Oh. The box was crammed full of vervain. There was

probably enough there to incapacitate a whole colony of vampires, if they could only figure out a way to rub it on them, or get them to eat it. At the very least, they'd all be able to protect themselves from being Influenced.

"Good," Stefan said briskly, recovering from his instinctive reaction to the vervain. "That should come in handy. Now, Matt, what can you tell us about the underground tunnels?"

Elena felt a little pulse of pride run through her as Stefan turned to Matt, quickly getting him to sketch out on paper what he remembered and what he had heard about the Vitales' safe house and network of tunnels. Stefan was nodding and asking questions, gently nudging Matt's memory, encouraging him to share even the smallest detail. Matt's eyes widened, his voice gaining strength as Stefan's questions continued, as if Matt was beginning to piece together the bigger picture in a new way.

Stefan had changed. When he had first come to Fell's Church, he had been so quiet and distant, reluctant to make any kind of mark on the humans who surrounded him. He had felt, Elena knew, like he was diseased, like he couldn't be among mortals without spreading death and despair.

Now he had the quality of a natural leader. As if he felt Elena's eyes on him, Stefan glanced up at her, his lips forming a small, private smile just for her. She knew this change in Stefan was due to her and to all that had happened in the past year. Surely, whatever Damon had done—even if he was sinking into violence again because of Elena—here in Stefan was something that she could be uncomplicatedly proud of?

"Couldn't we do something with all that vervain?" Bonnie asked suddenly. "Like, burn it, or make it a gas somehow and fill the tunnels with its smoke? If we blocked the other exits, all the vampires would go into the house. We could trap them and burn the house down, or at least get to all of them at once."

"That's a good idea, Bonnie," Stefan said. Zander agreed enthusiastically and Bonnie's face lit up with pleasure. It was funny, Elena thought, that they were all used to thinking of Bonnie as sort of the junior member of the group, the one who needed to be protected, and she really wasn't; she hadn't been for a long time.

"What other resources do we have?" Stefan asked thoughtfully, pacing back and forth across the room.

"I could get the guys to help out," Zander suggested. "We've been after the Vitale vampires for a while. We won't be as strong as we would be if it were the right lunar phase, and not all ten of us can transition without the full moon. But we work pretty well together . . ." His voice trailed off. "If you want us," he added. "I know you don't all feel comfortable with werewolves, and, to be honest, we're not usually big fans of vampires. No offense." He looked from Stefan to Meredith, who still held the knife against her leg.

Meredith, of course, was the one most likely to object to bringing a Pack of werewolves into their group. Bonnie had assured them that Zander's Pack was different than the werewolves they'd met before—that they were good, more like guard dogs than wild animals. But Meredith had been raised to hunt monsters.

Now she nodded slowly to Zander, though, and said only, "We can use all the help we can get." Bonnie and Meredith locked eyes across the room and Bonnie's lips tipped up in a tiny, satisfied smile.

"Speaking of 'all the help we can get,'" Meredith said. "Where's Damon?" She looked from Elena to Stefan when they didn't immediately answer. "This is one time when we can really use him. You should call him and get him in on the plan." Her expression was sympathetic but determined, and Elena realized that Meredith thought they were hesitating because Elena had almost-dated Damon while she and Stefan had been apart. *If only Meredith knew the truth*, she thought, *but she can't ever know. Stefan and I need to keep Damon safe.*

"Maybe you could call him, Elena?" Bonnie asked tentatively.

Elena's and Stefan's eyes met. Stefan's face was blank and controlled again, and Elena couldn't see the tiniest crack in his armor as he cut in, smoothly and casually, "No, I'll call Damon. I need to talk to him, anyway."

Elena bit her lip and nodded. She wanted to see Damon for herself—she was *desperate* to see him, to know what was wrong with him, wanting to fix it—but he wasn't taking her calls. Maybe what Damon needed right now from Elena was space. She hoped that Stefan, at least, could get through to him.

5

When Stefan knocked on the door of Damon's apartment, Damon opened it almost immediately, glared at Stefan, and tried to slam the door shut in his face.

"Stop," Stefan said, inserting his shoulder in the doorway. "You must have been able to sense that it was me."

"I knew you'd keep knocking or find a way in if I didn't answer," Damon said fiercely. "So I'm answering. Now *go away*."

Damon looked wrecked. Nothing could take away from the elegance of his features, but they were tense and drawn, the skin over his cheekbones white with strain. His lips were pale, his dark eyes bloodshot, and his usually sleek black hair disarranged. Stefan ignored his words and leaned closer, trying to make his brother meet his eyes.

"Damon," he said. "I found the girl in the woods last night."

Anyone who hadn't known Damon as long and as well as Stefan had—and so *anyone* except Stefan—would have missed the split second of stillness before Damon's face settled into cool disdain. "Have you come to preach to me, baby brother?" he asked. "I'm afraid I don't have the time just now, but perhaps another day? Next week sometime?"

He slid his eyes over Stefan, then glanced away dismissively. Just like that, Stefan felt like a child again, back home all those centuries ago, and his daring, charming, despicable, infuriating older brother was putting him in his place.

"She was still alive," Stefan said steadily. "I took her home. She's all right."

Damon shrugged. "How nice for you. Always the *parfait* knight."

Stefan's hand shot out and gripped Damon's arm. "Dammit, Damon," he said, frustrated, "stop playing with me. I came to tell you that you have to be *careful*. If you had killed that girl, it would have caught up with you."

Damon blinked at him. "That's it?" he asked, his voice the smallest bit less hostile. "You want me to be careful? Don't you have an overwhelming urge to scold me, little brother? Threaten me, maybe?"

Stefan sighed and slumped against the doorframe,

his urgency sucked away. "Would scolding you do any good, Damon?" he asked. "Or threatening you? It's never worked before. I just don't want you to kill anyone. You're my brother, and we need each other."

Damon's face tightened again, and Stefan reconsidered his words. Sometimes talking to Damon was like walking through a minefield. "*I* need *you*, anyway," he said. "You saved my life. Which, in case you didn't notice, you've done a lot this past year."

Damon leaned against the opposite side of the doorframe and studied Stefan, his face thoughtful, but remained silent. Wishing he knew what Damon was thinking, Stefan sent a questing tendril of Power toward his brother, trying to catch his mood, but Damon merely sneered, easily shutting him out.

Stefan bowed his head and kneaded the bridge of his nose between his thumb and forefinger. Was it always going to be like this, for the next long centuries together? "Look," he said. "There's enough going on with the other vampires on campus without you starting to hunt again. Ethan's still alive, and he's planning to try to bring back Klaus tomorrow night."

Damon's frown deepened for a moment, then smoothed out. His face could have been carved from stone.

"We can't stop him without you," Stefan continued, his mouth dry.

Damon's night-dark eyes gave nothing away and then he flashed his briefest, most brilliant smile. "Sorry," he said. "I'm not interested."

"What?" Stefan felt like he'd been kicked in the stomach. He had expected Damon's defensiveness and sarcasm. But after Damon had saved him from Ethan, the last thing he had expected was indifference.

Damon shrugged, straightening up and adjusting his clothes, brushing an imagined speck of dust from the front of his black shirt. "I've had enough," he said, his tone casual. "Meddling in the affairs of your pet humans has gone stale for me. If Ethan brings back Klaus, then he can deal with him. I doubt it'll go well for him."

"Klaus will remember that you attacked him," Stefan said. "He'll be after you."

Cocking one eyebrow, Damon smiled again, a quick, savage baring of his white teeth. "I doubt I'll be his first priority, little brother," he said.

And it was true, Stefan remembered. In that hideous last battle with Klaus, Damon had stabbed the Old One with white ash, keeping him from striking the final blow against Stefan. But *he* hadn't been responsible for Klaus's death. Stefan had engineered the fight against Klaus, had done his best to kill him. But, in the end, he had failed, too. It was Elena, bringing an army of the dead against the Original vampire, who *had* killed him.

"Elena," Stefan said desperately. "*Elena* needs you."

He was positive that would do it, that Damon's armor would crack. Damon *always* came through for Elena. But this time Damon's lip curled in a sneer. "I'm sure you can handle things," he said lightly, his voice brittle. "Elena's well-being is your responsibility now, not mine."

"Damon—"

"No." Damon held up a warning hand. "I told you. I'm done." And with one quick motion, he slammed the door in Stefan's face.

Stefan rested his forehead against the door, feeling defeated.

"*Damon,*" he said again. He knew Damon could hear him, but there was only silence from inside the apartment. Slowly, he backed away from the door. It would be best not to push Damon, not when he was in this mood.

In this mood, Damon might do *anything.*

"I'm so glad you came to see me, Elena," Professor Campbell said. "I was worried about you after"—he glanced around surreptitiously and lowered his voice, although they were alone in his office—"our last talk." He peered at her cautiously, his usually inquisitive and rather smug face clouded with uncertainty.

"I'm sorry I ran off like that, James," Elena told him, staring down into the cup of sweet, milky coffee he had given her. "It's just . . . when you told me I was a Guardian and the truth about what happened to my parents, I needed some time to think. Last summer, I *met* a few Guardians. They were powerful, but so inhuman."

She still couldn't accept that she was supposed to become like them. The whole idea was so big and horrifying that her mind kept scuttling away from it, focusing on solid and immediate concerns like the vampires on campus instead.

Elena's hands shook a little, making the coffee swirl and eddy. She carefully steadied her cup.

James patted her gently on the shoulder. "Well, I have been doing some research, and I think I have good news," he said.

"I could use good news," she said softly, almost pleadingly. "I don't really understand what a human Guardian would be like. Would I be different than a Celestial Guardian?"

James smiled for the first time since she had walked into his office. "After we spoke," he said, "I started to contact all my old colleagues who have studied mythology or magic, anyone who I thought might know something about the Guardians."

Now that he had information to impart, James lost his tentativeness and seemed to expand, his shoulders relaxing as he hooked his thumbs into his suit vest. "Legend has it," he said, his voice taking on its lecturing tone, "that human Guardians are rare, but there are always two or three in the world. Generally, their parents are recruited in the same way the Guardians recruited your parents, and then the children are handed over to the Guardians for training as they enter adolescence."

Elena closed her eyes for a moment, wincing. She couldn't imagine being given to the Guardians and losing her human life so young. But if she had been, her mother and father would still be alive.

"When the human Guardians reach young adulthood—about your age, Elena," James continued, "they're stationed where there are high concentrations of ley lines and, therefore, large amounts of supernatural activity."

"Like here," Elena said. "And Fell's Church."

James nodded. "The evidence shows pretty strongly that the Guardians recruit prospective parents from ley line–heavy places," he said. "So the human Guardians can stay near their homes."

"But what are the human Guardians for?" Elena asked. "What am I supposed to do?" She realized she was gripping her cup so tightly she might break it, so she put it down on James's desk and held on to the arms of her chair instead.

"The role of the human Guardians is to protect the innocent from the supernatural on Earth," James said.

"They maintain balance. And it seems that the Guardians develop different powers depending on what is needed where they live. So we won't know what your exact powers are until they begin to form."

"Protecting the innocent, I can handle," Elena said. She gave James a shaky smile. She wasn't so sure about "maintaining balance." In her opinion, the Guardians of the Celestial Court had been so obsessed with balance and order that they had forgotten about the innocent. Or perhaps the innocent were only the concern of the Guardians on Earth. But if that was true, wouldn't someone have looked out for her parents?

James smiled back. "That's what I thought. And," he said, with an air of having saved the best for last, "my colleague has located one of the other Guardians on Earth." He pulled a sheet of paper from a folder on his desk and passed it to her.

It was a printout of a color photograph, a little grainy. In it, a dark-haired man, maybe a year or two older than Elena, smiled at the camera. His brown eyes were narrowed in the sun's glare and his teeth were bright white against his tan skin.

"His name is Andrés Montez, and he's a human Guardian who lives in Costa Rica. My sources didn't have a lot of personal information about him, but they're going to try contacting him. I'm hoping he'll be willing to come to Dalcrest to teach you what he knows." James hesitated, then added, "Although, as a Guardian, I imagine he probably already knows all about you."

Elena traced Andrés's face in the picture. Did she want to meet another Guardian? Those dark eyes seemed kind, though.

"It would be good to talk to someone who could tell me what to expect," she told James, looking up. "Thank you for finding him."

James nodded. "I'll let you know as soon as I can get him here," he said.

Despite the news that there was someone else out there like her, someone who might understand, Elena's stomach lurched and she felt like she was falling, spiraling down into something deep and dark and unknown. Would Andrés be able to tell her what she most needed to know? Would she still be Elena once her fate caught up with her?

tefan, Elena, and five werewolves watched alertly from a hill overlooking the Vitales' darkened safe house. They were waiting for any sign that would indicate Meredith and her team's part of the plan was working and that the Vitale vampires were being driven through their secret tunnels and into the house.

When consulted over the phone, Alaric had suggested that the Vitale vampires would perform the resurrection ritual at midnight on the night of the equinox, so Stefan and Meredith had decided to go on the offense before sunset, when the vampires would be more likely underground and inside, avoiding the daylight. Now late afternoon sunlight reflected off the windows of the safe house, shielding any movement inside from view.

One of Zander's Packmates, Chad, a chemistry major, had been instrumental in making the gas out of Meredith's stash of vervain and the bomblike time-release gadgets that would unleash it into the tunnels. Somewhere beneath their feet, Stefan thought, Meredith and her team—Matt, Zander, and three more werewolves—were placing container after container of the gas, closing off one escape route after another until the vampires would have nowhere to go but the house. Bonnie, protected by another member of Zander's Pack, was at the library, working her spells and charms to keep the vampires from coming up through the tunnel there. Stefan shifted restlessly, wishing he was with the others beneath ground. He could hear distant explosions underfoot, although only someone with a vampire's hearing could have. By his side, Chad stirred, and Stefan amended his thought: a vampire's hearing, or a werewolf's.

Chad, like Zander, was one of the werewolves who could change form without the moon's influence. He was a wolf now, padding around silently past Stefan and Elena, eyes on the house. He whuffed gently through his nose and sat down, his ears twitching back.

"Chad says the vervain gas should have filled the tunnels by now," one of the other werewolves—this one in human form—said, translating the wolf's language. "We ought to see something soon."

Elena moved closer to Stefan and they shared a glance.

It was weird seeing the Pack at work: they'd changed from a bunch of scuffling, swearing, goofy boys into a serious, competent team. Each of the wolf-form werewolves was alert and active, their sleek, powerfully muscled bodies clearly attuned to every sound or scent coming toward them. And the human-form werewolves were swift to react to their wolf-brethren's every movement, acting as if there was a constant, silent communication among the Pack.

Maybe that was true. Stefan didn't know, but he thought that being a werewolf was probably a lot less lonely than being a vampire. If you had a Pack.

Chad rose to his feet, the hair along his back bristling, his ears pricked up.

"They're in," one of the human-form werewolves— Stefan thought his name was Daniel—said briefly, and Stefan nodded. He'd heard the trapdoor in the house's basement open, too, and the noise of Meredith, Matt, and the other half of the Pack climbing out of the tunnels. If the vervain bombs had worked, the vampires should have been herded into the house ahead of them.

"Let's go," Stefan said. Zander had ordered the Pack to defer to Stefan on this mission, and they fell in line behind him without argument, the humans shoulder-to-shoulder, the wolves ranging out beside them.

Elena nodded in reply to Stefan's questioning look: Stefan should hurry and leave her to follow. Meredith and the others were walking into a fight, and he should be with them. Stefan turned away from her with what felt like a physical wrench—she'd been in danger so often—but he knew he would hear her if she needed him.

Stefan channeled his Power and began to run. The werewolves kept up with him easily, men and wolves strangely alike with their long, loping strides. Their Power, so incomprehensibly different than his own, was strong and focused. The full blast of it, alive and wild and raw, wrapped around Stefan. It was exhilarating.

They stopped short in the clearing by the Vitale Society's safe house, isolated in the woods near campus. Something was wrong.

Chad cocked his head and gave a soft, low whine. The other wolves picked up on it as well, two anxiously pacing past the front of the house.

"They say the vampires aren't there," Daniel reported.

Stefan had already realized that. Listening hard, he could hear footsteps and muffled swearing as Meredith and her team walked through the small house. But nothing else. More than that, Stefan's Power should have been able to pick up on a group of vampires as large as the Vitale.

"Come on," Stefan said, heading for the front door. He was able to break the lock with a quick flick of his wrist, and entered easily—no human had lived here for a long time. The faint scent of vervain rising from the tunnel entrance in the basement clouded his head for a moment, but he shook it off.

"It's us," he called softly as their friends' feet hesitated upstairs, and one of the wolves curled a long lip as if he was laughing at him. They, of course, had no need to alert the others; their Packmates always knew exactly where they were.

The whole group trooped upstairs to meet the others, crowding the narrow hall of what had probably once been a hunting cabin. Zander, who had turned out to be a stunningly beautiful wolf, pure white with the same sky-blue eyes he had as a human, growled quietly, and his Pack moved closer to him while Stefan made his way to Meredith and Matt.

"The tunnels were empty when we went through," Meredith said grimly. "Either they had other exits we didn't know about, or they weren't there when we set off the gas."

"Do you think they're all out hunting?" Matt asked, his eyes wide and worried.

Stefan shook his head. "Even with their Vitale pledge pins protecting them from the sun, they wouldn't hunt during the day. The sunlight's too tiring for new vampires," he said flatly. "We're too late. They must have already left to begin the resurrection spell. Maybe they're doing it at moonrise instead of midnight." Frustrated, he turned and smashed his fist against the wall, leaving a long crack running through its plaster.

There was the sound of a brief startled movement somewhere on the other side of the now-cracked wall. All the wolves' heads went up at once, and Stefan stiffened with them.

"There's someone here," Daniel translated. "Zander says she's in the room at the end of the hall."

She. Not Ethan, then, but one of his followers.

Stefan led the way toward the door quietly, Zander padding at his side, Meredith just behind him with her stave ready. He was aware of Matt and the rest of the Pack, tense and alert, hanging back to give them room.

With a sudden brutal kick, Stefan burst through the door, raising his arms to fend off an attack.

At the end of the room farthest from the door, a curly-haired girl cowered, her arms up to protect her face, her eyes wide with fright. She looked so vulnerable that Stefan hesitated for a moment, even though he knew immediately what she was.

Meredith shot past him and held her stave to the girl's chest, right above her heart.

"No!" Matt shouted from the doorway, pushing his way through the crowd of werewolves. "Stop, you guys." He crossed the room and stopped in front of the girl. The girl lowered her arms, her face wondering.

"Matt?" she whispered.

"Oh, Chloe," Matt said mournfully. He raised a hand toward her but hesitated before making contact, his hand hanging in midair.

Matt's friend Chloe, Stefan remembered. Chloe, the first girl Matt had seemed to care about since he'd dated Elena, since before Stefan had met him.

Matt's hand dropped back to his side and Stefan wondered if Matt was remembering the vicious murderer his friend Beth had become, if he was already resigning himself to Chloe's fate.

"Where are the other vampires?" Meredith asked coldly, pressing the stave against the other girl's chest.

"They've gone to the woods," Chloe said in a small, terrified voice. "They're going to do the resurrection spell there."

Stefan shook his head. "Ethan can't do the resurrection spell without Damon's blood," he said, hearing the almost pleading tone in his own voice.

Chloe half shrugged, looking back and forth between him and the others. "I don't know," she said helplessly. "He said he had everything he needed."

Ethan had cut Damon during the fight. It was just possible that he had managed to collect some blood, or find enough after the battle, for what he needed. Stefan swallowed, his mouth suddenly dry.

"Why aren't you with them?" Meredith asked.

"I didn't want to go," the girl said, her voice shaking. Her gaze settled on Matt, and she frowned anxiously, as if it was important that Matt understand her. "I feel like . . . with part of me I feel like Ethan is the center of the universe, but with my *mind*, I know how terrible he is. I'm trying to fight it. I don't want to hurt *anyone.*" Her eyes were full of tears, and Matt clenched his jaw, looking miserable and uncertain.

"You're trying to fight off the sire bond," Stefan said gently. "It's hard, but it can be done. And your compulsion toward Ethan will wear off before long. You can reject this life if you really want to."

"I *want* to," Chloe said desperately. "Please. Can you help me?"

Stefan began to speak, but Matt broke in. "Stop," he said again. "Stefan, Beth said the same thing—that she didn't want to hurt anyone, that she needed help. But she was lying."

Zander, swift and silent, padded forward. Approaching Chloe slowly, he sniffed at her hands. He rose up on his back legs, placing his front paws on Chloe's shoulders. She cringed, but he nosed her face unconcernedly and, for a long moment, stared directly into her eyes.

"Is she telling us the truth?" Meredith asked.

The huge white wolf dropped back to all fours and

turned away, glancing at the human-formed members of his Pack.

"He says she's being honest," Daniel reported, "but that she's weak. Fighting her nature is almost too much for her."

Chloe sobbed, a rough, hopeless sound.

Meredith, still poised with her stave for the kill, raised a questioning eyebrow at Stefan, irresolute. Matt turned to him, too, his eyes shining with anxious hope. They were all looking to him, he realized, to make the decision.

"We'll help you," he said slowly, "but first you need to help us."

Matt let out a breath of relief and closed the distance between him and Chloe. She leaned against him gratefully but nodded at Stefan, tears running down her face. "If you want to stop Ethan," she said, "we'll have to hurry."

7

*A*s Elena and the others entered the woods, the sun was setting. She had caught up with her friends as they left the safe house and Stefan, his voice low, filled her in on what had happened as they followed Chloe's lead. They wandered in the dark woods for what felt like a long time, all of them tense and quiet.

Branches smacked Elena in the face and she wished for the night vision of a vampire or a werewolf, or for Meredith's well-honed hunter's instincts. Even Matt, tromping along stoically beside her, his eyes fixed on Chloe up ahead, seemed to be running into fewer things than Elena was.

She was on the verge of wishing her Guardian Powers would just kick in already; this was probably the kind of thing they'd be good for, never mind whether she actually *wanted* those Powers or not.

Finally, a sliver of flickering orange light appeared in the distance, and they headed toward it without speaking. Elena was jogging, her breath coming in harsh pants. At least now that Stefan and the Pack had slowed their pace to accommodate Meredith and Matt, she could just manage to keep up with the group.

As they got closer, she realized the flickering light was from a bonfire. The wolves ahead of her pricked their ears up. Then, suddenly, they and Stefan were running, long strides eating up the distance and leaving the humans behind. Chloe trailed a few paces after them.

Matt's and Meredith's strong hands closed over Elena's arms and they pulled her along between them, running after the others. She stumbled, a sharp pain shooting through her side, but they held her up and she kept moving.

A moment later, they could hear what Stefan and the Pack had heard. A heavy chant of many voices seemed to throb and reverberate through Elena's head. Above the murmur rose a single voice, calling out sharply.

She couldn't tell what language they were speaking, although it sounded ancient and guttural. Not Latin, she thought, but it could have been Greek or Old Norse or something much older, from the early days of the world. Sumerian, she thought wildly. Incan. Who knew?

As she broke into a clearing, her eyes stung from the smoke and light of the fire, and at first all she saw was a confusion of writhing dark shapes against the light. As her eyes adjusted, she saw Ethan, still looking incongruously like the preppy college senior he had been not long ago, leading the chant. His forehead was slightly wrinkled in concentration, and he held up a goblet full of rich, dark blood as if it was nothing more than wine.

Why aren't they stopping him? Elena thought, and then the struggling bodies before her came into focus.

Stefan, brutally graceful, was ripping into the throat of a tall, slightly stooped vampire. Elena recognized him vaguely as someone she'd seen around campus, before the Vitale Society pledges had all been changed into vampires. Nearby, the werewolves fought, too, the wolves flanking and protecting the humans as they battled together, each perfectly attuned to the others' positions. The vampires not currently locked in battle had formed a circle around Ethan, blocking him from attack as he continued his ritual.

Meredith pitched herself into the fight, the silver ends of her stave flashing in the firelight. Elena and Matt, all too aware of their lack of supernatural Power, hung back at the edge of the clearing. Chloe stood at a little distance from them, her eyes fixed on the battle. She was biting at her lip, her arms wrapped around herself, and Elena felt a sharp pang of sympathy for her: she remembered the anxious cravings of being a new vampire, and the way your sire's every move seemed to call out to you. It must be agony for

Chloe to keep from flinging herself into the fight.

Matt was watching Chloe, his forehead creased with worry, but he kept his distance, angling himself to protect Elena from Chloe as well as from the other Vitale vampires. *He must remember how volatile a new vampire could be, too.* Elena pressed his arm gratefully. Once again, she thought: *If I have to be a Guardian anyway, now would be a good time for some Powers to kick in.*

She tried to sense if anything might be changing inside her, feeling as if she was probing a loose tooth with her tongue, but she didn't feel any different. There was no sense of potential unfurling within her, as she had felt during the brief period after her resurrection, when she had been ripe with the mysterious and dangerous Wing Powers. Just mortal, everyday Elena, with no way to help now.

As she watched, a vampire gripped the sides of a huge white wolf—Zander—and with great agility and strength, tossed him aside. The wolf's body slammed heavily to the ground near the edge of the clearing and lay still. Elena's heart froze. *Oh, no,* she thought, stepping forward involuntarily, but Matt held her back. *Oh, Bonnie.*

The wolf lay still for a moment, and Elena couldn't see if he was breathing. Then, slowly, he clambered to his feet, his sides heaving. There were streaks of blood and mud on his pure white fur. Zander wavered on his feet, then seemed to find his balance and, snarling, threw himself back into the fight. With a sudden charge, he brought a vampire to her knees and Daniel, stake in hand, finished her off with one quick blow.

When Elena had arrived at the clearing, the fighters had seemed evenly matched, and there was no way to break through the wall of vampires to stop Ethan as he performed the ritual. But Meredith had gone in whirling like a dervish, her weapon flying, and the tide of the battle was slowly but clearly turning.

Meredith and Stefan exchanged a glance and she began to fight her way closer to the fire, moving steadily toward Ethan even as she angled her stave to strike a vampire, bringing him to the ground. Elena's eyes could barely follow her as she unsheathed a hunting knife from her side and, with one vicious swing of the blade, cut off his head. The body toppled backward, and suddenly a path opened through the crowd between Stefan and Ethan.

Stefan pushed away the vampire he had been fighting and leaped in one great bound over Meredith's head, landing on his feet in front of Ethan.

The chant stuttered to a halt. Stefan reached out and wrapped his hand around Ethan's throat just over the windpipe, tightened, and squeezed. The younger vampire choked and mouthed wordlessly, his hands desperately scrabbling at Stefan's. Reaching down with the hand not holding Ethan by the throat, Stefan felt at his side and brought out a stake. Ethan's golden eyes widened as Stefan pressed the stake against his chest. Elena heard Chloe whimper slightly, but the vampire girl didn't move.

"Good-bye, Ethan," Stefan said. His voice was quiet and matter-of-fact, not angry, but Elena heard, and so did the others. Everyone had paused in their fight, arms straining against one another, eyes turned toward Stefan and Ethan. It was as if they were all holding their breath. Then the vampires began to snarl and shriek, fighting to reach their sire. But the wolves moved faster than Elena could have imagined, flooding into the circle around Ethan and Stefan, holding the vampires back. Elena sucked in a long, relieved breath. Stefan had gotten there in time. The worst wouldn't happen. Klaus, the madman, the Original vampire, would stay dead.

Ethan glared at Stefan, but his lips slowly curled upward into a terrible smile.

Too late, he mouthed silently, and the glass in his hand toppled backward. Rich, red blood poured out onto the fire.

As soon as the blood touched the fire, it exploded into high blue flames. Elena cringed and shielded her eyes against the sudden burst of light. All around her, the others cowered, vampire, human, and werewolf alike.

The flames and the clearing filled with smoke. Elena was shaking, coughing, her eyes watering, and she could feel Matt wheezing and shuddering beside her.

As the smoke began to clear, a tall, golden-skinned figure took shape and stepped out of the flames. Elena knew him. She thought, as she had the first time she saw him, that he looked like the devil, if the devil were handsome.

He was naked as he came out of the fire, his body lithe and well muscled, and he held his head up proudly. His hair was white, his eyes blue. His smile was joyous and insane, and every move held the promise of destruction.

Lightning cracked overhead, and he threw back his head and laughed with what sounded like sheer malevolent pleasure.

Klaus had risen.

lena couldn't move. She felt numb, her limbs heavy and frozen. Her heart beat faster and faster, the rush of blood thundering in her ears, but she stayed still.

Before the fire, Klaus stretched and smiled, holding his hands out in front of him. He turned them slowly, examining them, admiring his long fingers and strong forearms.

"Unscarred," he said. He spoke softly, but his words resonated across the clearing. "I'm whole again." He tipped his head back to see the three-quarter moon high above him and his smile widened. "And back home," he said.

Ethan wriggled out of a shocked Stefan's loosened grip and dropped to his knees. "Klaus," he said worshipfully. Klaus glanced down at him with an indifferent sort of curiosity. Ethan opened his mouth to say more, his face ecstatic, but before he could, Klaus reached out, wrapped his strong, graceful hands around Ethan's jaw, and *pulled*.

With a terrible noise of tendons ripping, Ethan's head came away from his neck like a stopper lifting from a jar. His body slumped lifelessly to one side, abandoned. Klaus lifted up the head and held it above him as blood streamed down his arms. Around him, Ethan's followers quivered in fear, but none of them moved. Near Elena, Chloe gasped.

Stefan, his face spattered with Ethan's blood, was watching Klaus narrowly, angling his body to find a good position to attack. *No*, Elena thought, frightened, willing Stefan back. She hadn't forgotten how strong Klaus was. As if he'd heard her thoughts, Stefan eased back a little, darting an alert glance at their assembled troops, all watching Klaus now with horror.

Klaus gazed at Ethan's slack face for a moment, then tossed the head aside. Holding his right hand up to his mouth, he licked at Ethan's blood thoughtfully with a long pink tongue, and Elena's stomach turned uneasily. Seeing him kill Ethan so casually had been horrible enough, but there was something *obscene* in the thoughtless sensual pleasure he took in tasting the rivulets of blood.

"Delicious," Klaus said, his voice light. "I like the taste of human better than vampire, but that one was young and fresh. His blood was still sweet." He glanced coolly around the clearing. "Who's next?" he asked.

Then, across the firelit clearing, his eyes locked on Elena's, and his head went up like a dog catching a scent, his face changing from indifference to alertness. Elena swallowed, her throat dry, her heart still beating like a small, frantic bird trapped in her chest. His eyes were so blue, but not the kind light blue of Matt's or Zander's tropical sky blue. Klaus's eyes were like thin ice over dark water.

"You," Klaus said to her, almost gently. "I've wanted to see you again," and he smiled and opened his hands. "And here you are at my rebirth to welcome me. Come to me, little one."

Elena didn't want to move, but she staggered forward toward Klaus anyway, her feet shuffling forward without her consent, as if they were being operated by someone else.

She heard Matt's panicked whisper behind her— "Elena!"—and he gripped her arm, bringing her to a grateful halt. There was no time to thank him, though: Klaus was closing in.

"Should I kill you now?" he asked her, his tone as intimate as a lover's. "You don't seem to have your army of angry ghosts around you this time, Elena. I could finish you in seconds."

"No." Stefan stepped forward, his face hard and defiant. Meredith came up beside him and they stood shoulder-to-shoulder, glaring at Klaus. Behind them Zander and his Pack, both wolf and human, crowded closer, staying between Elena and Klaus. Zander was staring at Klaus, his eyes wide, his hackles raised and quivering. Slowly, his lips peeled back from his teeth and the werewolf growled.

Klaus looked at them all in mild surprise, then laughed in genuine amusement. "Still inspiring devotion, are you, girl?" he asked Elena across the crowd. "Maybe you have some of the spirit of my Katherine after all."

In one smooth movement, he reached forward and picked Stefan up by the throat, then tossed him aside as easily as he might have thrown a scarecrow. Elena screamed as Stefan landed with a heavy thud on the other side of the fire and lay still.

Meredith, poised and ready, instantly swung her stave toward Klaus's head. Klaus put one hand up and grabbed the stave from midair, ripping it from Meredith's grasp without even looking at her. He flung the stave aside as casually as he had thrown Stefan's body and waded quickly through the crowd, knocking Zander's Pack and Ethan's vampires aside with a brutal, careless efficiency.

On the other side of the fire, Stefan was climbing to his feet. But Elena knew that, even with his vampiric speed, he wouldn't be able to get to Klaus before Klaus reached Elena.

Before she could blink, Klaus was standing directly in

front of her, his fingers holding her jaw bruisingly tight. He tipped back her head, turning her face up toward him, forcing her to meet his icy, laughing eyes.

"I owe you a death, pretty one," he said, smiling. Elena could feel Chloe quivering beside her and Matt's hand on her arm, cold with fear but still holding tight.

"Leave her alone," Matt said, and Elena knew him well enough to know how hard he was working to keep his voice from shaking.

Klaus ignored him, his eyes fixed on Elena's. They stared at each other, and Elena tried to make her own eyes as defiant as possible. If Klaus was going to kill her now, she wouldn't go down weeping and begging for mercy. She *wouldn't*. She bit the inside of her cheek hard, trying to focus on the physical pain instead of her fear.

Then Stefan was suddenly there, wrenching at Klaus's arm with all his strength, but it didn't make any difference. Klaus's hand was as firm on her jaw as ever, his eyes steady on hers. The moment seemed to stretch out into years.

A new madness, more heated than Elena had seen before, bloomed in Klaus's eyes. "I *will* kill you," he said, almost affectionately, squeezing her face between his fingers so that Elena made an involuntary moan of pain and protest. "But not yet. I want you to be waiting for me, to think of me coming for you. You won't know when, but it *will* be soon."

Quickly, shockingly, he pulled her toward him and planted a soft, cold kiss on her mouth. His breath was rank, and the taste of Ethan's blood on his lips made her gag.

Finally, he opened his hand and released her. Elena stumbled back several paces, wiping at her mouth furiously.

"I'll see you again, little one," Klaus said, and then he was gone, faster than Elena's eyes could follow.

Matt caught Elena before she could fall. A moment later, Stefan's strong arms were around her, and Matt let her go.

Everyone was blinking and dazed, as if Klaus's exit had left a vacuum. The Vitale vampires were looking at one another uncertainly and, before Meredith and the rest could collect themselves enough to begin fighting again, the vampires were leaving, running away in a panicked, disorganized mob. Meredith reached for the stake in her belt, but it was too late. Frowning, she silently crossed the clearing to pick up her stave, turning it over in her hands to check for damage.

Zander, his fur bloody and bedraggled from the fight, lowered his head, and the rest of his Pack crowded around him anxiously. One of the other wolves licked quickly at his wound, and Zander leaned against him.

Chloe had not disappeared with the other vampires. Instead, she stood by Matt, biting at her lips with blunt teeth, staring at the ground. After a moment, Matt put his arm carefully around her and Chloe huddled close to his side.

Elena sighed wearily and let her head drop onto Stefan's shoulder. She could still taste Klaus's vile kiss, and tears stung her eyes.

Ethan was dead, but nothing was over. The fight was just beginning.

In a tree high above the clearing, a large black crow ruffled its feathers, eyeing the battleground below him. He had watched the fight critically, thinking that there were things he would have done differently, more aggressively. But no, this wasn't Damon's place anymore. He hadn't wanted to be seen, hadn't wanted to get involved with Elena and Stefan and all their problems. But the scent of blood and fire had led him here.

After everything, he still wanted to save Elena and Stefan, didn't he? That was what was pulling him to the fight, an almost unnatural urge to do what he was built to do: to kill. When he'd seen Klaus fling his brother aside, everything in him had tensed to attack. And when the arrogant Original vampire had dared to touch Elena—*Damon's* Elena, his heart still insisted—Damon had flown to the edge of the clearing, his normally slow pulse hammering with rage.

But they didn't need him, they didn't want him; he

was *done* with them. He'd tried—he'd done his best, he'd *changed*—all for Elena's love, and for the friendship he'd found with his brother at last. After centuries of caring for no one but himself, Damon had suddenly been caught in Elena's world, wrapped up in the lives of a handful of mortal teenagers. He'd become someone he barely recognized.

And it hadn't mattered. In the end, Damon was still left on the outside.

Klaus was gone and they were fine. This wasn't his fight. Not anymore. Now, all he had was the cloak of night and the cold comfort of once again relying on no one but himself.

Damon was, he told himself fiercely, *free.*

att craned to look over Stefan's shoulder and through the creaking door of the abandoned boathouse. It was dark and musty inside, and Matt's hand tightened automatically on Chloe's.

"This should be a safe place for now," Stefan told them.

Elena and the others had headed back to campus, shaken and quiet from the fight, but Chloe had nowhere to go. "I don't know what to do now," she'd said. "I can't go back to the Vitale house. Will you help me?"

Matt had taken her hand, feeling a wave of guilty compassion wash over him. If only he hadn't trusted Ethan. The other Vitale pledges had been innocent victims, but Matt had *known* vampires. Why hadn't he suspected? "Wherever you go, I'm coming with you," he'd said stubbornly. So Stefan had brought them here.

Matt rubbed the back of his neck and looked around. Safe or not, the old boathouse certainly was grim-looking. Stefan had said that students didn't come here anymore, and Matt could easily believe it.

This had once been the boathouse for the Dalcrest crew team, but new docks and a boathouse had been built closer to the river. Since then, the small artificial lake this boathouse fronted had silted up. Now algae-scummed, brackish water lay shallowly across the muddy lake bottom, and the boathouse itself had been left to rot. Foul-smelling water sloshed below damp, softened wood underfoot. Above their heads, the rotting roof let in glimpses of the night sky.

"I'm not sure Chloe should be living like this," Matt said slowly, not wanting to offend Stefan.

Stefan's lips curled up in a bitter smile. "The first lesson you both need to learn is that she's *not* living like this. She's not living at all—not anymore."

Next to Matt, Chloe hunched her shoulders protectively and crossed her arms. "I *feel* alive," she muttered. Matt waited for the wry, dimpling twist of her mouth he'd gotten used to from the human Chloe, but she just gazed down at her feet somberly.

"This is what it is, Chloe," Stefan said to her. His voice was dispassionate. "Until you can learn to survive without hurting humans, you can't stay near them. Any scent or sound might set you off. It takes a long time to get to the point where you can trust yourself, and until you do, you'll be skulking in the shadows, existing in the places where no human would go. Sewers. Caves. Places that make this boathouse look like luxury."

Chloe nodded, looking up at Stefan with wide, earnest eyes. "I'll do anything I have to," she said. "This is my second chance—I understand that. I'm going to fix myself."

Stefan gave her a small smile. "I hope so, Chloe," he said. Rubbing the bridge of his nose between two fingers in a familiar weary gesture, he turned to Matt. "There are things you can do to help her," Stefan told him. "She's young. It's important she have plenty of blood or she won't be able to think about anything else."

Matt started to speak and Stefan cut him off. "*Not* your blood. Animal blood. If you go with her into the woods when she's hunting, you can help keep her grounded and away from humans. You can bring her animals when she doesn't feel like she can go out." Matt nodded, and Stefan turned to Chloe. "You're fast and strong now; you'll be able to catch deer if you want to. If you concentrate, you should be able to call smaller animals—birds and rabbits—to you. You can try not to kill them if you want, but you probably will anyway, at least until you learn to control yourself."

"Thank you, Stefan," Chloe said solemnly.

"Practice deep breathing," Stefan told her. "Meditation. Listen to your own heartbeat, learn the new slower rhythm it has now that you've been turned. You're going to get pretty agitated sometimes, and you should find out how to calm yourself down. Do it with her, Matt. It'll help her focus."

"Okay." Matt wiped his sweaty hands against his jeans and nodded again. "We can do this."

His eyes met Stefan's, and Matt was surprised by the look on the vampire's face. Despite the matter-of-fact tone Stefan had been using, he could tell Stefan was concerned. "It's dangerous for you," Stefan said gently. "I shouldn't leave you with her."

"I wouldn't hurt him," Chloe said. Her eyes filled with tears and she angrily brushed them away with the back of her hand. "I'd never hurt Matt."

Stefan turned the same sympathetic gaze on her. "I know you don't want to hurt him," he told her, "but I also know you can hear the rushing of Matt's blood as his heart pounds, that you can smell the overwhelming sweet blood-scent of him all around you. It's hard to think straight when he's near you, isn't it? Part of you just wants to tear into him, to rip at that soft skin of his throat, to find the vein that's so full of rich, warm blood, just there below his ear."

Chloe clenched her jaw, but the white edge of a tooth slipped past the firm line of her mouth, cutting at her lip. With a shudder, Matt realized that Chloe's sharp vampire canines had descended while Stefan was talking, that she was ready to bite.

Steeling himself, Matt pushed down the instinct to run away from her and instead moved closer and put an arm across her shoulders.

"We'll get through this," he said firmly. Chloe took a deep, slow breath and then another, clearly trying to calm herself. After a moment, her shoulders relaxed a little and, looking at the looser set of her jaw, Matt thought that her teeth had gone back to normal.

"What else should we do?" Chloe asked Stefan, her voice determined.

Stefan shrugged and stuffed his hands into his pockets. He walked back to the doorway and looked out over the dark water of the lake. "In the end, the only thing that matters is that you really want to change," he said. "If you want it enough and if your willpower is strong enough, you will. I won't lie to you, it's not easy."

"I do want to," Chloe said, her eyes shining with tears again. "I won't hurt anyone. That's not who I am, not even now. These last few days—I can't be that *thing*." She closed her eyes, and the tears spilled over her lashes, running in silvery lines down her cheeks.

"You can't feed on anyone," Stefan warned her. "If Matt or anyone else gets hurt, even if you're sorry, I'll do what I need to do to protect the humans here."

"You'll kill me," Chloe agreed, her voice thin. Her eyes were still closed, and she hugged herself, wrapping her arms around herself defensively. "It's okay," she said. "I don't want to live like that."

"I'll take responsibility for her," Matt said, his voice sounding loud in his own ears. "I won't let anything bad happen."

Chloe inched closer to him, seeming to find comfort under his arm. Matt held on to her. Chloe could be saved; he knew it. He hadn't been careful enough, hadn't realized what Ethan was. But Chloe wasn't lost to him, not yet.

"All right," Stefan said quietly, looking between them. "Good luck." He shook hands with Matt and then he turned and was gone, faster than Matt's eyes could follow, no doubt headed back to Elena.

Chloe pressed against Matt's side and laid her head on his shoulder. He rested his cheek on the top of her head, her dark, curly hair soft where it touched his face. This was dangerous, a small unhappy knot in his stomach reminded him, and he didn't really know what he was doing.

But Chloe was breathing slowly beside him, and all he could think was: at least they had a chance.

"I'm fine, Bonnie," Zander said, half laughing. "I'm tough, remember? Supertough. I'm a hero." He tugged on her hand, trying to pull her onto the bed beside him.

"You're hurt is what you are," Bonnie said sharply. "Don't try that macho stuff on *me*." She pulled her hand away and shoved an ice pack at him with her other hand. "Put that on your shoulder," she ordered.

They'd met up outside the library a little while after dawn, and she'd immediately seen that Zander was wounded. Back in his human form, he had seemed *almost* as graceful as always, running along with his Pack with his usual easy, loping stride, but he'd held himself aloof from the rest of the guys' playful shoving and tussling, the rough hands-on affection that was their default mode when they weren't on duty. As he'd stepped lightly out of range of Marcus's and Enrique's grappling arms and ducked away from Camden's headlock, Bonnie had realized Zander must be hurting.

So she'd taken him to the cafeteria and filled him up with eggs and bacon and the sugary cereal he loved. They'd come back to Zander's dorm room and she'd gotten him to take his shirt off so she could examine the damage. Normally, Bonnie would have been happily ogling Zander's chiseled abs, but right now, the purple-black bruise beginning to bloom on his shoulder and stretch down his side was ruining the view.

"I'm not really hurt, Bonnie," Zander insisted. "You don't have to baby me." He lay back on the bed, though, and didn't try to get up, so Bonnie figured that Zander was feeling a lot worse than he was willing to admit.

"I'll get you some ibuprofen," she said, and he didn't

argue. She rummaged through his desk until she found the bottle and rattled the last couple of pills out into his hand, then brought him a bottle of water. Zander hitched himself up onto his elbows to swallow the pills and winced.

"Lie down," Bonnie told him. "If you promise to stay in bed and try to nap, I could go get you some of my special healing tea."

Zander grinned at her. "Why don't you lie down with me?" he suggested. "I bet I'd feel a lot more comfortable with you here." He patted the mattress next to him.

Bonnie hesitated. That was actually pretty tempting. She was about to snuggle up to him when a brisk knock came on the door.

Bonnie waved Zander back onto the bed as he started to rise. "I'll get it," she told him. "It's probably one of the guys." Not that Zander's Packmates bothered to knock much, but maybe they were using their best manners, assuming Bonnie would be there.

Another sharp tap came as Bonnie crossed the room. "All right, hold your horses," she muttered, opening the door.

In the hallway, her hand raised to knock yet again, stood a complete stranger, a girl with hair cut in a long blond bob. Her small, precise features mirrored Bonnie's own surprise.

"Is Zander here?" the girl asked, frowning.

"Um," Bonnie said, feeling thrown. "Yeah, he's . . ."

Then Zander came up behind her. "Well, hi, Shay," he said, his voice slightly unsure. He was smiling, though. "What're you doing here?"

The girl—*Shay*, Bonnie thought, what kind of name was that?—glanced at Bonnie instead of answering, and Zander flushed. "Oh," he said. "Yeah, Bonnie, this is Shay, who's a friend from back home. Shay, this is my girlfriend, Bonnie."

"Nice to meet you, Bonnie," Shay said coolly, raising one eyebrow. Her eyes traced over Zander's naked chest, lingering for a moment on the purpling bruise, and his cheeks flushed pink. "Been busy?" she asked.

"Come on in," he said, and backed away from the door, reaching for his shirt. "I, uh, was just putting some ice on my shoulder."

"Nice to meet you, too," Bonnie said, a little late, as she made room for Shay to pass her. Since when did Zander *have* female friends? Other than Bonnie, and Bonnie's friends, he lived in an exclusively male world.

"I need to talk to you. Alone," Shay said to Zander, shooting him a meaningful look and then cutting her eyes sharply to Bonnie.

Zander rolled his eyes. "Subtle, Shay," he said. "But it's okay. Bonnie knows about me and the rest of the Pack."

A second eyebrow climbed up Shay's forehead to join

the first. "Do you think that's wise?" she asked.

Zander's lips quirked into the half smile Bonnie loved. "Believe me, it's not the weirdest thing Bonnie knows," he said.

"O-*kay*," Shay said slowly. She fixed Bonnie with a long, speculative look and Bonnie stuck out her chin defiantly and glared right back at her. Finally, Shay shrugged. "I guess I lost my right to give you advice a while back," she said, then lowered her voice, as if she was afraid someone might be eavesdropping from the hallway. "The High Wolf Council sent me," she said quietly. "They're not happy with what they're hearing about the vampires at Dalcrest. They thought maybe I could help you guys find some direction."

Zander's jaw tightened. "Our direction's fine, thanks," he said.

"Oh, don't be like that," Shay said. "I'm not trying to Alpha you." She reached out and touched his arm lightly, letting her hand linger on it. "It was a good excuse to come visit," she said, even more softly. "I was sorry about how things ended the last time we saw each other."

Bonnie glanced down at herself. Shay was so focused on Zander that Bonnie had started to wonder if maybe she had disappeared and left them thinking they were alone together. But nope, same solid Bonnie.

"Oh," she said, startled, as everything Shay had said

suddenly clicked into place. "You're a *werewolf.*"

She should have seen it immediately: despite Shay's neat, swinging bob and feminine features, she moved the same way Zander and his Pack did, with a kind of solid grace, as if she was completely aware at all times of her body, without even having to think about it. And she had touched Zander the way he touched the guys in his Pack, easy and as if her body was almost part of his own.

He didn't touch Bonnie that way. Not that Bonnie had any complaints at all about the way Zander *did* touch her, which was sweet and sure and as if she was the most precious thing he'd ever held. But still, it wasn't quite the same.

There was no one there to overhear, but Shay pinned Bonnie with a glare. "Keep your voice down," she whispered fiercely.

"Sorry," Bonnie said. "I just didn't know there were girl Original werewolves."

Shay's lips curved into a smirk. "Sure," she said. "Where do you think all the little Original werewolves come from?"

"The High Wolf Council usually divides younger wolves up into Packs of either guys or girls when they send us out to keep an eye on things," Zander told Bonnie. "They think mixing together distracts us from our jobs."

"Apparently they're not considering the *other* ways

some of us can get distracted," Shay said acidly. Her eyes were cold on Bonnie's, but Bonnie hadn't been through hell and back in the last year to let any bossy and self-important werewolf girl push her around.

Bonnie was just opening her mouth to tell Shay that she'd better lose the attitude when Zander, seeming to sense her reaction, grabbed hold of Bonnie's hand.

"Listen, Shay, I really need to get some rest," he said quickly. "We'll catch up later, okay? Call me or one of the other guys and we'll get together." Bonnie had a brief impression of Shay looking startled, and then Zander hurried Shay right out of the room and shut the door behind her.

"So . . . friend from back home?" Bonnie asked after a moment. "I don't think you've mentioned her before."

"Um," Zander said. His gorgeous long lashes brushed his cheeks as he looked down, away from Bonnie, and she might have been distracted by how sweet that made him look. Except that Zander also looked distinctly *guilty*.

Bonnie suddenly felt her stomach sink. "Is there something you're not telling me?" she asked. Zander shifted uncomfortably from one foot to the other, his cheeks flushing, and Bonnie's stomach plummeted even further. "No more secrets, remember?"

Zander sighed. "I just think this is going to sound like a bigger deal than it is," he said.

"*Zander*," Bonnie said.

"The High Wolf Council wanted Shay and me to be together," Zander confessed. He glanced up at her tentatively through his lashes. "They, um, I guess thought we'd be like mates? Get married, maybe, and have werewolf children together when we finished school. They thought we'd make a good team."

Bonnie blinked. Her brain felt numb, she realized. Zander and Shay had thought about getting *married*?

"But we couldn't get along," Zander said hurriedly. "I swear, Bonnie, we just never clicked. We fought, like, all the time. So we broke up."

"Uh," Bonnie said. She was so blindsided by this, it felt like a huge effort to even put words together. "So the High Wolf Council controls who you marry?" she asked finally, picking the most general of the questions swarming her mind.

"They *try*," Zander said, looking at her anxiously. "They can't . . . they can't make me do anything I don't want to do. And they wouldn't want to. They're fair." His sky-blue eyes, that heavenly tropical blue, caught hers, and he smiled tentatively, his hands warm on her shoulders. "You're the one I love, Bonnie," he said. "Believe me."

"I do believe you," Bonnie said, because she *did*; it was shining out of Zander's eyes. And she loved him, too. Zander flinched a little as she hugged him, and Bonnie loosened her arms, mindful of his bruises. "It's okay," she said softly.

But even as she turned her face up to Zander's kiss, Bonnie couldn't help the word that resounded in her mind, making her twitch with anxiety.

Uh-oh.

Stefan and Elena curled together on his bed, her head on his shoulder. Stefan let himself relax under her touch, feeling the softness of her hair against his cheek. It had been a seemingly endless day. But Elena was safe, for now. Just for this moment, she was in Stefan's arms and nothing would hurt her. He tightened his hold on her.

"Is Chloe going to be all right?" Elena asked.

Stefan bit back an incredulous little laugh and the corners of Elena's lips turned up in response. "What?" she said.

"You're worried about Chloe," Stefan said. "Klaus has promised to kill you, and you want to hear if Chloe, who you barely knew when she was human, is going to be all right." He should have known, though. Elena had a core of steel running through her. And nothing was more important to her than protecting her friends, her town, the world.

Maybe, Stefan thought, *she's always been a Guardian.*

"I haven't stopped thinking about what Klaus said," Elena told him, and Stefan felt her body shudder against his. "I'm afraid. But I can't stop caring about everyone else, either. Matt needs Chloe, so she matters to me, too. I worry that there might not be a lot of time left. We should all be with the people we love." She kissed Stefan, just a light brush of her lips on his. When she spoke again, her voice trembled. "We just found each other again, Stefan. I don't want to miss anything. All I want to do is hold on to you."

Stefan kissed her, more deeply this time. *I love you*, he told her silently. *I will protect you with my life.*

Elena broke the kiss and smiled at him, her eyes full of tears. "I know," she said. "I love you, too, Stefan, so much." She pulled her hair back and tilted her head invitingly, exposing her long slender throat. Stefan hesitated—it had been so long, not since before they broke up and came back together—but she drew his mouth down to her throat.

The rush of Elena's blood—so intoxicating, so full of vitality that it was like champagne and sweet nectar at the same time—made Stefan light-headed, flooding him with warmth. There were no barriers between them, no walls, and he felt a great wonder at the steadfast tenderness that he found in Elena.

They fell asleep wrapped around each other. Darkness threatened them on all sides, but for this night, they would be together, be each other's light.

10

"A headless body found in the woods near Dalcrest College last week has now been identified as Dalcrest senior Ethan Crane," announced the pretty newscaster on the TV morning show, her forehead crinkling seriously. "Police have not yet released a statement on whether Crane was the victim of a murder or a freak accident, but judging from the difference in wounds, Crane's death appears unrelated to the most recent animal attacks in the woods."

As the newscaster went on to another story, Meredith flipped off the TV, hissing in irritation.

"They must think everyone who watches the news is a moron," she muttered. "How could someone lose their head in a freak accident in the woods?"

Even though the student lounge was empty except for

the five of them—Elena, Bonnie, Meredith, Stefan, and Zander—Elena lowered her voice and glanced around before answering. "They don't want people to panic any more than they are already."

The empty lounge was a sign of how frightened everyone already was, Elena thought. The first couple of weeks of school, the lounge had been packed in the evenings, guys and girls hanging out to watch TV or flirt or even study.

Now, though, everyone was wary, sticking to their rooms in case one of the friendly faces on campus was masking a killer. Elena was constantly on edge, too. She and her friends checked and rechecked their weapons, tried to anticipate what Klaus might do. And yet he'd done nothing, as far as they could tell.

"My psychology class was canceled this week," Bonnie told the others. "And there's hardly anyone left in my English section. A lot of people have left." She hesitated, her wide brown eyes flicking between Elena and Zander. "My father wants me to come home and see if we can get the tuition refunded. He says I could come back next year if they get to the bottom of all the attacks and disappearances," she confessed.

"You're not going home, are you?" Elena asked her. Bonnie's dad had always been superprotective of Bonnie and her older sisters, so Elena wasn't surprised by this news.

"Of course I'm not going," Bonnie said stoutly. "You guys need me here." She snuggled closer to Zander and tipped her head back against his chest to smile up at him. He smiled back, wide and warmly, and Elena found herself smiling, too. Zander was such a guy's guy, not really Elena's type at all, but it was wonderful to see Bonnie with someone who liked her so much that pure contentment just shone out of him whenever they were together.

Stefan cleared his throat to get their attention. "I don't know where Klaus is feeding, but I don't think the bodies that have been found in the woods are people he killed. The news reports are saying they look like animal attacks, and, uh"—he looked down at his feet, his face slightly embarrassed—"I compelled a police officer to find out what the police have seen. The kills are really sloppy; they look like an animal actually *is* attacking people, so it's not just a cover story as far as the police are concerned."

"So you think it's the new vampires who are killing people, not one as experienced as Klaus," Elena said. Stefan met her eyes and she knew he was thinking the same thing she was: *not Damon, either.* A great wave of relief broke over her.

If Damon crossed that line, if he started killing again, she didn't know what they would do. She couldn't imagine that they'd betray him, turn him over to the others, or hunt him down. So much had changed between Stefan and

Damon. Elena knew Stefan would protect his brother now, choose him over anyone else except perhaps Elena herself.

But it hadn't come to that yet. It never would, Elena told herself fiercely. Damon might have lost control once, but no lasting harm had been done. The girl was fine. And it was the new vampires, the ones Ethan had turned, who were killing.

Meredith was watching her, her gray eyes sympathetic. "People are still dying, even if the killer is not Klaus," she said gently. With a start, Elena realized that she'd given away her relief that it wasn't Damon. Luckily, Meredith had misinterpreted Elena's reaction. "We can't guess what game Klaus is playing or what his plans are until he reveals himself," Meredith went on. A lock of dark hair fell over her cheek and she tucked it back behind her ear. "But we can target the Vitale vampires. Gassing the tunnels didn't work, and we can't make more gas unless we can get a lot more vervain than we have now. We should be patrolling regularly to keep the students safer."

She dug into her backpack and pulled out a campus map, carefully annotated in red ink, and traced an area on the map with one finger. "I've marked their hunting grounds here, and I think we can focus our patrols on the woods and on the playing fields on the edge of campus. We need to organize and make sure we've got nightly patrols that have enough strong fighters in them to take down a group of young vampires."

"What about during the day?" Bonnie asked, frowning and reaching for the map. "They've all got lapis lazuli, don't they? So they could be out hunting anytime."

Stefan stirred restlessly next to Elena on the couch. "Even though the sunlight doesn't kill them, they'll be laying low during the day," he explained. "Sunlight bothers vampires even with the lapis lazuli. Night is a vampire's natural habitat, and they won't leave it unless they're forced to."

Elena looked at him in surprise, but said nothing. Stefan lived in the day with her, slept at night. Did it hurt him, too? Had he changed so much, just to be with Elena?

"So nighttime patrols ought to be enough, at least for now," Meredith said.

Zander examined the map closely, his white-blond head close to Bonnie's red one. "I can organize the guys to take some of the patrols," he offered. Stefan nodded to Zander in acknowledgment. Meredith turned to Elena, her gray eyes sharp. "What about Damon?" she asked. "We could really use him."

Elena hesitated. Beside her, Stefan cleared his throat. "My brother isn't available right now," he said, his voice expressionless. "But I'll let you know if anything changes."

Meredith's lips tightened. Elena could imagine what was going through her friend's head: Damon, irritating but always *there*, had finally, over the past summer and fall, proven himself as a worthwhile ally, only to disappear when the campus was falling into chaos around them?

If that was what Meredith was thinking, she didn't say anything, just narrowed her eyes and let out a long sigh, then asked, "What about you, Bonnie? Are there any spells that will help the patrols?"

"There are a few protection spells I already know that could be useful," Bonnie said thoughtfully. "I'm going to call Mrs. Flowers and see what else she recommends."

Elena smiled across at her friend. With the discovery of her talent for witchcraft, Bonnie had found a new confidence. Bonnie looked up and caught her eye, then smiled back.

"We'll beat them, won't we, Elena?" she said softly. "And Klaus, too, when he shows up again."

"We did before, after all," Elena said lightly. Bonnie's expression sobered, and Meredith picked up the map again, turning it over thoughtfully in her hands. Next to Elena, Stefan reached to take her hand in his. They all knew just what it had taken to beat Klaus the first time they had faced him: Damon and Stefan united, and an army of the dead of Fell's Church, rising up from the land where they had fallen in battle. Not something they could duplicate. And even then, they had barely survived.

"We're stronger now," Bonnie said uncertainly. "Right?"

Elena forced herself to smile. "Of course we are," she said. Meredith's hand took hold of Elena's, and Elena felt comforted and strengthened by Stefan, her love, on one side, and Meredith, her friend, on the other. Bonnie raised her head proudly, her small face defiant, and Zander straightened beside her.

"We're invincible when we're together," Elena told them, and looking around at their resolute faces, she almost believed it.

11

Elena was pulling on her sturdiest boots—perfect for a night of tromping through the woods—when her phone rang.

"Hello?" she said, glancing at the clock. In less than five minutes, she was supposed to be meeting Stefan and three of Zander's Packmates to patrol the campus. She tucked the phone between her ear and her shoulder and hurriedly finished lacing up the boots.

"Elena." James's voice came through the phone, sounding exuberant. "I have good news. Andrés has arrived."

Elena stiffened, her fingers fumbling on her bootlaces. "Oh," she said faintly. The human Guardian was *here* at Dalcrest? She swallowed and spoke more firmly. "Does he want to meet with me right now?" she asked. "I'm on my way somewhere, but I could . . ."

"No, no," James broke in. "He's exhausted. But if you come here around nine tomorrow morning, he'd be delighted to talk to you." He dropped his voice, as if not wanting to be overheard. "Andrés is extraordinary, Elena," he said happily. "I can't wait for you two to meet."

Pulling her hair back into a tight, businesslike ponytail, Elena thanked James and got off the phone as quickly as she could. *Extraordinary*, she thought apprehensively. That could mean a lot of different things. The Celestial Guardians she had met had been extraordinary, and they had taken away her parents and Power, crippling her. Still, James clearly thought Andrés was good.

She tried to push her thoughts about the Earthly Guardian away as she jogged across campus to join the others. There was no point in worrying about him now; she'd meet him soon enough.

Stefan and the werewolves were waiting for her on the outskirts of the woods. Tristan and Spencer had already changed into their wolf forms and were restlessly sniffing the air, ears cocked for any sound of trouble. Shaggy-haired Jared, in human form, stood with Stefan, his hands stuffed into his pockets.

"There you are," Stefan said as Elena came up to them, and pulled her close to him in a brief embrace. "Ready?"

They set off into the woods, Tristan and Spencer pacing on each side of them, their heads and tails up, and their eyes alert. There had been too many attacks on and near the campus, and Elena knew the Pack felt that they were failing in their responsibility to keep the Dalcrest students safe. She and her friends felt the same way: they were the only ones who really knew what supernatural horrors were out there, and so were the only ones who could keep other people safe.

Bonnie, Meredith, Zander, and two more of his Packmates were patrolling the playing fields, trying to keep another section of the campus safe. Elena would have liked to have Matt's quiet, stubborn strength beside her, but he was still sequestered away with Chloe. Stefan had been checking on them daily, and said Chloe was making progress, but that she was still not ready to be near anyone else.

It was a clear, starry night, and everything seemed peaceful so far.

"Sorry I was late," Elena told Stefan, linking her arm through his. "James called just as I was leaving. He said Andrés is here. I'm going to meet him tomorrow."

Stefan opened his mouth to say something when the wolves stopped, their ears cocked, and stared into the distance. Stefan's head swung up, too. "Check it out," he told them, and Spencer and Tristan were gone, racing into the forest. Stefan and Jared stood still, alertly tracking their progress, until a howl came in the distance.

"False alarm," Jared translated, and Stefan relaxed. "An old scent."

The two wolves came trotting back through the woods, their tails arched high over their backs. Despite being very different as humans, Tristan and Spencer made similar wolves, sleek and gray and not as large as Zander was in wolf form. Only the black tips of Spencer's ears made it possible to tell them apart.

Watching them come back, Jared hunched his shoulders and shoved his long bangs out of his eyes. "I need to learn to change without the moon," he said irritably. "I feel blind trying to scout as a human."

"How does that work, anyway?" Elena asked curiously. "Why can some of you change without the moon, but not all of you?"

"Practice," Jared said glumly, letting his hair flop back over his face. "It's hard, and it takes a long time to learn, and I haven't managed to do it yet. We can learn how to stop ourselves from changing when the moon's full, too, but that's even harder, and they say it hurts. Nobody does that unless it's really necessary."

Spencer sniffed the breeze again and gave a short bark. Jared laughed, not bothering to translate. Stefan turned to follow their gaze, and Elena wondered what Stefan and the wolves—even Jared—could sense in the night that she couldn't. She was the only true human here, she realized, and so the blindest of them all.

"Do you want me to come with you?" Stefan asked as they started walking again. "To meet Andrés?"

Elena shook her head. "Thanks, but I think I should do this by myself." If she was going to become something new, she had to be strong enough to face it alone.

They patrolled the woods throughout the night without finding any vampires or any bodies. As dawn began to break over the horizon, Elena could see the two wolves plodding along next to her in the dim light, their heads hanging low. She was so sleepy, she held on to Stefan's arm for support and just focused on moving one foot in front of the other. Then Spencer's and Tristan's heads snapped up and they began to run, lean muscles stretching under their gray fur.

"Did they smell vampires?" Elena asked Jared, alarmed, but he shook his head.

"It's just the others," he said, and then he was running, too, faster than Elena could go.

As she and Stefan came over the next small hill, Elena could see the edge of the woods and the campus stretching out ahead of her again. She'd been so tired that she hadn't realized they'd looped back around. Halfway down the hill, Spencer and Tristan were greeting the great white wolf that was Zander and another gray wolf, their tails wagging, as Jared hurried toward them. Bonnie, Meredith, and another human-form member of Zander's Pack watched.

Bonnie said something and waved them off. The werewolves, human and wolf, turned as one and ran back into the woods, Zander in the lead.

"What's that about?" Elena asked, as she and Stefan came up to Bonnie and Meredith.

"Oh, since patrol's over, they have to go change back and do Pack stuff," Bonnie said casually. "I told Zander we'd be fine. Did you find anything?"

Elena shook her head. "Everything was quiet."

"For us, too," Meredith said, swinging her stave jauntily as they turned and began to head back toward their dorm. "Maybe the new vampires have made it through the blood-craze of changing and they'll lay low for a while."

"I hope so," Stefan said. "Maybe we can find them before someone else dies."

Bonnie shivered. "I know it's stupid," she said, "but I almost wish Klaus would do whatever he's going to do. I'm on edge all the time. It's like he's watching me from the shadows."

Elena knew what Bonnie meant. Klaus was coming after them all. She knew it: she could still feel the ghostly sensation of his cold lips on hers like a promise. *We've defeated Klaus before*, she tried to tell herself. But a new conviction nagged at her. It was as if something inside her knew, beyond all arguing, that the life she'd lived was coming to an end.

"I'm sorry," she said impulsively to Bonnie. "Klaus wants to punish me, and so we're all in danger. This is my fault, and I don't even have any Power now to protect you all."

Bonnie stared at her. "If it weren't for you, Klaus would have destroyed us all long ago," she said dryly.

Stefan nodded. "No one thinks this is your fault," he said.

Elena blinked. "I guess you're right," she said uncertainly.

Bonnie rolled her eyes. "And we're not total wimps, in case you hadn't noticed," she said.

"If you want to be ready to fight Klaus, maybe you should start developing your Guardian Powers," Meredith told her.

Warm sunlight was beginning to spread over the campus, and Elena instinctively slowed and straightened, tipping her face back to the sun. Meredith was right, she realized. If she wanted to help keep her friends safe, to keep the campus safe, she needed to be stronger. She needed to be a Guardian.

After only a few hours of sleep, Elena staggered across the quad, clutching a cup of coffee. She was heading for James's house just off campus, and trying to remember the little she knew about Andrés. He was twenty years old, James had told her, and had been taken from his family by the Guardians when he was twelve.

What would that do to a person? Elena wondered. The Guardians she had met, the ones of the Celestial Court, had taken their duties seriously. Surely Andrés would be well versed in all the Powers and responsibilities of Guardianship, everything Elena herself didn't know, and would have been adequately cared for, at least physically.

But how would it affect a human child to be raised by creatures as cold and emotionless as the Guardians? Her skin crawled at the idea.

By the time she got to James's door, Elena was anticipating a cold-eyed, unemotional greeting from an Earthly Guardian who would teach her exactly as much as *he* thought Elena should know.

Well, he would have to learn that he couldn't push her around. The Celestial Court full of Guardians at the peak of their Power hadn't been able to make Elena obey them, and there was only one of Andrés. Elena rang James's doorbell with determination.

James's face was serious, but not apprehensive, when he opened the door. He looked wide-eyed and solemn, as if, Elena thought, he was witnessing something momentous he didn't fully understand.

"My dear, I'm glad you could come," he said, ushering her in with little beckoning waves of his hand and taking her empty coffee cup. "Andrés is in the backyard." He escorted her through his small, extremely neat house, and showed her out the back door.

The door closed behind her and, with a start of surprise, Elena realized James had sent her out alone.

The yard was lit in gold and green by sunlight filtering through the leaves of a large beech tree. On the grass beneath the tree sat a young, dark-haired man who raised his head to look at Elena. As she met his eyes, the nervousness drained out of her and she felt a great peace settle on her. Without even meaning to, she found herself smiling.

Andrés rose unhurriedly and came to her. "Hello, Elena," he said, and wrapped his arms around her.

At first, Elena tensed in surprise at the hug, but then a calming warmth seemed to flow through her, and she laughed. Andrés let go of her and laughed, too, a pure note of joy.

"I'm sorry," he said. His English was fluent, but he had a slight South American accent. "But I've never met another human Guardian before, and I just . . . felt like I knew you."

Elena nodded, hot tears pricking at her eyes. She could feel a connection between them, humming with energy and joy, and she realized with happy surprise that it wasn't just emotions sent to her by Andrés. They were coming from her as well, her own happiness rushing toward him. "It's like I'm seeing family for the first time in ages," she told him. They couldn't seem to stop smiling at each other.

Andrés took her hand and tugged her gently over to the tree, and they sat down beneath it together.

"I had a Guide, of course," he said. "My beloved Javier, who raised me. But he passed away last year"—Andrés suddenly looked ineffably sad, his brown eyes liquid—"and since then I have been alone." He brightened again. "But now you are here, and I can help you as Javier helped me."

"Javier was a Guardian?" Elena asked, surprised. Andrés had loved Javier, clearly, and *love* was not something she associated with the Guardians.

Andrés gave a mock shudder. "God forbid," he said. "The Guardians wish the world well, but they are cold, yes? Imagine one of them in charge of a growing child. No, Javier was a Guide. A good man, a wise man, but fully human. A priest, actually, and a teacher."

"Oh." Elena thought for a while, carefully plucking a blade of grass and pulling it to pieces, looking down at her hands. "I thought that the Guardians themselves raised the human children they took. I don't—my parents didn't want to let me go. I guess I would have had a Guide if I had gone with them when I was little."

Andrés nodded, his face solemn. "James has told me of your situation," he said. "I'm sorry about what happened to your parents, and I wish I could offer some kind of explanation. But since you don't have a Guide assigned to you, I hope I can help you with what I know."

"Yes," Elena said. "Thank you. I mean, I really do appreciate it. Do you—" She hesitated, ripping another blade of grass apart. There was something she had wondered. It wasn't something she could imagine asking a stranger, but that curious, happy connection between them made her relax enough to turn to Andrés. "Do you think it would have been better if my parents had let them take me? Are you *glad* the Guardians took you away from your family?"

Andrés leaned his head back against the tree and sighed. "No," he admitted. "I never stopped missing my parents. I wish they had tried to keep me with them. But they saw me as a child who belonged to the Guardians, not to them. They're lost to me now." He turned to look at her. "But I did come to love Javier, and I was glad to have someone with me when I went through the transformation."

"Transformation?" Elena asked, sitting up straight and hearing her own voice go high and panicky. "What do you mean, *transformation?*"

Andrés smiled at her reassuringly, and despite herself, Elena instinctively relaxed a bit at the warmth in his eyes.

"It will be all right," he said quietly, and part of Elena believed him. Andrés sat up, too, wrapping his arms around his knees. "It's nothing to be afraid of. When your first task as a Guardian comes up, a Principal Guardian will come and explain to you what you must do. Your Powers will start developing when you have a task. Until you've finished your task, you won't be able to think of anything else. You'll feel this overwhelming *need* to complete it. The Principal Guardian returns when the task is done and releases you from your compulsion." He shrugged, looking self-conscious. "I've only had a few tasks, but when they ended, I couldn't wait for the next one. And the Powers I've developed for a task, I've kept over time."

"Is that the transformation you're talking about?" Elena said dubiously. "Developing Powers?" She wanted the Power to defeat Klaus, but she didn't like the idea of changing, of something *making* her change.

Andrés smiled. "Working as a Guardian makes you stronger," he told her. "It makes you wiser and more powerful. You'll still be you, though," he said.

Elena swallowed. This was the crux of her plan. With Klaus out there, *Powers* would be more than useful, but she needed to access them now rather than waiting around until a Principal Guardian decided to appear.

"Is there any way to wake up these Powers before I have a task?" she asked. Andrés was opening his mouth to ask her why, a puzzled frown forming on his face, and she pushed forward with her explanation. "There's a monster here," she said. "A very old, very cruel vampire, and he wants to kill me and my friends. And probably a lot of other people. The more we have to fight him with, the better."

Andrés nodded, his expressive face earnest. "My Powers aren't very warlike, but they may be useful, and I will help you however I can. No two Guardians have the same Powers. There's got to be some way to find yours, though, and to turn them on."

A glow of excitement shone through Elena. If she could access the Powers the Guardians gave her by herself, she wouldn't be their tool; she'd be a weapon. Her own weapon. "Maybe you could tell me about the first time you accessed yours?" she prompted.

"Okay." Andrés sat up straighter and let his knees fall so that he was sitting cross-legged on the grass. "The first thing you have to understand," he said, "is that Costa Rica is very different from here." He waved an arm around, indicating the little yard and house, the rows of houses beside and behind them, the sunshiny but chilly autumn skies. "Costa Rica has a great deal of unspoiled land, land that is protected by our country's laws for the animals and plants. The people of Costa Rica have a phrase we use a lot: *pura vida*—it means *pure life*, and when we say that—at least when I say it—we're talking about our connection to the natural world."

"I'm sure it's beautiful there," Elena said.

Andrés chuckled. "Of course it is," he said. "And you're wondering why I'm talking about ecology when I should be talking about Power. Watch."

Closing his eyes, he seemed to gather his strength, then placed both his hands flat, palms down, against the ground.

A gentle rustling noise began, so quiet at first that Elena barely noticed it, but soon grew louder. She glanced up at Andrés's face, which was closed off and intent, still listening to something she couldn't hear.

As she watched, the grass where his hands rested grew longer, the blades poking up between his fingers and rising higher to frame his hands. Andrés's mouth opened a tiny bit and he breathed harder. From above them came a creaking and Elena looked up to find new leaves unfurling from the beech tree's branches, their fresh spring green strange among the yellow-tinted autumn leaves already there. There was a soft thump behind her, and Elena turned to realize that a small pebble had rolled closer to them. Looking around, she saw a ring of pebbles and small stones, all gently sliding toward them.

Andrés's hair rose lightly, individual strands crackling with energy. He looked powerful and benevolent.

"So," he said, opening his eyes. Some of the intensity in his posture faded. The sounds of the quickly growing plants and the movement of the pebbles stopped. There was still a sense of expectant energy in the air around them. "I can tap into the power of the natural world and channel it to defend against the supernatural. If I need to, I can make boulders fling themselves through the air, or tree roots drag my enemies down to the ground. My strength feeds nature, and nature increases my strength. It's more effective in Costa Rica, because there are so many more uncultivated places and therefore so much more wild energy than there is here."

"It looks like your talents are pretty strong even here," Elena said, picking up a smooth, white pebble from the ground and turning it over curiously in her fingers.

Andrés grinned and ducked his head modestly. "Anyway," he said, "my first task came to me when I was seventeen. Javier had been teaching me for about five years, and I was dying to prove myself. A creature was killing young married women in the town where we lived, and a Principal Guardian—who was quite terrifying in her way, very powerful and focused—came to me and told me my job was to track and kill it."

"How did you find it?" Elena asked.

Andrés shrugged. "The beast was easy to find. Once I had my assignment, something in me drew me toward it. It turned out to be a demon in the shape of a black dog. A pure demon, not a half creature like a vampire or a werewolf. It was attracted by guilt, especially the guilt of adultery. Javier had taught me the principles of accessing my Power, but the first time I actually did it, I felt like I was sucking the whole world into myself. I was able to call a wind and *blast* the black dog away." He smiled again shyly at Elena.

"Maybe if I try to tap into nature the same way, it'll help unlock whatever my Powers are," Elena said.

Andrés knelt directly in front of Elena. "Close your eyes," he said, and Elena did as she was told. "Now," Andrés continued, and Elena felt him gently touch her cheek, "take deep breaths and concentrate on your connection to the earth here. Your talents won't be the same as mine, but they'll be rooted in this land, the place where you began, just as mine are."

Elena breathed deeply and slowly, concentrating on the ground beneath her, the warmth of the sunlight on her shoulders and the tickle of the grass against her legs. It felt comfortable, but she didn't sense any mystical connection between herself and the world around her. She gritted her teeth and tried harder.

"Stop," Andrés said soothingly. "You're too tense." His hand left her cheek and she felt him sit beside her, his thigh touching hers, and take her hand. "Let's try it this way. I'll channel some of my connection with the earth into you. At the same time, I want you to visualize sinking deeper into yourself. All the doors that are usually shut inside you will open and let your Power flow through."

Elena wasn't quite sure how to "visualize sinking deeper into herself," but she took another slow breath and tried to imagine it, consciously making herself relax. She pictured herself walking along a passageway of closed doors, the doors flying open as she passed them. Her hand felt pleasantly warm and tingled slightly where it touched Andrés's hand.

But when she had possessed the Power of Wings, before the Guardians had taken them, she had felt a lot more than this, hadn't she? There had been the feeling of amazing potential inside her, of these tightly furled, powerful *things* that were part of her, and that she could release when the time was right.

She wasn't feeling anything special now. The doors flying open were only in her imagination, nothing more. Elena opened her eyes. "I don't think this is working," she told Andrés.

"No, I don't think so either," he said regretfully, opening his eyes to look at her. "I am sorry."

"It's not your fault," Elena said. "I know you're trying to help me."

"Yes." Andrés tightened his hold on her hand and looked at her thoughtfully. "I don't think that relaxation and visualization are really your strengths," he said. "Let's try something else. Instead, we will work with your protective instincts."

This sounded more likely.

"Close your eyes again," Andrés went on, and Elena

obeyed. "I want you to think about evil," he said. "Think about the evil you have seen in your adventures, the evil that you—that both of us—must fight."

Elena opened her mind to her memories. She remembered Katherine's pretty, half-mad face twisting as she screamed with rage and tore at Damon's bleeding chest. The dogs of Fell's Church, vacant-eyed and snarling, turning on their owners. Tyler Smallwood's teeth lengthening into fangs and the glee in his eyes as he tried to attack Bonnie. Klaus gathering the lightning in his hands and throwing it at her friends, his face alight with vicious glee.

Images spun through her mind faster and faster. The *kitsune*, Misao and Shinichi, cruel and careless, laughing as they turned the children of Fell's Church into savage killers. The phantom that set Stefan and Damon tearing at each other's throats, mad with jealous fury, their mouths full of blood. Ethan, foolish Ethan, raising the cup of blood above his head, calling Klaus back to life.

Golden, terrifying Klaus stepping out of the fire.

And then different faces, other scenes, flooded her mind. Bonnie giggling in her ice-cream-cone pajamas. Meredith, her slim body graceful in a perfect swan dive. Matt holding her in his arms at their junior prom. Stefan, his eyes soft, taking Elena in his arms.

Elena's lab partner. The girls in her dorm. Strange faces

from the cafeteria, others she'd glimpsed only in class. All the people Elena needed to protect, her friends and innocent strangers.

Meredith's vampire-hunter friend Samantha, fierce and funny, until the Vitale vampires had killed her. Matt's sweet roommate Christopher, murdered on the campus quad.

The girl Damon had left in the woods, dazed and frightened, blood streaming from the bites on her neck.

Inside herself, Elena felt something unfurl, not swinging open like a door or spreading like Powerful wings, but gently blossoming, like a flower.

She opened her eyes slowly, and saw Andrés close beside her. A glow of pure green light surrounded him, and Elena's chest tightened. The light was so beautiful, and without knowing exactly how she knew it, she knew the light was *good* in the simplest, most definite sense.

"It's beautiful," she said, awed. Andrés opened his eyes and smiled back at her.

"Something?" he said, an undercurrent of excitement running through his voice.

Elena nodded. "I can see light around you," she said.

Andrés almost bounced with happiness. "This is wonderful," he told her. "I've heard of this. You must be seeing my aura."

"Aura?" Elena said skeptically. "Is that really going

to help us fight evil?" It seemed like a flaky, New Agey power.

Andrés grinned. "It will help you sense if someone is good or evil right from the start," he said. "And with practice, I've heard you can use it to track and seek out your enemies."

"I guess I can see how that might be useful," she agreed. "Not as useful as blasting away evil things with my hands like you can, but it's a start."

Andrés stared at her for a moment and then began to laugh. "Maybe you'll get to the blasting part soon," he said.

Unable to stop herself, Elena laughed, too, and leaned against him helplessly, giggling. She was so relieved, so simply, fiercely *glad*. She had found a Power without having to wait for a Principle Guardian to give her a task. And now that she had accessed one, she thought that she could feel more Power curled up inside her, more flowers waiting to open.

This was just the beginning.

By the central gates to the campus, Meredith paced, her sneakers making tracks in the dust at the edge of the road. In the past, she'd always been able to school herself into calm, but since she'd moved from training as a vampire hunter to actually using her skills to fight vampires, she'd gotten more and more restless. She always wanted to be moving, wanted to be doing something—especially now when she knew monsters haunted the campus. She knew that with Samantha gone—a part of her still choked at the memory—she was one of the only protectors left. Her skin was tingling and tight with the sense of something evil, something *wrong*, just out of sight.

She couldn't wait to see Alaric.

As if that thought had conjured him up, there was Alaric's little gray Honda turning down the road toward campus at last. Meredith waved to him as he parked, and started to run toward the car, aware that she was grinning like an idiot but not caring.

"Hey," she said, coming up to him as Alaric stretched and got out of the car, and then she kissed him hard. She knew they needed to strategize and plan—that with luck, Alaric had found something in his research that could help them fight Klaus. But for now, she just treasured the feeling of Alaric solid and real in her arms, his lips soft on hers, the smell of him that was made up of leather and soap and something sort of herbal and just essential *Alaric*.

"I've missed you," he said, resting his forehead against hers for a moment after they finally broke the kiss. "Talking on the phone isn't the same."

"Me too," Meredith said, and she had, so much. "I love your freckles," she told him inconsequentially, and brushed her lips across the golden spots on his cheek.

They headed into the campus, holding hands as they walked. Meredith pointed out sites of interest: the library, the cafeteria, the student center, her dorm. The few people they passed hurried by in groups, heads down, not making eye contact.

When they came to the gym, Meredith hesitated before stopping in front of it. "This is where I train. It's hard . . . I used to come here with Samantha," she told Alaric. "She was so competitive and smart. She pushed me, in a really good way." She leaned against Alaric for a moment, and felt him drop a kiss on the top of her head.

They walked on, but Meredith couldn't stop thinking about Samantha. Before Samantha, Meredith had never met anyone else from a family of hereditary vampire hunters. Her parents had left the hunter community behind. Because Samantha's parents had been killed when she was young, she hadn't really known any other hunters either.

They had taught each other so much. Meredith loved Elena and Bonnie—they were her best friends, her sisters—but no friend had ever understood as much about Meredith as Samantha had.

And then Ethan and the Vitale vampires had killed her. Meredith had been the one to find Samantha's body. She had been ripped apart so violently that her room had been soaked in blood.

Meredith felt her face twist, and her voice came out

thick and fierce. "Sometimes I feel like it's never going to stop," she told Alaric. "There's always more monsters. And now Klaus is back, even though we killed him. He should be *gone*."

"I know," Alaric said. "I wish I could make things better. Klaus destroyed your family, and you defeated him. You're right, this should have ended then." They paused by a bench underneath a clump of trees, and he sat, pulling Meredith down beside him. Taking her hand, he looked into her eyes, his face filled with love and concern. "Tell me the truth, Meredith," he said. "Klaus destroyed your family. How are you feeling?"

Meredith caught her breath, because that fact was exactly what she had been avoiding ever since Klaus stepped out of the fire.

Klaus had attacked Meredith's grandfather and driven him into madness. He had kidnapped her twin brother, Cristian, and made him into a vampire. And he had made Meredith herself into a living half vampire, something every hunting family had a right to loathe.

And then the Guardians had changed everything, making a reality out of what would have happened if Klaus had never come to Fell's Church. Cristian was a human now— Meredith didn't remember ever meeting him, but he had grown up with her in this reality—and in army boot camp in Georgia. Their grandfather was happy and sane, living in a retirement village down in Florida. And Meredith didn't need blood, didn't have sharp kitten teeth. But she and her friends still remembered the way things used to be. No one else in her family remembered, but she did.

"I'm terrified," Meredith confessed. She twisted her hand around, playing with Alaric's fingers. "There's nothing Klaus wouldn't do, and knowing that he's out there somewhere, waiting, planning something, is . . . I don't know what to do with that."

She clenched her jaw and looked up, meeting Alaric's eyes. "He has to die," she said softly. "He can't start over, not now."

Alaric nodded. "Okay," he said, shifting from sympathetic to businesslike. "I have some good news, I think." He unzipped the black messenger bag he'd been carrying over his shoulder and pulled out his notebook, flipping over a few pages until he found the information he wanted. "We know that white ash wood is the only wood deadly to Klaus, right?" he asked.

"That's what they say," Meredith told him. "Last time, we made Stefan a weapon of white ash, but it didn't turn out to be that useful." She remembered Klaus tearing the white ash spear out of Stefan's hand, breaking it, and using it to stab at Stefan himself. Stefan's screams as a thousand deadly splinters had torn into him had been . . . unforgettable. He had almost died.

Damon had wounded Klaus with the spear of white ash after that, but in the end, Klaus had managed to pull the bloody wood out of his own back and had stood triumphant, still powerful, still able to bring Stefan and Damon to their knees.

And this time, we don't even have Damon, Meredith thought bleakly. She'd given up on asking Elena and Stefan where Damon was. He'd always been unpredictable.

"Well," said Alaric with a little smile, "there's an Appalachian folk legend I found in my research that says a white ash tree planted at the full moon under certain conditions is more powerful against vampires than any other wood. A white ash with that kind of magic in its origins ought to pack a real punch against Klaus."

"Sure, but how are we going to find something like that?" Meredith asked, and then she cocked an eyebrow. "Oh. You already know where one is, don't you?"

Alaric's smile grew wider. After a second, Meredith wrapped her arms around his neck and kissed him. "You're my hero," she said.

Alaric blushed, the pink rising from his neck to his forehead, but he looked pleased. "*You're* the hero," he said. "But with luck, we'll have a real weapon against Klaus."

"Road trip," Meredith said. "But not until we've made sure the campus is as safe as we can get it. Klaus is lying low and we don't have any leads on where he is, so we have to focus on the newly made vampires for now." She smiled ruefully at Alaric, scuffing her sneakers below the bench. "It's important to face the immediate threat first. But this is good."

Alaric pressed her hand between both of his. "Whatever you need, I'll help," he said earnestly. "I'll stay here as long as I'm useful. As long as you want me."

Despite the seriousness of their problems, despite the gory mess that was her past and the almost definite horror of her future, Meredith had to laugh. "As long as I want you?" she said, flirting, glancing up at him through her lashes, basking in Alaric's smile. "Oh, you're never getting away from me now."

12

Chloe stalked silently through the forest, every move precise. She tilted her head alertly, her eyes tracking some near-invisible movement in the undergrowth.

Matt followed her, messenger bag slung over his shoulder. He was trying to walk quietly, too, but sticks and leaves crackled under his feet, and he winced.

Stopping, Chloe blinked for a moment, sniffed the air, and then stretched her hands out toward the bushes to their left. "Come on," she murmured, almost too low for Matt to hear.

There was a rustling, and slowly a rabbit nosed its way out from between the leaves, staring up at Chloe with wide, dark eyes, its ears quivering. With a quick swoop, Chloe snatched it up. There was a shrill squeak, and then the little animal was still and docile in her arms.

Chloe's face was buried in the rabbit's light brown fur, and Matt watched with a sort of detached approval as she swallowed. A drop of blood made a long, sticky track down the animal's side before dripping to the forest floor.

Waking from its doze, the rabbit spasmed once, kicking out with its hind legs, and then lay still. Chloe wiped her mouth with the back of her hand and laid the rabbit onto the ground, looking down at it mournfully.

"I didn't mean to kill it," she said, her voice low and sad. She pushed back her short ringlets of hair and looked up at Matt beseechingly. "I'm sorry. I know how gross and weird this is."

Matt opened his messenger bag and pulled out a bottle of water to hand to her. "You don't have to apologize," he said. Yeah, watching her feed on animals was sort of weird and gross, but less so now than the first time he'd seen it. And it was a hundred percent worth it: Chloe hadn't relapsed at all, seemed content with drinking animal blood instead of hunting humans. That was all that mattered.

Chloe rinsed out her mouth, spitting pink-tinged water into the bushes, then took a drink. "Thanks," she said shakily. "It's been hard, I guess. Sometimes I dream about blood. Real human blood. But the things I did, in those days with Ethan, I can't really forgive myself for. I don't think I'll ever be able to. And Ethan—why did I ever trust him?" Her Cupid's-bow mouth trembled.

"Hey." Matt caught her arm and shook it lightly. "Ethan had us all fooled. If Stefan hadn't saved me, I'd be in the same situation you are."

"Yeah." Chloe leaned against him. "I guess you're saving me, too."

Matt tangled his fingers with hers. "I wasn't ready to lose you."

Chloe tipped her face up to his, her eyes widening. Matt brushed his mouth against her cheek and then her mouth, just a light brush of lips at first, and then more deeply. Matt closed his eyes, feeling the softness of her lips against his. He felt like he was falling. Each day he spent with Chloe, helping her turn toward the light, seeing her strength, he loved her just a little more.

Meredith stretched and groaned quietly to herself. The room was dark, except for the light of her laptop screen. Elena and Bonnie were fast asleep in their beds, and Meredith glanced longingly at her own bed. Nights of patrolling and days spent at the gym meant that she had been collapsing gratefully into deep dreamless sleep as soon as she lay down lately.

But unlike many of the classes on campus, her English section was still meeting, and Meredith had a paper due. She'd been a straight-A student in high school, and her

000512386
8497
Transited:
July 18,
2018 8:11
PM

pride wouldn't let her miss the deadline on a paper or do a shoddy job, no matter how tired she was. Forcing herself back into student mode, Meredith yawned and typed: *From their first encounter Anna and Vronsky's relationship is clearly doomed to end in mutual destruction.*

Student mode or not, she was still a hunter, still an exquisitely balanced weapon, still a Sulez, and she snapped to attention as soon as Bonnie's voice rose from her bed on the other side of the room.

"He doesn't like to be alone," Bonnie said abruptly. Her usually expressive voice had that flat, almost metallic quality that signaled one of her visions.

"Bonnie?" Meredith said tentatively. Bonnie didn't answer, and Meredith turned on her desk light to illuminate the rest of the room, careful not to shine it directly in Bonnie's face.

Bonnie's eyes were shut, although Meredith could see them moving beneath their lids as if she were trying to wake, or trying to see something in her dreams. Her face was strained, and Meredith made a soothing sound in her throat as she crept across the room and shook Elena gently by the shoulder.

Elena gave a half-asleep *mmph* rolling over, and muttered, "What? *What?*" in irritation before she blinked all the way awake.

"Shh," Meredith told her, and said gently to Bonnie,

"Who doesn't like to be alone, Bon?"

"Klaus," Bonnie answered in that same deadened voice, and Elena's eyes widened in comprehension. Elena sat up, her golden hair tousled with sleep, and reached for a notebook and pen on her desk. Meredith sat down on Bonnie's bed and waited, staring at the smaller girl's sleeping face beside her.

"Klaus wants his old friends," Bonnie told them. "He's calling for one now." Still sleeping, she raised one thin, white arm out above her and crooked her finger, beckoning into the darkness. "There's so much blood," she added in that flat voice, as her hand flopped back down by her side. The skin on Meredith's arms pebbled into goose bumps.

Elena scribbled something in her notebook and held it up: in big letters she'd written *ASK HER WHO*. They'd found in the past that it was better for just one person to question Bonnie when she was seeing visions, to keep her from getting confused and snapping out of her trance.

"Who is Klaus calling for?" Meredith asked, keeping her voice calm. Her heart was pounding hard at the idea, and she pressed one hand against her chest as if to calm it. Anyone Klaus considered a friend was definitely dangerous.

Bonnie's mouth opened to answer, but she hesitated. "He calls them to join his fight," she said after a moment, her voice hollow. "The fire's so bright, there's no way to tell who's coming. It's just Klaus. Klaus and blood and flames in the darkness."

"What is Klaus planning?" Meredith asked. Bonnie didn't answer, but her eyelids fluttered, her lashes looking thick and dark against the paleness of her cheeks. She was breathing more heavily now.

"Should we try to wake her up?" Meredith wondered. Elena shook her head and wrote on the pad again. *ASK HER WHERE KLAUS IS.*

"Can you tell where Klaus is right now?" Meredith asked.

Restlessly, Bonnie moved her head back and forth against the pillow. "Fire," she said. "Darkness and flames. Blood and *fire*. He wants them all to join his fight." A thick chuckle forced its way out of her mouth, although her expression did not change. "If Klaus has his way, every-thing will end in blood and fire."

"Can we stop him?" Meredith asked. Bonnie said noth-ing, but grew more restless. Her hands and feet started to drum against the mattress, lightly and then more heavily, a rapid patter. "Bonnie!" Meredith said, and leaped to her feet.

With a great gasp, Bonnie's body stilled. Her eyes flew open.

Meredith grabbed the smaller girl's shoulders. A second

later, Elena was beside them on the bed, reaching out and taking hold of Bonnie's arm.

Bonnie's brown eyes were wide and blank for a moment, and then she frowned and Meredith could see the real Bonnie flooding back in.

"Ow!" Bonnie complained. "What are you doing? It's the middle of the night!" She pulled away from them. "Cut it out," she said indignantly, rubbing at her arm where Elena had grabbed her.

"You had a vision," Elena said, shifting back to give her some room. "Can you remember anything?"

"Ugh." Bonnie made a face. "I should have known. My mouth always tastes funny when I come out of one of those. I *hate* that." She looked at Elena and Meredith. "I don't remember anything. What'd I say?" she asked tentatively. "Was it bad?"

"Oh, blood and fire and darkness," Meredith said dryly. "The usual sort of thing."

"I wrote it down," Elena said, and handed Bonnie her notebook.

Bonnie read Elena's notes and paled. "Klaus is calling someone to come to him?" she asked. "Oh, no. More monsters. We can't—there's no way this is good for us."

"Any guesses about who he might be calling?" Elena wondered.

Meredith sighed and stood, beginning to pace between

the beds. "We don't really know that much about him," she said.

"Thousands of years of being a monster," Elena added. "I imagine Klaus has a lot of evil in his past."

Despite her quick strides across the room, a cold shiver ran down Meredith's back. One thing was certain: anyone Klaus wanted to join him would be the last person they would want here. Decisively, she clicked her laptop closed and went to her closet to pull out the weapons trunk. There was no time to be a student now. She had to prepare for war.

13

"I think I can see better in the dark now," Elena told Stefan as she pushed back a tree branch and held it so that he could pass.

The night seemed alive with sounds and motion, from the rustle of leaves to the scurry of some sort of tiny rodent in the undergrowth. It felt so different from the last time she and Stefan had patrolled the woods together. Elena didn't know if this new awareness was directly linked to the Power she could feel spreading steadily inside her, or if knowing she had the Power just made her more alert to everything else.

Stefan smiled, but didn't answer. She could tell that he was focused on sending out his own Power, looking for vampires in the woods.

When she concentrated, she could see that Stefan's

aura was a beautiful clear blue, shot with tendrils of soft gray that she thought might be the doubts and guilt that never fully left him. But the living blue was so much stronger than the gray. She wished that Stefan could see his aura for himself.

She reached out and touched it, her hand hovering right above his skin. The blue enveloped her hand, but she couldn't feel anything. She wiggled her fingers, watching Stefan's aura flow around them.

"What're you doing?" Stefan said, turning his hand to thread his fingers between hers. He still looked out at the darkness around them.

"Your aura—" Elena said, and then stopped.

Something was coming.

Stefan made a soft questioning noise and when Elena drew a breath to speak again, something dark and clammy swept over her, chilling her as thoroughly as if she'd been swept beneath an icy river.

Evil. She was sure of it.

"This way," she said urgently, and pulling Stefan by the hand, started to run through the forest. Branches slapped at her as she pushed past them, one leaving a long stinging scratch on her cheek. Elena ignored it. She could feel something tugging at her, its urgency claiming all her attention.

Evil. She needed to stop it.

Her feet slipped and skidded on the dead leaves under-foot, and Stefan caught her by the arm before she could fall, pulling her upright. She stood still for a moment, gasping to catch her breath.

Ahead, she could see streaks of a dirty rust-red cut with sickly bile-yellow. Nothing like the soothing colors of Stefan's or Andrés's auras, not at all. As Elena watched, the rust-red—the color of dried, old blood—contracted and expanded around the bilious yellow in a steady pulse. Two auras, she realized—one dominating the other. Elena's sense of urgency grew.

"I can see it," she said desperately. "Something bad is happening. Come on."

They ran on. Elena could tell when Stefan's Power picked up on what she was sensing, because he suddenly sped up, pulling her on instead of following her.

A vampire was pressing his victim back against a tree; the two figures huddled together into one dark, hulking shape. The pulsating auras wrapped around them, almost nauseating to watch. Elena barely had a moment to realize she'd found what she'd been hunting when Stefan yanked the vampire off the human and snapped his neck with one efficient twist of his hands. Then he tore a branch from the tree and staked him through the chest.

The vampire's victim fell to his hands and knees with a muffled thump. His yellowish aura lost its sickly tint almost immediately, but dimmed to a thin gray as the guy slumped down into the heap of leaves beneath the tree.

Elena dropped to her knees beside him and dug out her flashlight to check him over as Stefan dragged the vampire's body—one of the Vitale pledges—away into the bushes. The victim had very short black hair and was pale, but his pulse was steady, and his breathing shallow but regular. Blood trickled from a bite on his neck, and Elena pulled off her jacket and used it to put pressure against the wound.

"I think he's okay," she told Stefan when he came back to stand beside her.

"Good work, Elena," he told her, and then inhaled deeply. "There's blood still flowing somewhere on him, though."

Elena ran the flashlight over the guy. He was wearing pajama pants and a T-shirt and his feet were bare. The soles of his feet were bleeding.

"The vampire must have compelled him out of his dorm," she realized. "That's how he ended up in the woods."

"They're getting more skilled," Stefan said. "We'll organize more patrols around campus. Maybe we can stop some of them before they catch their victims in the first place."

"For now, we'd better get this guy back home," Elena

said. The black-haired guy whimpered as Stefan and Elena gently pulled him up. The grayness of his aura began to fill with agitated strands of color, and Elena could tell he was starting to wake. "It's all right," she said soothingly, and felt a whisper of Stefan's Power as he began to murmur to him, calming him for the trip back to his dorm.

She couldn't focus on helping him, though. Her skin itched and she felt a tugging deep inside. There was still something out there. Evil, close by. Elena let Stefan take the full weight of the vampire's victim and stepped away, reaching out with her Power to try to sense in what direction the evil lay.

Nothing. Nothing specific, anyway—just that heavy, dreadful certainty that something was *wrong*, not too far away. She strained her senses, looking and feeling for a trace of some aura.

Nothing.

"Elena?" Stefan asked. He was supporting the vampire's victim easily and giving her a questioning look.

Elena shook her head. "There's something," she said slowly. "But I don't know where." She stared out into the darkness for a moment, but there was still no clue to tell her where the oppressive feeling was coming from. "We should call it a night," she said finally.

"Are you sure?" Stefan asked. At her nod, he hiked the guy higher on his shoulder and turned back toward campus. As Elena followed him, she took one last uneasy glance around. Whatever it was, it was shielding itself from her and from Stefan better than the young vampires could.

Something old, then. And evil. Was Klaus nearby? If he wanted to, he could kill them right now, Elena realized with a dizzying flare of panic. He was stronger than Elena and Stefan were. The woods around her looked darker, more ominous, as if Klaus might be lurking behind any tree. She walked faster, sticking close to Stefan, eager to see the lights of campus ahead.

Bonnie kept hold of Zander's hand as they followed Meredith around the edge of the soccer field. They hadn't seen any vampires tonight, but the stars were incredibly bright above them.

"I like patrolling with you," she told him. "It's almost like a romantic stroll, except for, you know, the possibility of being attacked by vampires."

Zander grinned down at her and swung their clasped hands. "Don't you worry yourself, little lady," he said in a terrible imitation of a western drawl. "I'm the toughest werewolf in this here town and I'm looking out for you."

"Is it weird that I find that voice sexy?" Bonnie asked Meredith.

Meredith, striding along ahead of them, looked back

to raise an expressive eyebrow at Bonnie. "Yes," she said simply. "Very weird."

A long, drawn-out howl echoed from the direction of the hills just outside of campus and Zander cocked his head, listening. "The guys haven't found anything," he said. "They're heading out to get some pizza once Camden changes back."

"Do you want to meet up with them?" Bonnie asked.

Zander pulled her closer, putting his arm around her shoulders. "Not unless you do," he said. "I thought maybe we could hang out in my room, watch a movie or something."

"Passing up food, Zander?" a dry voice said behind them. "It must be true love." Meredith whipped around, and Bonnie knew she was kicking herself for not sensing the girl coming up to them.

"Hi, Shay," Bonnie said resignedly. "Meredith, meet Zander's old friend Shay." *Werewolf*, she mouthed to Meredith when she was sure Shay wasn't looking.

"I hope you don't mind me catching up with you," Shay said, falling into step with them on Zander's other side. "Spencer told me you'd be patrolling over here."

"The more the merrier," Bonnie told her, very consciously *not* gritting her teeth.

"I'd love to get some fighting in," Shay said, rolling her shoulders. "Feels like I've been doing nothing but sitting around since I got here. Zander could tell you how restless we get when we're cooped up."

"Yeah, I've noticed," Bonnie said. Zander had sped up his pace to match Shay's quicker one, and his arm dropped from Bonnie's shoulders. She took his hand again, but found herself having to hurry to keep up.

Meredith hesitated, glancing between them, and was just opening her mouth to say something to Shay when Shay suddenly stopped.

"Hear that?" she said, and Zander, Meredith, and Bonnie all stopped and listened, too.

Bonnie didn't hear anything, but Zander smiled and nudged Shay with one elbow. "White-tailed deer on the ridge," he said.

They shared a private smile.

"What are you guys talking about?" Bonnie asked.

Shay turned to Bonnie. "The High Wolf Council divides us into Packs-to-be when we're children, and we grow up playing together. When Zander and I and the others were about fifteen, our Pack spent a week roaming the mountains near where we grew up." She grinned at Zander, and Bonnie tensed at the intimacy that was clear between them.

"Anyway," Shay went on, "on this trip, after we'd been out running with the Pack all night, Zander and I went to drink from a pond tucked away in the pinewoods. We found deer there, and we could have killed one of them easily—we were wolves right then, and it's natural for us to hunt in that form—but they just looked at us, the sun coming up behind them. And"—she shrugged—"they were beautiful. It was like that moment was just for us." She smiled, and for once, it didn't seem like she was trying to needle Bonnie. Shay was just remembering. She tipped her face into the breeze. "Smell that?" she asked Zander.

Bonnie didn't smell anything, but Zander sniffed the breeze and shot Shay another nostalgic smile. "Pine," he said. Shay grinned back, her nose crinkling.

After a moment, Meredith cleared her throat and they started walking again, scanning the area for trouble, and Zander squeezed Bonnie's hand. "So," he said. "Movie?"

"Sure," Bonnie said, distracted. She couldn't help seeing the similarities in Zander's and Shay's movements and how, even when Zander was talking to her, he had one ear cocked for faraway sounds Bonnie would never be able to hear. There was a distance between Bonnie and Zander, she thought, that they might never be able to cross.

Maybe Bonnie would never belong in Zander's world. Not like Shay.

14

Elena turned over restlessly in her bed, the sheet wrapping around her, and flipped her pillow over so that she could rest her cheek on the cooler side. Across the room, Meredith muttered something in her sleep and then quieted.

Elena was exhausted, but she couldn't sleep. It had taken so long to maneuver the guy the vampire had attacked from the woods back to his dorm, and longer still for Stefan to Influence him to forget what had happened. And they didn't know if Stefan's Power had entirely worked on the guy: Stefan's animal-blood diet kept his Power from being as strong as that of other vampires his age who fed on humans.

It wasn't that worry, though, keeping Elena awake now. She couldn't sleep because she couldn't shake the sense she'd had in the woods, of something dark and evil pulling at her, her Power trying to lead her somewhere.

If anything, that sense was stronger now. Something insistent tugged at the center of her, telling her *now* and *hurry*.

Elena sat up in bed. The Power inside her wanted her to go out after the *wrong* that was out there, wanted her to make things right. She had to—there was no question about it.

She glanced over at Meredith's and Bonnie's beds. Meredith lay on her back, one slim arm thrown across her eyes, while Bonnie was curled up tightly on one side, a hand tucked under her cheek, looking impossibly young.

They would want her to wake them, to take them with her.

She discarded the idea almost immediately. She thought of Stefan, a few floors above, probably reading or sitting on his balcony watching the stars, but she reluctantly pushed away the idea of calling to him, too. Whatever was out there, her Power was telling her it was just for her. She trusted her Power: Andrés had told her that her skills would unlock as she needed them. Her Power would keep her safe.

Elena slipped out of bed, careful to move so quietly that even Meredith wouldn't wake, and pulled on jeans and a sweater. Picking up her boots to put on in the hall, she tiptoed out the door.

It was very dark as she crossed the quad, the moon hovering low over the roofs of campus. Elena hurried, not sure if it was the chill in the air or the tingling feeling urging her on that was making her shiver.

That pull got stronger as she left campus and ventured into the woods. Even without switching on the flashlight in her pocket, Elena found herself as sure-footed as if it were broad daylight.

The sense of *wrongness* grew stronger and stronger. Elena's heart was pounding. Maybe she should have told someone what was going on, she thought. At least she could have left a note. Would Stefan be able to find her if she didn't come back? What if, alone in the forest, she met Klaus? Could her Power protect her then?

Suddenly, with a sharp shock, the pulling feeling in her chest became intense, suffocating, and just as suddenly, left her. Something moved in the darkness in front of her, and Elena switched on her flashlight.

Seated on a log in the middle of the forest, in the dark, was Damon. His eyes glittered beetle-black in the glow of the flashlight.

Damon. Seeing him was like a kick in the stomach, and Elena gasped. *Damon.* She'd spent more than a year wrapped up with him, focused on Damon and Stefan and herself and the twisted, complicated relationships between them all. Then, with no warning, he'd been gone.

And now, here he was.

He looked . . . well, he looked as touchable as always, all smooth skin and sleek hair, powerful, lean muscles. Like a wild animal she wanted to stroke while knowing it was too dangerous to touch. She'd made her choice between the brothers and she was purely, simply *glad* about it: Stefan was the one she wanted. But that didn't mean she was blind to Damon's beauty.

But, touchable or not, Damon's face looked as hard now as if it had been carved from white marble. He turned his unfathomable eyes toward her, raising a hand to block the flashlight's beam.

"Damon?" Elena asked uncertainly, lowering the flashlight. Usually, something in Damon seemed to soften when he saw her, but now he stiffened and stayed silent.

After a moment, she reached inside herself, pulled at that new Power she'd found, and tried to see Damon's aura.

Oh. This was really bad. There was a dark cloud around Damon. It wasn't simple evil, but there was evil in it, and pain, and something else—a sort of dull distance, as if he was numbing himself against some hurt. Black and gray and a curious dull blue swirled around him, tendrils shooting out unexpectedly and then pulling back in so close to his body she could barely see him. Damon wasn't moving a muscle as he stared at her, but his aura was agitated.

And winding through everything was a fine net of that

same dried-blood color that had permeated the aura of the vampire Stefan had killed earlier that night.

"Were you just feeding on someone?" she asked him abruptly. Would that explain the strength of the pull, the wrongness, she'd felt on the way here?

Damon smirked a little and cocked his head, studying her. When the pause had gone on long enough that Elena was sure he wasn't going to answer, he shrugged one shoulder indifferently and said, "It doesn't really matter, does it?"

"Damon, you can't just—" Elena began, but Damon cut her off.

"This is who I am, Elena," he said in the same flat, indifferent voice. "If you've thought differently, you were lying to yourself, because I never lied to you about it."

Elena sank down on the log beside him, resting the flashlight between them, and took Damon's hand. He stiffened, but didn't immediately pull away. "You know I care about you, right?" she asked him. "No matter what. I always will."

Damon stared at her, his dark eyes cold, and then deliberately began untangling his fingers from hers, his hands cool and firm as he pushed her away. "You've made your choice, Elena," he said. "I'm sure Stefan's waiting for you."

Elena shifted away from him, since that was what Damon seemed to want, and put her hands in her lap.

"Stefan cares about you," she told him. "I love Stefan, but I need you, too. We both do."

Damon's mouth twisted. "Well, you can't always get everything you want, can you, princess?" he said, a mocking bite to his words. "Like I told Stefan, I'm done."

She stared at him and pushed herself, trying to see his aura again. Using her new Power so much today was like straining muscles she'd never known she had. When she managed it once more, she flinched: Damon's aura had gotten darker as they talked, and was now a stormy gray shot with red and black, a sullen cloud thick around him. The blue had been swallowed by the darker colors.

"I can see your aura, Damon," she said. "I've got Power now." Damon frowned. "It's dark, but there's still good in you." Surely there must be. She didn't know if she could read it in his aura—she didn't know enough about auras yet; she needed to learn—but she *knew* Damon. He was complicated and selfish and mercurial, but there would always be good in him. "Please, come back to us."

Damon's face was still turned away from her, his eyes fixed on something out in the darkness that Elena couldn't see. Sliding to her knees next to the log, Elena put her hands on his cheeks and turned his face toward her. The ground was freezing and there was a stone digging into her leg, but it didn't matter. "Please, Damon," she said. "You're the one doing this. It doesn't have to be this way."

He glared back at her mutely. "Damon," she said, her eyes stinging. "Please."

Damon stood up abruptly, pushing her away, and Elena lost her balance, falling backward onto the hard ground. Scrambling up, she brushed herself off and grabbed the flashlight. "Fine," she said. "I'll go, if that's what you want. But listen to me." She made an effort to soften her voice again. "Don't do anything you'll regret, no matter how angry you are at me. When you're ready, we'll be waiting for you. We *love* you. Stefan and I both love you. And it may not be the way you want me to care about you, but it's worth something."

Damon's eyes glistened again in the flashlight's glow. She thought for a moment that he was going to speak, but he only stared at her, his face hard and defiant.

There wasn't anything left to say, really. "Good-bye, Damon," Elena said, and backed away a few paces before turning to find her way out of the forest.

There was a huge, hard mass of sobs building in her chest and she needed to get home before it overwhelmed her. If she started to cry now, she might never stop.

15

Dear Diary,

I can't stop worrying about Damon.

Meredith and Bonnie have gone to the mountains in pursuit of the blessed white ash tree, and our room is too quiet. When I'm alone in here, the empty space fills up with thoughts of how angry and distant Damon seemed when I found him in the woods last night. His aura was so dark that it frightened me.

I haven't told Stefan yet about my Power leading me to Damon. I'm going to tell him, though, as soon as we're alone—I've learned my lesson at last about letting secrets come between us.

But Stefan's been so busy. He's pulling us all together: sparring with Meredith, researching with Alaric, and now that Zander's gone to the mountains with them and Bonnie, Stefan's been working with the Pack, too. He's determined to protect me from Klaus, to protect us all.

Wherever Klaus is, his plan is working—I'm always on edge now. I know he wants me to be afraid; he even told me so—but I can't stop myself from jumping at every shadow. Every day I get more frightened, and angrier at myself: I don't want to feel the way Klaus intends me to. But when I'm with Stefan, we can slide into our private world. Despite the danger that hovers near us, it's safe there. In Stefan's arms, I feel like maybe we can defeat Klaus. Sometimes I believe we can do anything, together. We can save ourselves, and save Damon, too, even if he doesn't want to be saved.

A knock came at the door of Elena's room, and she slipped her journal back under her mattress and ran to let Stefan in. He'd been with the Pack most of the day, since Zander and the others had left, and how much she'd missed him sank in as soon as she finally saw him.

His curly dark hair was hanging over his forehead and he had a streak of dried mud over one eye. "What's this?" Elena asked, brushing a finger across it.

Stefan grimaced. "Apparently being accepted by a werewolf Pack means they try to knock you down a lot," he told her. "Shay pushed me into a bush."

Elena tried to keep a straight face, but she couldn't help giggling at the mental image, and Stefan's face lightened, too, the weary lines around his mouth disappearing.

"I think she's mad about Zander leaving town with Bonnie," Elena told him, and reached past him to close the door.

As soon as the door was shut, Stefan pulled her against him. He drew back Elena's hair and kissed her softly on the throat, just above her pulse point. She arched back, leaning into him as he wrapped his arms around her waist.

"Did you work the patrol routes out with the Pack in between wrestling matches?" she asked him. "Can we manage without the others until they get back?"

"Mmhm, I think so," Stefan answered, gently tracing her cheek with one finger, his eyes intent on her face. "I just wish that we had some idea where Klaus was," he went on, his voice growing somber. "He could be anywhere, ready to strike."

"I know." Elena shivered. "I feel like there's this black cloud hanging over us all the time. I just wish I could figure out all my Guardian Powers. If I'm going to have real Power, why won't they let me have it now? We're all in danger, and it's so *frustrating* knowing that I ought to be able to protect everyone, but I can't."

"What about the evil you sensed in the woods yester-day?" Stefan asked. "Have you felt it since?"

Elena hesitated. Now was her chance. She'd promised herself she would tell Stefan what had happened as soon as they had a moment alone. But she didn't want to hurt him, didn't want to tell him how angry and distant his brother seemed. "I felt it again last night," she said finally, "but I don't feel it now."

"You did?" Stefan asked. "Did you get more of an idea where it might be coming from?" When Elena still hesi-tated, he gently tipped her face up to look at him. "Elena, this is important. These feelings could be our first real clue as to where Klaus is. Is there something you're not telling me?"

Elena felt herself flinch, but Stefan just waited patiently, his mouth soft and serious. "What is it, love?" he asked.

"I followed it into the woods late last night," she told him, nervously fiddling with the bracelet on her arm. "I, um, I found the source." With the feeling of jumping off a cliff, she told him, "It wasn't Klaus, or the Vitale vampires. It was Damon."

"But you were sensing *evil*," Stefan said, sounding confused.

"Yeah." Elena sighed. "Maybe not entirely evil. Damon's not, I know that. But he's not doing well. I don't think that girl we found is the only one he's attacked. His aura was . . . violent. Angry."

Stefan's shoulders slumped, and he leaned against her desk. "I know," he said. "I told you what he was like when I tried to talk to him. I think we need to give him some space. You can't push Damon. He's just going to do exactly what he wants, especially if you try to control him."

"There must be something we can do," Elena said. Her voice sounded scratchy to her own ears, rough with misery.

Crossing the space between them in one step, Stefan took her hand and looked down at her, his eyes dark and troubled. "It's never going to be just us, is it?" he said sadly. "Damon will always be standing between us, even when he's not here."

"Stefan, no!" she said fiercely. Stefan cast his gaze down sadly at their entwined fingers. "Look at me!" she urged. He slowly raised his eyes to meet hers again. "I love you, Stefan. I care for Damon, he's part of me now, but that's nothing compared to what I feel for *you*. It's just us, you and me, and that's how it's going to be. Always."

Elena pulled him closer, desperate to show him this truth. Their lips met in a long kiss.

Stefan, she thought, *oh, Stefan*. Elena let herself open fully to him. Exposed and vulnerable, she showed Stefan the love she had for him, her joy at having come back to him at last. Wonderingly, Stefan gradually took in her emotions. She could feel him pushing gently at the walls she'd always kept in her mind, the little shameful secrets, the part of herself she'd always wanted to hide from him. But Elena pulled the barriers down, showing him that there was nothing there but love for him, only him.

Stefan sighed against her lips, a tiny exhalation of breath, and she felt peace flood through him as he understood that, at last, he was the only one for her.

As the couple inside clung to each other, a large crow clenched its claws tightly around a tree branch in the darkness outside the dorm room's window. It wasn't as if he had been holding out hope, though. He had tried his best with Elena, had given her what he thought she wanted, had shown her what he had to offer. He had changed himself for her.

And she had turned away from him and chosen Stefan. She still felt *nothing* for him, not compared to her feelings for Stefan.

Fine. Damon should have known better than to care. What he had told Stefan, what he had told Elena, was right: he was done with them, done with all of them. Why should he follow around one human girl when there was a wide world out there waiting for him?

Damon spread his wings and pitched himself off the tree branch and into the night. Riding the soft breezes over campus, he tried to think about where he should go next. Thailand, maybe. Singapore. Japan. He had never spent much time in Asia; perhaps it was time to conquer new places, to be the mysterious, cold-eyed stranger again, to feel the rushing sea of humanity surging all around him while he held himself separate and alone.

It will be good to be alone again, he told himself. Vampires weren't pack animals, after all.

As he pondered his future, he watched the paths of the campus and then the streets of the town beneath him in an absentminded, habitual way. A lone female jogger, young and blond, was running along below him, hair pulled into a ponytail, earbuds in place. *Idiot*, he thought scathingly. *Doesn't she know how dangerous this place is right now?*

Without letting himself consider what he intended, Damon glided down and resumed his human form, landing silently on the sidewalk a few yards behind the jogger. He stopped for a moment and fastidiously adjusted his clothing, long-ago words of his father's echoing in his mind: *a gentleman can be told by the care he takes of his appearance and by the precision of his dress.*

Then he moved quickly and gracefully after the girl, letting loose a little Power so that he was faster than any human could be.

He jerked her off her feet as easily as plucking a flower from its stem, and pulled her into his arms. She gave one sudden, aborted squeak and struggled briefly as he sank his sharp canines into her throat, then grew still. He had no reason to stop himself, not now.

It was so *good*. He'd been soothing his girls, making it painless for them for so long, and the pure adrenaline of her fear rocketed through his system. It was even better than the girl in the woods, who had already been dizzy and pliant with blood loss when he let the calming compulsion drop.

Damon drank down deep gulps of blood, feeding his Power. Her heart slowed, staggered, and he felt that dizzyingly sweet moment when her slackened pulse matched the unnatural pace of his own. Her life flowed into him steadily, warming his cold bones.

And then everything—her heartbeat, the blood flow—stopped.

Damon let her body drop to the sidewalk and wiped his mouth with one hand. He felt drunk on her, buzzing with the energy he'd taken into himself. *Here I am*, he thought with sour triumph, *the real Damon, back again.*

On the back of his hand was a smear of the girl's blood. He licked it off, but it tasted wrong, not as sweet as it should have. As the sheer physical pleasure of taking the blood, of taking it all the way to death, wore off, Damon could feel a sharp ache just below his breastbone. He pressed one hand to his chest.

There was an empty place inside him: a hole in his chest that all the blood, all the blood of the prettiest girls in the world, could never fill.

Unwillingly, he looked down at the body at his feet. He would have to hide it, he supposed. He couldn't leave her here, exposed on the sidewalk.

The girl's eyes were open in a flat, unseeing stare, and she seemed to be gazing back at him. She was so young, Damon thought.

"I'm sorry," he said, his voice small. He reached down and carefully pressed her eyes closed. She seemed more peaceful that way. "I am sorry," he said again. "It wasn't your fault."

There didn't seem to be anything else to say or do. With an effortless swoop, he picked up the girl's body and walked on, into the night.

16

"Okay," Alaric said, panting a little. "According to these directions, the white ash tree should be on the bank of a stream, only about half a mile farther from here."

"Is it all still uphill?" Bonnie moaned, pushing sweaty red ringlets out of her eyes. They'd spent the previous night in a dingy motel and started out on their trek early that morning. By now, it felt like they'd been on this narrow mountain trail *forever*. It had been fun at first; it was a beautiful sunny day and a bright blue jay had flown from tree to tree before them for a while, which seemed like a good omen. But after several hours she was hot and thirsty and they *still* had to keep going.

"Come on, Bonnie," Meredith said. "Not far now." Meredith was striding cheerfully along at the front of the group, looking as cool and comfortable as if she was taking a little stroll down one of the paths on campus. Bonnie scowled at her back: sometimes Meredith being in such good shape was utterly infuriating.

Defiantly, Bonnie stopped for a minute and drank some water from her canteen as the others waited for her.

"So, once we find this magic white ash tree, what's the plan?" Zander asked, shifting restlessly from one foot to the other as he waited.

Shay wouldn't have had to stop to rest, Bonnie thought sourly. Then Zander nudged her companionably with his elbow as he took out his own canteen, and she felt a little better.

"Well, we can't chop down the tree," Alaric said seriously. "It's got a lot of spiritual significance and gives protection to this area as well as being the only weapon that might be effective against Klaus. But it's a pretty big tree, reportedly, so we should be able to take several branches without doing too much damage."

"I brought an axe," Meredith said enthusiastically as they started walking again. "We'll make as many stakes as we can, and distribute them to everyone." She glanced at Zander. "Everyone who's not going to be a wolf when we fight Klaus, anyway."

"Hard to hold a stake with paws," Zander agreed.

"We should gather leaves, too," Bonnie said. "I've been

looking through spell books, and I think we could use the ash leaves to make potions and tinctures that might help us get some protection from Klaus. Like the effect vervain has on a regular vampire's Powers."

"Good thinking," Zander said, throwing an arm around her shoulders. Bonnie leaned against him, letting him take some of her weight. Her feet hurt.

"We're going to need all the help we can get," Meredith said, and she and Bonnie exchanged a glance. Of the four of them on this mountainside, they were the only ones who had fought Klaus the first time, and the only ones who knew how much trouble they were really in.

"I wish Damon were working with us," Bonnie said fretfully. "He'd give us much better odds in a fight." She had always felt a special bond with Damon, ever since the days when she'd had a crazy, embarrassing crush on him. When they had traveled through the Dark Dimension together, they had looked out for each other. And Damon had sacrificed himself for her, pushing her out of the way and taking the fatal blow from the tree on that Nether World moon. The locks of hair Bonnie and Elena had left with his body had helped to remind Damon who he was when he was resurrected. It ached that he had turned his back on her now.

Meredith frowned. "I've tried to talk to Elena about Damon, but she won't tell me what's going on with him.

And Stefan just says Damon needs time and that he'll come around."

"Damon would do *anything* for Elena, wouldn't he? If she just asked him," Bonnie said, biting her lip. Damon had been obsessed with Elena for so long; it was weird and disturbing to have Elena in danger and Damon nowhere to be found.

Meredith just shook her head. "I don't know," she said. "I've never understood him."

"Almost there," Alaric said encouragingly. "It should be right up ahead." Bonnie could hear the rushing of a stream.

Zander stopped. "Do you smell that?" he said, sniffing the air. "Something's burning."

Just around the next bend in the path, a long finger of black smoke spread across the sky. Bonnie and Meredith exchanged alarmed glances and broke into a jog, Bonnie forgetting all about her aching feet. Alaric and Zander sped up, too, and as they rounded the corner, they were all running.

Alaric stopped first, his face devastated. "That's it," he said. "That's the white ash tree."

It was engulfed in roaring flames and already charred black. As they watched, a branch fell heavily to the ground, shooting up sparks as it landed, and crumbled into soot. Alaric stripped off his shirt, soaking it with his water bottle as he ran forward, toward the flames.

Bonnie rushed after him. She had the impression of two figures ducking away down the path and Zander and Meredith running after them, but she couldn't focus on that now: she had to try to save the tree. As she got nearer, the heat was incredible, almost like a wall forcing her away. Gritting her teeth, she stamped at the small flames springing up in the grass around the burning tree. Smoke stung her eyes and seeped into her mouth, so that she coughed and wheezed.

Her arm burned painfully and she brushed away the hot ash that had fallen on her. Closer to the trunk, Alaric beat at the flames with his wet shirt and then stumbled backward, choking, his face streaked black. They weren't having any effect on the fire at all.

Bonnie grabbed his arm and pulled him farther back, her heart dropping. "It's too late," she said.

When she turned around, she saw Zander and Meredith shepherding two people back up the path toward them. Zander had a firm grip on a beefy dark-haired guy as Meredith held her stave across the throat of a girl. She looked familiar, Bonnie thought dazedly. After a moment, the sense of familiarity sharpened into certainty, and then Bonnie was flooded with outrage.

The tall girl with the long auburn hair had once been as close to her as Meredith and Elena were: Caroline. They'd celebrated each other's birthdays, gotten dressed for high school dances together, spent the night at each other's houses.

But then Caroline had changed. She'd betrayed them all, and the last time Bonnie had seen her, Caroline had been pregnant with werewolf twins and infected by the kitsune demons, vicious and insane.

Bonnie started forward, a hot ball of anger in her stomach. How *dare* Caroline turn up now, after all that had happened, and *still* be working against them?

Then the beefy guy yanked away from Zander, who wrenched him back onto the path. Bonnie saw his face for the first time. She stopped, the hot anger turning to ice. She could remember those thick features twisting grotesquely into a snarling, feral snout. He'd been a killer. He'd leered at her, called her names, and wanted to *eat* her.

Tyler Smallwood. The werewolf who had killed Sue Carson and run away from Fell's Church, leaving Caroline pregnant. The werewolf who had helped Klaus.

"Stop! Meredith, stop," Caroline begged. Meredith could see one side of Caroline's face from where she held her, and tears were running down it, cutting clean tracks through the soot from the fire.

What was left of the trunk of the tree crashed to the ground, sending up more sparks and thick black smoke, and Meredith felt Caroline start at the sound. Slowly,

Meredith released her grip on Caroline, pulling the stave away from her throat so she could look Caroline in the eye. Caroline took a deep, sobbing breath and turned to face Meredith fully. Her cat-shaped green eyes were wide with terror.

Meredith glared at her. "How could you help him, Caroline?" she asked fiercely. "Don't you remember how Klaus kidnapped you?"

Caroline shook her head. "You're crazy," she said, and Meredith was amazed that bedraggled, tearful Caroline could still sound so disdainful. "I'm not helping anyone."

"So you just decided to burn down a tree today?" Meredith asked, her voice dripping with sarcasm.

"I . . . guess," Caroline said, frowning. She crossed her arms defensively across her chest. "I think it was an accident."

There was something wrong here, Meredith realized. Caroline didn't look guilty or defiant. Freaked out, absolutely, but it seemed like she was being honest. Meredith sighed. It would be nice to get her hands on someone responsible for the destruction of their only weapon, but she was beginning to suspect Caroline wasn't that person.

Beside them, Zander growled, tussling with Tyler.

"Let him go, Zander," Meredith said. "I need you to tell me if Caroline's telling the truth."

Zander snarled again, kneeing Tyler in the chest and

knocking him onto the ground. Meredith stared at him. She'd never seen the easygoing Zander like this: his white teeth bared in fury. He even looked bigger, and somehow more feral, his hair disordered as if it was trying to stand on end.

Zander had once told her, Meredith remembered, that those who had been turned into werewolves didn't smell right to him, not like Original werewolves.

From behind her, closer to the fire, Bonnie spoke, her voice rough from the smoke. "Zander," she said. "Zander, let him go."

Zander heard Bonnie as he hadn't seemed to hear Meredith, reluctantly releasing Tyler and standing up. He was tense, though, poised to attack again as Tyler slowly climbed to his feet, brushing dirt from himself. They watched each other carefully.

"All right," Zander said. He backed away from Tyler slowly, his lips still pulled back in a snarl, and looked at Caroline. Zander got close to her, close enough to sniff at her neck. "Tell me what you're doing here," he said.

Caroline pulled away indignantly, but Meredith took her arm and forced her back toward Zander. "Why are you here, Caroline?" she asked sternly.

The auburn-haired girl glared at them. "I don't have to explain myself to you," she said. "We're just camping. The fire was an accident."

"So Klaus didn't send you here?" Bonnie asked skeptically. "You've never been the camping type, Caroline."

"This doesn't have anything to do with Klaus," Caroline said steadily.

"What about you, Tyler?" Meredith asked. "Did your old master send you here?"

Tyler shook his head hurriedly. "I don't want anything to do with that guy," he said.

"Well, Zander?" Meredith asked quietly.

"They're telling the truth, as far as they know it," Zander said. "But there's something wrong. They smell . . . off."

"Klaus compelled them," Meredith said flatly. "They only know what Klaus told them was true. And Klaus must have told them to go camping here. We can't hold them responsible for burning down the tree. It's not their fault."

"That's ridiculous," Caroline said. "No one compelled us to do anything." But her voice sounded nervous and unsure, and Tyler wrapped his arm around her protectively.

"It's not a big deal," Tyler assured her. "Even if we'd meant to burn down that tree, it's just a tree. Why would Klaus even care?"

Meredith let her stave rest loosely against her leg. She wasn't going to fight anyone here. The Tyler she'd known back in the worst days in Fell's Church might have deserved killing, but judging by the way he was trying to shield Caroline, that wasn't who he was now. "It was a pretty important tree," she said quietly.

"I'm sorry," Caroline said. Caroline had never been good at apologies, Meredith remembered. "You've got no reason to believe me, to believe us, but I wouldn't have done anything to hurt you, not even kill a tree. If the memories I have of Fell's Church are real, we used to be friends. *Real* friends," she said, looking from Meredith to Bonnie, "and I ruined it all."

"Yeah, you did," Bonnie said bluntly. "But it's in the past now." Caroline gave her a crooked half smile, and, after a moment, Bonnie smiled back awkwardly.

"What *do* you remember? About Fell's Church?" Meredith asked them.

Tyler visibly swallowed and pulled Caroline closer to him. "The monsters and everything, that's the truth?" he asked, his voice shaking.

Bonnie nodded. Meredith knew she couldn't even bear to put all that history into words.

A drop of blood rolled down Tyler's forehead from a scrape Zander must have inflicted, and he wiped it away with the hand that wasn't holding on to Caroline. "One day I woke up, and I remembered normal life, but I also remembered this crazy story where I was a werewolf and did, uh . . ." His cheeks flushed. "Bad things."

"The bad things happened, but then everything

changed," Meredith told him. "Most people don't remember, but everything you think you know is true." It would be too complicated to explain to them how Elena had saved Fell's Church by blackmailing the Guardians into changing the events of the last year. For almost everyone, their senior year had been completely normal: no vampires, no werewolves, no kitsune. But a handful of people, all with supernatural Powers or Influences of one kind or another, could remember both timelines.

"Do you remember Klaus?" Alaric asked. "Did you see him at all after you left Fell's Church? Maybe in your dreams?"

Meredith glanced at him approvingly. Klaus could dream-travel; they knew that. Maybe Tyler or Caroline would have some residual memory that could help them, even if they couldn't remember being Influenced.

But Tyler shook his head. "I haven't seen him since Fell's Church," he said.

"Not since you kidnapped Caroline to help bring Stefan to him, you mean?" Bonnie said tartly. "How did you two end up together again, anyway?"

Tyler was blushing miserably and Caroline took his hand, folding his meaty fingers in her long, elegant ones. "I was still expecting Tyler's babies. Both sets of memories were sure about that. So when we found each other we decided that the best thing we could do was try to raise our family." She shrugged. "All that stuff—Klaus and everything—it just seems like a dream now. We've been staying with my grandmother, and she's been helping to take care of the twins." And *that*—picking the version of events that was most convenient for her and sticking to it—was just like Caroline, Meredith realized. She'd never had any imagination.

"You know, Tyler," Bonnie said, "you should get in touch with your cousin Caleb. He was looking for you in Fell's Church, and he seemed really worried."

That was one way of putting it, Meredith supposed. Caleb had stalked them, put glamours on them, and cast spells to sow discord between Elena and the others, all because he suspected them of being behind Tyler's disappearance and his own dual memories.

Caroline put her hand on Tyler's shoulder, and Meredith noticed something. "You cut your nails off," she said. Caroline had always had long, perfectly polished nails, ever since they had stopped making mud pies and started talking about boys.

"Oh," Caroline said, glancing at her hands. "Yeah, I had to cut them short so they wouldn't scratch the twins. They like to suck on my fingers." She added hesitantly, "Do you want to see pictures?"

Bonnie nodded curiously, and Meredith joined her to look at Caroline's cell-phone pictures of two tiny babies.

"Brianna and Luke," she told them. "See how blue their eyes are?"

That was when Meredith decided she might as well forgive Caroline and Tyler. If Caroline had changed enough that she cared more for her babies than her looks, and Tyler wasn't trying to throw his weight around, they were probably no threat. True, they had ruined everything by destroying the white ash, but they hadn't done it maliciously.

They exchanged a few more words, and then parted ways. Caroline and Tyler headed back down the trail, Caroline's long hair swinging against her tanned shoulders. It was strange, Meredith thought as she watched them. Caroline had been such a close friend, and then such a despised enemy, and now she felt nothing for her.

"That was the only lead I'd found in any of the references about defeating Klaus," Alaric said mournfully, looking at the heap of ash and scorched pieces of the blessed ash tree.

"Could we gather up the ashes and use them for something?" Bonnie asked hopefully. "Maybe make a salve and put it on a regular stake?"

Alaric shook his head. "It wouldn't work," he told her. "Everything I've read makes it clear that it's got to be undamaged wood."

"We'll find something else," Meredith said, gritting her

teeth. "There has to be something he's susceptible to. But at least one good thing that came out of this."

"What?" Bonnie asked. "I hope you're not talking about Caroline, because a few pictures aren't going to erase everything that she's done. And those babies are clearly going to look more like Tyler than like her."

"Well," Meredith pointed out, "remember how we told you that when you were having your vision in our room, you said Klaus was calling an old friend to help him?" She waved a hand toward the retreating figures down the path. "If it was Tyler, he's not a threat after all. We're not facing a second enemy."

"Yeah," Bonnie said thoughtfully, and wrapped her arms around herself. "*If* the vision was talking about Tyler."

17

Meredith moodily picked at the mud in the grooves of her hiking boots, flicking the little pieces of dirt onto the floor of the car.

Beside her, Alaric was driving them back to campus. There was a thoughtful crease between his eyebrows, and Meredith knew he was turning over possibilities, trying to approach the Klaus problem from every angle he could think of. She felt a wave of affection for him wash over her, and she reached over to squeeze his knee. Alaric glanced at her and smiled.

Turning to look into the backseat, she saw Bonnie fast asleep, her head on Zander's shoulder. Zander had cuddled her close, his cheek resting against her hair.

But as Meredith watched, Bonnie's peaceful face grew agitated, her mouth pinching together and her eyebrows drawing down into a worried frown. She twisted in her seat, pulling her legs up under her and burying her face in Zander's chest.

"No," she said, the word muffled against Zander.

Zander grinned and tightened his arm around her. "She's dreaming," he told Meredith. "It's so cute how she talks in her sleep."

"Alaric, pull over," Meredith said sharply. Alaric pulled the car onto the side of the road, and Meredith quickly rummaged through the glove compartment. Thank goodness Alaric carried paper and pens in the car.

"What is it?" Zander asked, alarmed. Pressed against him, Bonnie shook her head hard, her curls spreading across his chest, and murmured small noises of distress.

"She's not just dreaming, she's having a vision," Meredith told him. "Bonnie," she said, keeping her voice low and soothing, "Bonnie, what's happening?"

Bonnie moaned and thrashed, her body arching away from Zander. Eyes widening, Zander grabbed at her, trying to hold her still.

"Bonnie," Meredith said again. "It's okay. Tell me what you're seeing."

Bonnie sucked in a breath, and then her wide brown eyes flew open and she began to scream. Alaric jerked in surprise, banging his elbow on the steering wheel.

The scream went on and on, filling the car with noise.

"Bonnie, stop it!" Zander was pulling Bonnie to his chest, trying to calm her and to keep her from falling off the seat as she struggled.

Finally, she grew still, and the screams died off into whimpers. Then she looked around at the others. "What's going on?" she said thickly.

"You were having a vision, Bonnie," Meredith said. "Everything's okay."

Bonnie shook her head. "No," she whispered, her voice cracked and strained from screaming. "It wasn't a vision."

"What do you mean?" Alaric asked.

"It was a dream." Bonnie was visibly calmer, and Zander gingerly released her from the tight hold he had on her arms and took her hand instead.

"Just a dream?" Meredith said doubtfully.

Bonnie shook her head again, slowly. "Not exactly," she said. "Do you remember the dreams I had when Klaus was holding Elena prisoner? After . . ." She hesitated. "After Elena died. The dreams she sent me? That Klaus invaded? I think Klaus was sending me this dream."

Meredith exchanged a look with Alaric. "If he can get inside her mind like this, how are we going to protect her?" she asked quietly, and he shook his head.

"What happened in the dream?" Zander asked, stroking Bonnie's arm.

"It was . . . it was like a military camp or something,"

Bonnie said, frowning, clearly trying to remember. "There were trees everywhere. Klaus had a whole group of people around him. He was standing in front of them, telling them how strong they were and that they were ready."

"Ready for what?" Meredith asked quickly.

Bonnie grimaced. "He didn't say exactly, but nothing good, I'm sure," she said. "I couldn't see how many people there were or make out what they looked like exactly. But it seemed like there were a lot of them. It was all sort of clouded and vague, but I could see Klaus as clearly as anything."

"He's gathering an army," Meredith said, her heart sinking. They had no ash tree, no weapon against Klaus. And he wasn't alone.

"There's more," Bonnie said. She hunched her shoulders, curling into herself protectively, pressing closer to Zander. She looked miserable and frightened, her face sickly white and her eyes rimmed with red. "After he finished his speech, he looked right at me, and I knew he'd brought me there. He reached out like he was going to take my hand and just brushed it with his fingers." She reached her own hand out in front of her and stared at it, her lips trembling. "His hand was so cold. And he said, 'I'm coming, little one. I'm coming for you.'"

18

Stefan pushed Elena behind him as he launched himself at a vampire, ripping into its throat with his elongated fangs. Beside him, Spencer, in wolf form, cannoned into another of the Vitale vampires and knocked her sprawling, only to be thrown violently into a row of bookshelves as the vampire regained her footing. The shelves wobbled and collapsed on top of the werewolf, blocking him from Elena's sight.

Elena gripped the stake in her hand firmly and gritted her teeth. She could sense evil all around her, pulling her to hurry, to do something about it. She didn't have the supernatural strength of Stefan or the werewolf, or of the vampires they were fighting against, but if she was quick and lucky, maybe she could take one or two of them out.

They hadn't really expected to find any vampires in

the library at all. If they had, they would have been better prepared, weapons in hand, and would have brought more members of the Pack with them. They had been doing a quick after-hours sweep of the library, making sure the Vitale Society's meeting room was still chained up. And here, just a floor above the entrance to that room, they'd found what must be—Elena glanced around, calculating—all the remaining vampires of the Vitale Society, except for Chloe, still safely hidden with Matt.

Eight vampires. Until now, they'd been tracking down one vampire at a time, finding them alone midhunt. They'd had no idea the vampires were still allied, because it seemed like they had scattered. If they had known they were still working together, Elena and the others would have been more careful, or somehow managed to track them more closely.

Spencer was up again now, and snarling as he tore at the side of one of the vampires, who struggled frantically against him. Stefan was stronger than these younger vampires, and two bodies already lay at his feet, but they were still outnumbered. Two grabbed Stefan by the arm and swung him around so that another could pin him by the shoulder, stake held high.

"No!" Elena shouted, panic ripping through her. She charged toward the vampires holding Stefan, but a hand clamped down on her shoulder, and she turned to see a tall, dark-haired guy she was pretty sure had been in her chemistry class, back at the beginning of the year.

"No interfering, now," he said mockingly. "I think we can keep each other company." Elena struggled, but she couldn't move her arm, and he fisted his other hand in her hair, pulling her head back slowly to expose her neck.

Out of the corner of her eye, Elena saw Stefan fling one of the vampires off him, only to be pinned again. He was still fighting, though, not staked yet. The vampire holding her smiled, his canines descending, bigger and sharper, as she strained against him.

This can't be how it ends, she thought, dazed. *I won't die like this.* Elena wrested one of her hands free just as she heard a sudden clattering on the stairs, the sound of feet and bodies in motion. Another set of shelves fell, books skidding across the floor. The vampire holding her looked up and then released her, falling backward as a great splotch of blood bloomed on his chest.

Behind him, stave extended, was Meredith.

"Thanks," Elena said, her mouth dry with fear.

"Anytime," Meredith said, grinning savagely. "Just remind me to cut off his head later." Then she was gone, spinning through the room, stave raised. A huge, white wolf—Zander, of course—had joined Spencer on the other side of the room, and they were fighting side by side, snarling and tearing at their enemies' flesh. Alaric rushed past Elena, stake raised, and behind him stood Bonnie, her hands extended in front of her, chanting a spell of protection.

Alaric staked one of the vampires holding Stefan, and Stefan was able to take care of the others who had been restraining him. In a few minutes, the fight was over.

"You arrived just in the nick of time," Stefan said. "Thank you."

"It was Zander. He heard the fight when we drove past the library," Meredith said, looking up from where she and Alaric were dragging vampire bodies across the floor to pile neatly in the corner. "We'll have to burn these bodies, but it looks like this is the end of Ethan's vampires. Other than Chloe, of course."

"Thank goodness," Bonnie said. She'd pulled an assortment of herbs from her bag and was tracing patterns, casting charms of distraction and misdirection, in the hopes that no one would come near the bodies until they could dispose of them. "But we've got something bigger to deal with."

"Klaus," said Elena, her shoulders slumping.

"We couldn't get the wood. And Bonnie had a vision," Meredith said.

"A dream, not a vision," Bonnie interrupted sharply.

"Sorry, a dream," Meredith corrected herself. "She thinks Klaus was reaching out to her, threatening her, and from what he said, it sounds like he's ready to attack."

"I don't understand why he'd warn us, though," Zander said. He and Spencer were both human-form again, and as he spoke, Zander wrapped a bandage around Spencer's shoulder where he'd been hit by the row of shelves.

Meredith and Elena exchanged a look. "Klaus likes to taunt his victims," Meredith said. "It's all a game to him."

"Then maybe we should try to turn the tables on him," Elena suggested. Stefan nodded, guessing what she was planning, and gave her a subtle half smile. He'd been encouraging her to explore her new Powers more thoroughly. "I can try again to sense him," she told the others. "If we can find where he and his allies are hiding, maybe we can find out what he's doing, who he's working with, catch him off guard."

"Can you do it now?" Alaric asked, watching her with professional interest.

Elena nodded. Relaxing her body, she took a deep breath and closed her eyes. At first, she felt nothing special. Slowly, she became aware that the sense of evil that had been overwhelming when she was surrounded by the fight wasn't gone. There was still an insistent, low-key tugging, a feeling that something was *wrong* and that she had to fix it. That sense filled her, and she opened her eyes again.

Tendrils of black-and-rust-red aura hung smokelike in the air before her. Elena raised a hand toward them, but the colors swirled around her fingers without substance, the same way that Stefan's aura had. Her powers must be getting stronger: what had been just a feeling was now solid, a trail of black and red leading up the stairs and out of the library. She could picture it going farther, over the quad and across the athletic fields behind the campus. Elena followed the wisps of color, and the others followed her.

"The woods again," Bonnie said from behind Elena, but Elena barely heard her. The colors weren't leading her into the woods; they were stretching across the field and around an equipment shed. The pounding in Elena's head, the feeling of something being *wrongwrongwrongwrongwrong* intensified.

"Klaus is hiding back here somewhere?" Zander said, sounding confused. "Isn't it kind of exposed?"

No, Elena thought, *not Klaus*. And suddenly, she realized what a huge mistake she'd made. The trail, the feeling of wrong she got, was familiar. *Damon*. She was leading everyone right to him.

There was a split second between when Elena realized this and when the whole group rounded the corner of the equipment shed. Her steps faltered, but it was too late to change their direction.

Damon was feeding, another fair-haired girl pulled tightly against his chest, his mouth open against her neck, his eyes tightly shut. Blood ran down both their necks, making a gory, wet patch on Damon's black shirt.

There was a moment when everyone, even Meredith, froze. Without consciously thinking about it, Elena moved, throwing herself between the others and Damon.

"No," she said, directing her words at Meredith. Meredith was the one who mattered here, the one who wouldn't hesitate to kill Damon. "You can't," she told her. She glanced quickly at Damon, who opened his eyes briefly and gave her an irritated look, the look of a cat interrupted at its food dish. Then he closed his eyes again, working his fangs deeper into the girl's throat. Bonnie gave a soft, horrified moan.

"What the *hell*, Elena?" Meredith shouted. "He's killing her!" Balanced on the balls of her feet, she dodged to the side, stave raised, and Elena shifted quickly to stay between her and Damon. Someone was slipping past Elena on the other side, and she half turned to try to stop them, but it was Stefan, who pushed Damon away from his prey. Damon snarled but didn't try to grab her again. Stefan watched his brother tensely as he supported the girl and passed her carefully to Alaric.

"Meredith, please," Elena said, her voice thin and desperate to her own ears. "Please stop. There's something wrong with him. But it's *Damon*, he's saved us before. He's fought on our side in so many battles. You can't kill him. We have to figure out what's going on."

Stefan had hold of Damon by the arms now, but his brother shrugged him off with an irritated twitch of his shoulders. As Elena looked over at them, Damon straightened up and settled his clothing into place, shooting Elena a brilliant, unfriendly smile. There was still blood streaking his mouth and chin. "I don't need you to protect me, Elena," he said. "I've taken care of myself for a long time now."

"Please, Meredith," Elena said again, ignoring his words, and stretched out her hands to her friend pleadingly.

"Oh, yes," Damon said mockingly, turning his sharp smile on Meredith. "*Please, Meredith.* Are you sure about who your allies are here, hunter?"

Meredith had lowered her stave a couple of inches, but her eyes were flat and hard as she glared at Elena. "You and Stefan jumped in to protect him awfully quickly," she said coldly. "How long has this been going on?"

Elena flinched. "I've known for a few days that Damon was hunting again," she said. "The girls were all right at the end, though." She knew how weak that protest was. Worse, she wasn't sure she quite believed it—Damon had abandoned the girl she and Stefan found in the woods; she could have died. What else had he done?

But she couldn't let Meredith kill him.

"I'll take responsibility for him," she said quickly. "Stefan and I. We'll make sure he doesn't hurt anyone else. Please, Meredith." Stefan nodded, his hand tight again around his brother's arm, as if he was restraining a disobedient child. Damon sneered at them both.

Meredith hissed through her teeth with frustration. "What about you?" she said, jerking her chin at Damon. "Do you have anything more to say for yourself?"

Damon tilted his chin and gave her a cool, arrogant smile, but said nothing. Elena's heart sank: Damon had clearly decided to be as irritating as possible. After a moment, Meredith jabbed the stave at Elena, stopping well short of touching her.

"Don't forget," she said. "This is *your* problem. *Your* responsibility, Elena. If he kills anyone, he'll be dead the next day. And we're not done talking about this."

Elena felt Stefan, pulling Damon with him, move up behind her, a strong, supportive figure at her shoulder. "We understand," he said solemnly.

Meredith glared at them all, shaking her head, and then turned and walked off without a word. Alaric and Bonnie followed her, supporting Damon's victim between them, her choking sobs the only sound Elena could hear. Zander and Spencer gave Elena and the Salvatore brothers long, thoughtful looks before following the others. Elena trembled inwardly: the Pack could be a dangerous enemy, if it decided Elena wasn't on the right side.

As soon as her friends had rounded the bend in the path and were out of sight, Elena whirled angrily to face

Damon. But Stefan, still clutching Damon by one arm, spoke before she could.

"You idiot," he said coldly, punctuating his words with a little shake of Damon's arm. "What were you thinking, Damon? You want to undo all the good you've done?" With each question, he shook his brother a little more.

Damon shoved Stefan's hand away, the mocking smile he'd worn dropping off his face. "I was thinking that I'm a *vampire*, little brother," he said. "Clearly a lesson you still have to learn." He wiped the blood from his mouth.

"Damon—" Elena said in exasperation, but Damon was already turning away. Quicker than her eyes could see, he was gone. A moment later, from a tree on the other side of the athletic field a large crow flew up, letting out a raucous caw.

"We might not be able to save Damon," Stefan said in a troubled voice, taking her hand. "Not this time."

Elena nodded. "I know," she said. "But we have to try." Her eyes followed the bird, just a dot in the sky now, as it flew above the campus. Regardless of what she had promised Meredith, she didn't know if she could stop Damon from doing anything he wanted. But she and Stefan wouldn't let Damon die. Somehow, at some point, saving him had become more important than anything else.

19

Elena had been no stranger to battle in the past year. Her younger self would never have dreamed about weapons practice and defensive maneuvers. That Elena had focused on trips to France and beautiful dresses. But now, the fight against evil was what gave Elena a thrill, as much as she hated to admit it. Now, she walked united with her friends and allies, all looking to her for guidance.

Usually they were all united and looking to her for guidance, anyway. Since she and Stefan had defended Damon, Meredith had been distant. The Pack had been eyeing them so suspiciously that Elena could almost see the hair bristling on their heads as they shied away from her. Elena had turned the other day to find Shay staring at her menacingly. Even Bonnie had seemed to be avoiding her for the last few days. Only Andrés, although she'd told him what had happened, remained unchanged in his attitude toward Elena. They'd worked together the previous day, trying to unlock more of Elena's Powers, but hadn't been successful yet.

The fact that her other friends were suddenly suspicious of her *hurt*. The night after they found Damon feeding, Elena had been with Stefan in his room. "We're doing the right thing, aren't we?" she had asked him, hot tears stinging the corners of her eyes. "Even though our friends are scared, we can't abandon Damon."

Stefan had dragged a heavy, comforting hand across her back. "Everything will be okay," he said, but Elena could hear the doubt and pain in his voice, mirroring her own.

Elena had to beg Meredith to follow her again as she tried to locate Klaus. But finding Klaus before he attacked was the best plan, Elena was sure, and this time they had all the fighters they could bring together. Klaus was so powerful; maybe the element of surprise would give them some advantage. Although a small comfort, they hoped that the daylight might also work in their favor.

The sunlight certainly seemed to be bothering Chloe, Elena thought. The curly-haired girl's dimples were nowhere in sight as she clung close to Matt's side, her head bowed. She looked strained and miserable, and Matt, although standing straight and alert as a soldier, seemed weary, his features sharper and paler than they'd been just a couple of weeks before.

Zander and his Pack of Original werewolves, on the other hand, were hyped up and practically bouncing off the walls. As Elena watched, Zander grabbed tall, shaggy Marcus in an armlock and forced him to his knees, both of them laughing and swearing as Marcus kicked at him. Even Shay, who usually seemed a little removed from the rest of the Pack, was getting in on the act, gleefully screeching from her perch on Jared's shoulders as he spun around and around, trying to dislodge her. Tonight would be a full moon, and the werewolves, sensing the change coming, were high on adrenaline.

Stefan was moving among their friends, calmly offering instructions and words of encouragement. The werewolves quieted to listen to him, their expressions alert. Bonnie and Alaric, looking through a book of spells Alaric had located, turned to show Stefan what they had found, obviously asking his advice. They might be angry at him for protecting Damon, Elena realized with a surge of pride, but when push came to shove, they all trusted Stefan.

Meredith remained silent as she prepared for the battle. She sharpened her knives and polished her stave with her face tight and closed off, refusing to look at Stefan or Elena. Impulsively, Elena started toward her hunter friend. She didn't know what she could say, but Meredith understood loyalty: she'd be able to forgive Elena even if she didn't agree with her. But before she made it more than a few steps, Elena felt a hand on her arm. She turned and there was Andrés, smiling tentatively at her.

"You came," she said, simple pleasure bubbling up inside her.

"You called me," he answered. "We have to stick together against the evil things of this world, yes?"

"Absolutely," Stefan said as he joined them. Elena introduced Stefan and Andrés, watching as Andrés frowned and pulled back a little, clearly realizing for the first time that the Stefan she'd told him about was a vampire. But then he shook Stefan's hand enthusiastically, and Elena relaxed. She'd thought Andrés would see through to the good person Stefan was, vampire or not, but she hadn't been entirely sure. The Guardians of the Celestial Court had not, after all, not really.

After greeting Andrés, Stefan turned back to Elena. "I think we're all good to go," he told her. "Are you ready?"

"Okay," Elena said. Closing her eyes, she breathed deeply, feeling Andrés feed her his Power, opening herself up to let it stream into her.

"Think of protection," Andrés told her, his voice barely more than a whisper. "Think of defending those you love against Klaus." Elena concentrated, and as before, it was like blossoms unfolding within her, one by one.

She felt the familiar ominous gray and blue of Damon's aura off across campus, and pushed it away, concentrated harder. *Klaus. Klaus.* There was something else, greasy and dark, like a pall of foul smoke. Worse than Damon's aura, much worse.

Her eyes snapped open. "This way," she said.

Even to Meredith, who was easily the best human hiker in the group, it felt like they'd been trekking for hours. They were deep into the woods now, and the sun had passed overhead and was hanging above the horizon; they were going to lose the advantage daylight would have given them. But Elena still walked on, as straight and certain as if she was following a clearly laid-out road through the trees.

Meredith pulled the hair off her neck into a ponytail, trying to cool off, and continued after Elena, pushing away the memory of the last time she'd let Elena lead them, of Damon's vicious feeding. A good warrior focused on the battle ahead of her, not conflicts within her own army.

The ground was growing swampy, their steps leaving little puddles of water seeping through the mud behind them, when Elena suddenly halted and gestured the others to come closer to her.

"We're almost there," she said. "Just through that next stand of trees."

"Are you sure it's Klaus?" Meredith asked, and Elena shook her head.

"It's a big group of vampires, anyway," she said. "I can sense that. Who else could it be?"

Stefan nodded. "I feel them, too."

Now that everyone knew where they were going, Elena dropped back to walk with Alaric and Bonnie, who began muttering spells of protection and concealment, their hands extended. Andrés, breathing deeply and seeming to draw Power into himself, joined them. It was time for the fighters to take the lead.

Stefan and Meredith moved side by side, Meredith balancing her stave. Stefan was poised on the balls of his feet. His mouth was slightly ajar, and Meredith could see that his sharp canine teeth had descended in anticipation of their attack. She felt a slight, unexpected pang: not long ago, Damon had fought beside her and he had been a worthy comrade, quick and brave and relentless. Stefan was all of that; but he didn't take the same pleasure in a fight that Damon did. If only Damon could be trusted.

Zander, Shay, and the four other Pack werewolves who could shift without the full moon at its peak had changed, and they flanked Stefan and Meredith. Moving quietly, they paced ahead with their tails held out straight behind them and their ears pricked forward, lips pulling back in silent snarls. Zander and Shay, leading the Pack on each side, moved in tandem, each one's step perfectly in time with the other's. The five remaining werewolves, who would not be able to change until the moon rose, walked behind them, as alert and focused as their lupine family. Matt and Chloe came next, halfway between the warriors and the others.

They shouldered their way through the last grove of trees, placing their feet carefully to avoid making noise. Bonnie and Alaric mouthed quiet spells, muffling their approach.

But when they came at last into the open, they found Klaus, dressed now in the shabby raincoat Meredith remembered with a stab of terror from their encounters in Fell's Church, his face alight with terrifying good humor, laughing. There was a huge group of vampires there, easily outnumbering their own forces, and every eye was already fixed upon them.

In that frozen moment, Meredith could see all the vampires in sharp definition. Her brain snagged on a face and stopped in confusion. *Elena.* But Elena was behind her, and Meredith had never seen Elena's face hold so much malice. Then she realized: the paler gold of the hair, the lighter blue of the eyes, the slightly mad glee in the pretty face. This wasn't Elena. It was Katherine, somehow reborn.

And then, just behind Katherine, Meredith saw another face she knew, and her heart froze. It couldn't be Cristian.

Her brother was human now; the Guardians made sure of that. Didn't they?

But there was Cristian, his face familiar only from the pictures at home, and he smiled at her intimately across the clearing, his vampire canines visible. For a fraction of second, Meredith's hands loosened on her stave and she swayed on her feet. But then she tightened her grip again and took a fighting stance. She'd thought her family was safe, that Cristian had been returned to them. Everything was crumbling again at this very moment, but she still had a battle to fight.

20

People were rushing past Elena on all sides,
buffeting and banging against her, so she flat-
tened herself against a tree. The noise was
overwhelming—shouts and groans and bodies slamming
together.

Klaus's army was too big, but her friends were holding
their own. Stefan, his face a mask of fury, was grappling
with a slim, fair-haired girl. When Elena caught a glimpse
of the girl's face, her heart seemed to stop for a second.
Katherine.

Elena had seen Katherine die, seen lines of fire crack
her face open as she screamed. How could she be here?
Katherine raised a hand and scratched at Stefan's face, her
fingers bent into claws, and he twisted her arm viciously,

snarling and knocking her to the ground, where they were lost to Elena's view.

Meredith was sparring with a handsome, dark-haired guy whose face was vaguely familiar to Elena. They were evenly matched, each blocking the other's blows with deadly speed and efficiency. Meredith looked tense and serious, without the gleeful expression she often had in battle.

Matt and Chloe had squared off against a female vampire, Chloe shielding Matt with her body and yanking the vampire's head back, trying to turn her so that Matt could stake her through the heart. The vampire snarled and twisted in Chloe's hands.

A wild howl came from one side of the clearing, making the hair on the back of Elena's neck stand up on end, and her eyes shot to the horizon: the sun was hanging low and a full moon had just risen. The rest of the werewolves had changed as they fought, and now the vampires who had been battling them in human form fell back as the Pack leaped eagerly upon them. Zander and Shay, who was easily identifiable by the reddish tint of her fur, pulled a vampire down together, their heavy bodies pinning him as they tore at his flesh.

Bonnie and Alaric were chanting in Latin, their voices steady but strained. Beside Elena, she could hear Andrés muttering softly in Spanish. She glanced at him, and his aura was so clear she could see it without even trying: a circle the color of beech leaves in spring was spreading out from him, touching on their allies in the fight. She realized that like Bonnie and Alaric, Andrés was using all the Power he could call on to protect her friends.

They were fighting hard, but there were so *many* of the vampires, at least twenty. Both men and women of different races and ethnicities, but all young, all beautiful. All with a certain mad savagery in their expression that echoed Klaus's. Their faces were wild with hate and with anticipation. They wanted to fight, Elena could tell, wanted to kill. One, a golden-haired boy who looked younger than Elena herself, high-school age maybe, wrestled a werewolf to the ground laughing, his face smeared with blood.

Katherine is here. The words repeated in Elena's brain as if they had significance beyond the fact that Klaus had resurrected her oldest enemy. Katherine was here . . . and Ethan had used the blood of the vampires Klaus had made to resurrect him.

Klaus had been calling upon old friends. With a sickening twist, Elena wondered: Could these all be vampires Klaus had turned, all gathered together like some kind of vicious tribe, some kind of *family*? And had Klaus used their blood to resurrect Katherine, to raise his most beloved child as he had been raised?

Through the brutally battling crowd, Klaus was coming

toward her, his face gleeful. He was so handsome, she thought irrelevantly, and so terrifying. His ice-blue eyes were wide, and his golden skin glowed in the moonlight. His allies—his *children*—moved out of his way so that his path was effortless. Something shone in his hand. With a chill, Elena realized that he held an unsheathed dagger.

Elena couldn't move. She felt as if she were in a dream as Klaus came closer and closer, smiling and gliding easily through the crowd, until he was so close she could smell the coppery scent of blood on him. He took her arm rather gently, and his smile grew wider. He held her effortlessly still with his Power, and as she slid her eyes to the side, she saw Andrés, his mouth open in horror, and realized Klaus was holding him still as well. Stefan, too, was fighting against Klaus's Power, desperate to reach Elena before it was too late.

"Hello, pretty one," Klaus said, his voice soft and intimate. "I think the time has come, don't you? I'm ready to taste you."

The dagger's blade flashed in the setting sunlight as he raised it to her neck. Elena, with the sharp focus of terror, saw its hilt gleaming with runes and patterns. From below the blade, a curious wry-faced beast, something like a lizard, grinned at her cruelly. And then she couldn't see the dagger anymore, because Klaus had pressed it to her throat.

Stefan, Elena thought. She could see him across the clearing, his face frozen in despair. Even though she was becoming a Guardian, she'd always thought things would work out so that she could be that normal, happy girl with him. His heart would break without her, she realized, and she had just a moment of pure sorrow for him and for what they could have had together.

She felt the freezing cold blade cross her throat, and then the heat of flowing blood. Klaus leaned closer, his breath cool and rank, then suddenly pulled back. The blood had stopped, Elena realized. And she couldn't feel the pain anymore. She was healing almost as fast as Klaus could cut her.

Klaus's blade couldn't kill her. Was this because she was a Guardian? she wondered dazedly.

Klaus growled in fury and slashed at her neck again. Elena felt a shock of pain, but again, the wound seemed to heal. The others were seeing what was going on now, although Klaus's Power must have been holding them at bay. Elena met Stefan's horrified eyes as Klaus shoved her away from him.

"Your magician and witch have found a way to protect you, have they?" Klaus sneered. He glowered at Bonnie and Alaric, who both took an automatic step backward, their faces white with fear, and then he turned back to

Elena. "Don't worry, pretty one, it won't stop me from having you." His voice dropped to an insinuating whisper and he reached out with one finger to trace the line of Elena's upper lip. He smiled, but his eyes were furious. "I'll figure out a way around whatever they've done, believe me."

He raised his voice again, looking slowly around the clearing. "We like it here, my children and I," he announced. "All the fresh, young blood—it's a continual feast." A ragged cheer came from some of the vampires. He smiled again, his sharp, white canines gleaming in the last rays of the setting sun, and his hand tightened around Elena's jaw, dragging her forward. "In the end," he said, his voice low and intimate, "not one of your friends will survive us."

Klaus turned away, striding across the clearing. As he passed the Pack, frozen still and silent by his Power, he grabbed up the closest wolf in one smooth, quick move— *Chad*, Elena realized, recognizing his wiry frame and the white blaze at his throat—and threw him easily into a tree. Elena heard Chad's bones crack and then the wolf collapsed limply at the bottom of the tree, motionless.

Klaus grinned and lightning cracked across the sky. "He's only the first. I'll see you all soon." He sauntered slowly and carelessly into the woods. His vampires melted into the night after him. As Klaus's army vanished, Elena felt his Power release her at last, and she slumped to her knees. The Pack, the first to spring back into motion, raced to Chad's side.

Gazing across the clearing, Elena saw Stefan. He was pale and still, and as their eyes met, Elena saw a mirror of her own fear.

21

"Elena, oh Elena," Stefan said, stroking her hair, feeling the urge to pull her to him and never, never let her leave his side again. "I was so afraid that I'd lost you. That I'd failed you."

As soon as Klaus had left the clearing, releasing the compelled stillness he'd held them all under, Stefan had raced to Elena, taking her in his arms. They were still on the battlefield, everyone nursing their wounds all around them, but he couldn't let go of her even for a moment.

"I'm okay," Elena said, grasping his hand and holding it against her cheek, letting him feel how warm and alive she was. She sounded bewildered. "How can I be okay, though? Klaus *cut my throat*."

"Do you know, Andrés?" Stefan said, turning to the Guardian beside them. Behind him hovered Meredith,

Alaric, and Bonnie. Bonnie was watching the werewolves across the clearing as they gathered around Chad's body, but she lingered with the other humans, giving them some space. A few steps away, Matt and Chloe stood half in the clearing, half below the trees, murmuring quietly to each other.

"I don't know for certain what protected her," Andrés said slowly.

"You must have a pretty good idea," Stefan said sharply. "Tell us." He knew he should treat Andrés more gently; he was, after all, the only one who could help Elena through her transition to Guardianship. But Stefan was still terrified, feeling sick and hollowed out from the moment when he had seen Klaus draw his dagger across Elena's throat. And he was *sure* that Andrés knew more than he had told them.

"I have heard that, sometimes, Guardians who have very dangerous assignments are given special protections as well," Andrés said. The full moon lit up the clearing and he looked pale and worn in its light. "Most commonly, they are safeguarded against death by paranormal means. The Power—the Guardian Powers—can't make them immortal, because they have to stay in tune with nature. Elena could be run over by a car or die of disease, but, if this is what's happened, she can't be killed by a vampire's bite or a spell, or"—he waved a hand in the direction that

Klaus and his family had retreated—"by a magical dagger."

"If Klaus and his vampires can't kill her," Meredith said, starting to grin a wild, delighted grin, "then we have a weapon. Elena's safe."

Andrés frowned. "Wait," he said. "They can't kill her *by supernatural means.* If Klaus figures that out, he could kill her with a rope or a kitchen knife." Stefan flinched, and Andrés looked at him sympathetically. "I'm sorry," he said. "I know. It's hard to love someone as fragile as a human."

A long, drawn-out howl, echoing with misery and loss, rose from the foot of the tree where Chad had fallen. The wolves had, as a Pack, raced to Chad's side as soon as the Power holding them in place had lifted. They had been nosing at the fallen wolf's shaggy body, whimpering and growling, trying to confirm what Stefan had known since Chad hit the ground: Chad was dead.

Not just humans, Stefan thought bleakly. *Anyone mortal is so vulnerable to death.*

"We need to take a vow," he said, looking around at the humans' stricken faces. "No one can know about Elena's Powers, or about her being a Guardian. Not anyone. If Klaus finds out, he'll find a way to kill her." He felt sick and dizzy with panic. If Klaus found out Elena's secret . . . He looked wildly around. With the Pack here, there were so many now who might slip and give her away.

Meredith met his eyes challengingly. "I will never tell,"

she said. "On my honor as a hunter and a Sulez."

Matt nodded fervently. "I won't tell anyone," he promised, and Chloe, her eyes wide, nodded along with him.

Bonnie, Andrés, and Alaric all promised, too. Stefan held Elena close to him and kissed her again before, with almost a physical wrench, letting go and walking across the clearing. Approaching the circle of mourning wolves, he called softly, "Zander." The huge white wolf had laid his head alongside Chad's and, at Stefan's approach, jerked his head up to snarl a warning.

"I'm sorry," Stefan said. "It's very important. I wouldn't interrupt you if it weren't."

Zander pressed his muzzle to the top of Chad's head for a moment, and then stood and left the circle of wolves. Shay moved automatically in to take his place, laying next to Chad's body as if she could comfort the dead wolf.

When Zander was standing before Stefan, he stiffened and then writhed, his muscles contracting and expanding. Patches of bare skin began to show between the tufts of his thick fur, and he staggered up onto his hind legs as the direction of his joints reversed with a cracking noise. He was changing back into a human, Stefan realized, and the transformation looked painful.

"It hurts to change back when the moon is still full," Zander said gruffly, once he was standing before Stefan in human form. His eyes were reddened with grief, and he drew his hand roughly across his face. "What do you want?"

"I am so sorry about Chad," Stefan said. "He was a loyal member of your Pack and a valuable ally to the rest of us."

Chad had been a nice kid, Stefan thought, earnest and cheerful. His chest tightened as he remembered that Chad's death was ultimately Stefan's fault: Klaus had come to this part of the world to avenge Katherine, who had followed Stefan. Years of Stefan's own history, leading to the death of a skinny, friendly nineteen-year-old werewolf who had never done anyone harm.

"It's a risk we take when we fight—we all know it," Zander said shortly. His usually open face was closed off: Pack mourning was not for outsiders. "Is that all?"

"No, I need your word. Elena's Guardian Powers are the only reason Klaus couldn't kill her tonight," Stefan said. "I need you and your Pack to promise not to tell anyone she's a Guardian."

"Wolves are loyal," Zander said. "We won't tell anyone." He turned away from Stefan and took two long strides back toward the circle of wolves, his body changing as he went.

Huddled together at the edge of the clearing, Matt took Chloe's hand and noticed she was trembling, a small, tight shiver running through her body. He was cold, but vampires didn't get cold, did they?

"Are you okay?" he asked quietly.

Chloe pressed her free hand against her chest, as if she was having trouble breathing. "It's just that there were so many people," she said. "It was hard to concentrate. The blood—I could smell everyone's blood. And when the wolf died . . ."

Matt understood. Fresh blood had leaked from Chad's nose and mouth as he died, and Matt had felt Chloe stiffen beside him. "It's okay," he said now. "Let's head back to the boathouse. You just weren't ready to be around such a big group yet, especially with everyone's pulses pounding from the battle."

Watching Chloe closely, he saw her jaw shift shape as her canines involuntarily descended. *No talking about pounding pulses*, he thought.

Chloe turned her head aside, trying to hide her lowering canines, and Matt noticed something else. There was a long streak of blood along Chloe's jaw, near her mouth. "Where's that from?" Matt asked, hearing the sharpness in his own voice as he let go of Chloe's hand.

"What?" Chloe asked, alarmed, skating her fingers over her own face. "I don't . . . I don't know what you mean." She was looking away, though, avoiding Matt's eyes.

"Did you feed?" Matt asked, trying to calm down, to not scare Chloe. "Maybe from Chad after he died? I know it wouldn't have seemed as bad with him in wolf form, but werewolves are still people." *And jeez, when did that become something I believed?* he wondered.

"No!" Chloe's eyes flew open wide, the whites showing all the way around her pupil. "No, Matt, I wouldn't do that!" She wiped roughly at her face, trying to erase the mark. "We were together the whole time!"

Matt frowned. "Not the whole time," he contradicted. "I lost sight of you during the fighting for a while." Chloe knew they'd been separated. Why would she say differently?

Chloe shook her head hard. "I didn't feed from anyone," she insisted. But her eyes jittered nervously away and, with a sickening swoop of his stomach, Matt realized he had no idea what to believe. Chloe sighed. "Please, Matt," she said quietly. "I promise I'm not lying to you." Tears shone in her big brown eyes. "I'm not going to do that. I'm not going to become something to be afraid of."

"You won't," Matt promised her. "I'll keep you safe." Chloe leaned her face against his, forehead to forehead, and they stayed that way for a while, breathing quietly. *I will*, Matt promised himself silently. *I can help her.*

tefan held Elena close to him, ran his fingers through her silky hair, and felt her heart beating against his chest. When their lips met, he could feel her fear and weariness, as well as her wonder at her new Powers. Elena was sensing his own mixture of love and fear, and his delight at the new protection Elena had. She was sending him a constant stream of love and reassurance, which he returned in kind.

It was a marvel to him always, the way the world stopped, however bad things were, when Elena was in his arms. This human girl was his light and his touchstone, the one thing he could rely on.

"Sleep well, my love," he said, reluctantly releasing her. Elena kissed him one more time before going into her dorm room and shutting the door. Stefan hated to see her go; he couldn't erase the image of Klaus slicing her throat. Still, Bonnie and Meredith would be there. Elena had always been strong and independent and now she had Power of her own. He would be only a couple of floors above if she needed him.

Stefan trudged up the two flights of stairs between Elena's room and his own and unlocked his door. His room was dark and peaceful and he thought that although he would not sleep, he might lie down and let the world turn without him for a few hours.

As he closed the door behind him, he caught sight of a flash of white out on the balcony.

Katherine. His slow-beating heart seemed to stop for a moment. She was leaning gracefully against the balcony's railing, looking deceptively young and delicate in a long, white dress. She must have flown up, and waited for him just outside.

His first thought was to barricade the door to the balcony, to keep her out. His second was to arm himself with a stake and attack her. But she could have easily come in already: he wasn't alive; there was no barrier preventing a vampire from entering his room. There was no point in attacking her when she would see him coming, her eyes steady on his through the glass of the balcony door.

"Katherine," he said, stepping out onto the balcony, keeping his voice neutral. "What do you want?"

"Dear Stefan," she said mockingly. "Is that any way to

greet your first love?" She smiled at him. He didn't know how he could ever have thought she and Elena looked alike. Their features were similar, certainly, but Elena's were firmer, her hair more golden, her eyes a deeper blue. Katherine seemed waiflike and frail in the style of her times, Elena more muscular and strong. And the love and warmth he saw in Elena's eyes was nothing like the malice Katherine's held.

"Did Klaus send you?" he asked, ignoring her comment.

"Where's Damon?" Katherine asked, playing the same game. She tilted her head flirtatiously. "You two were getting along so well the last time I saw you. Trouble in paradise already?" Stefan didn't answer, and her smile grew. "Damon should have taken my offer. He would have been happier with me."

Stefan shrugged, refusing to let Katherine see she'd gotten under his skin. "Damon didn't love you anymore, Katherine," he said, adding vindictively, "You weren't the one he wanted."

"Oh, yes, *Elena*," Katherine said. She came closer to Stefan and traced her fingers along his arm, glancing up at him through her eyelashes.

"Leave her alone," Stefan snapped.

"I'm not mad at Elena anymore," she said softly. "I had a lot of time to think. After she killed me."

"Really," Stefan said dryly, stepping away from

Katherine's lingering touches. "So being dead gave you time to get over your jealousy of Elena?"

Seeing that he wasn't responding to her pseudoinnocent flirtations, Katherine straightened up, her face hardening. "You'd be surprised how much you learn, being dead," she said. "I saw *everything*. And I see what's going on with Elena and Damon. In fact"—she smiled, her long, pointed canines shining in the moonlight—"it seems Elena and I have more in common than I ever knew."

Stefan ignored the pang he felt thinking of Elena and Damon together. He trusted Elena now, and he wasn't going to fall for Katherine's games. "If you hurt her, or any of the innocent people here, I'll find a way to kill you," he said. "And this time, you'll stay dead."

Katherine laughed, a soft, bell-like sound that took him back for a moment to the gardens of his father's palazzo, many lifetimes ago. "Poor Stefan," she said. "So loyal, so loving. I've missed your passion, you know." She reached up and brushed one soft, cool hand across his cheek. "It's good to see you again." Stepping backward, she changed, her delicate form rippling in her white dress until a snowy owl spread its wings on the railing and quickly rose into the night.

Bonnie stared out the window of Zander's dorm room. It had been a long night, but now dawn was breaking, pink and gold, over the quad. She had come over an hour before, as soon as Zander had called her to tell her he needed her. When Bonnie had arrived, Zander had taken her in his arms and held her close, his eyes tightly shut, as if he was blocking everything else out, just for a moment.

Now the rest of the Pack was gone and Shay and Zander were hunched over Zander's desk behind Bonnie, sketching battle plans on scraps of paper.

"Tristan's not as strong as he should be," Shay was saying. "If we flank him with Enrique and Jared, they can compensate for his weak left forefoot."

Zander made a low, thoughtful sound. "Tristan pulled a hamstring back at the beginning of the year, but I thought he was almost healed. I'll work out with him and see if he can get back up to speed."

"Until then, we'll need to make sure he's covered," Shay said. "Marcus is strong, but he has a tendency to hesitate. What should we do about that?"

Before tonight, Bonnie hadn't quite understood what it meant that Zander was the Alpha. The Pack had mourned Chad tonight, first as wolves and then, as the moon set, as people. There had been howling and, later, speeches and tears, remembering their friend. And throughout, Zander had taken charge, guiding his friends and supporting them through their grief.

And now, the night over, he and Shay were strategizing

the best ways to keep their Pack safe in the future. They were always focused on the good of their Pack.

Bonnie now understood exactly why the High Wolf Council had chosen an Alpha female for Zander when they were younger, not just as a mate, but as a partner.

Bonnie turned as Zander stood up. "Okay," he said, rubbing his eyes. "Let's call it a night. We'll get the guys together this afternoon, see how they're doing."

"I'll head back and call you in a few hours when I'm up," Shay said, getting to her feet. They hugged and she clung to him for a minute. Separating from Zander, she gave Bonnie a stiff nod. "Later, Bonnie," she said coolly.

As the door closed behind Shay, Zander stretched out his arms to Bonnie. "Hey there," he said, and gave her his long, slow smile. Even paired with the pain in his eyes, that smile was devastating, and Bonnie went to him, twining her arms around him.

But even as she held him close, it didn't feel quite right. Zander must have sensed a stiffness in her because he pulled back, his wide, blue eyes searching hers. "What's up?" he said softly. "Are you okay? I know things are really hard."

Bonnie's eyes stung, and she had to let go of Zander with one hand so that she could wipe at them. It was just like Zander: his friend was dead, he'd spent the night comforting and protecting his Pack, and now he was worried about how *Bonnie* was doing?

"I'm fine," she said. "Just tired."

Zander caught her hand. "Hey," he said. "Seriously, what is it? Tell me."

Bonnie sighed. "I love you, Zander," she said slowly, and stopped.

Zander's eyes narrowed and he half frowned. "Why does that sound like there's a *but* at the end?" he asked.

"I *love* you, but I'm not sure that I'm good for you," Bonnie said miserably. "I see you and Shay together . . . taking care of each other, fighting side by side, looking out for the Pack together, and I can't do that. Maybe the High Wolf Council is right about what you need."

"The High Wolf . . . Bonnie, what do they have to do with this? They don't decide what I want," Zander said, his voice rising.

"I can't be that for you, Zander," Bonnie said. "I don't know. Maybe we both need some time to figure out what the future holds. What's best for us. Even if it's not . . ." Her voice broke, and she swallowed hard before continuing. "Even if it's not being together." She was looking down at her clutched hands, twisting them, unable to look Zander in the eye. "I do love you," she said desperately. "But maybe that's not all that matters."

"Bonnie," Zander said reasonably, stepping between her and the door. "This is ridiculous. We can figure this all out."

"I hope so," Bonnie said. "But for right now, I know I'm not the one you need by your side." She was trying to sound reasonable, but she heard her voice crack as she spoke.

Zander grunted a denial and reached out for Bonnie again, but she ducked away. She had to leave his room before she lost her nerve. She was sure that this was the right thing, the best thing—Zander had responsibilities, he needed someone who could understand them and be a true partner for him—but if she didn't leave right now, she was going to fall flat on the floor and wrap her arms around his legs, begging him not to let her go.

"*Bonnie,*" Zander said as she pushed by him. "Stay." She kept moving toward the door without answering. After a moment of silence, she heard Zander sit heavily on the bed.

Bonnie tried not to look back, but she couldn't help sneaking a glance at Zander as she closed the door behind her. He was hunched over, miserable, as if he was protecting himself from a blow. Maybe she was doing the right thing, or maybe she just ruined the best thing that had ever happened to her. She just didn't know.

tupid Guardians, Elena thought, hurrying away from the gym. *If they want something from me, why can't they just tell me?* She and Meredith had been sparring before Meredith's morning class and now she was in a rush to get back home. Being alone on campus made her nervous, and she wasn't sure if it was paranoia, but something felt close to Elena. Too close.

The Guardians were game players; that was all there was to it. Not straightforward, not honest. *Nothing like me,* she told herself fiercely. *Not anymore, not for a long time.* Andrés certainly wasn't like them, anyway, which was a reassuring fact.

She caught a glimpse of a figure out of the corner of her eye, just the barest impression of movement. All across campus she'd had the creeping sensation of being watched. Someone was following her.

Elena whipped around, but where she had been sure she'd seen another person, there was no one.

The back of her neck prickled, and she hunched her shoulders unhappily. Was Klaus out there? She tried to sense him, but felt nothing. She couldn't see an aura anywhere.

She pulled out her phone and tried to call Stefan. She didn't want to take her chances, and she would feel much safer if she weren't alone. Where *was* everyone? It was the middle of the morning—although the campus had gotten emptier and emptier as the students got more nervous and classes were canceled, there should have been someone else *somewhere* around.

Stefan didn't pick up. Shoving the phone back into her bag, she walked faster.

Just as she reached her dorm, a cool, commanding voice spoke behind her. "Elena Gilbert."

Elena froze and then, slowly, turned around. "Yes?" she said.

The tall woman standing behind her was serious and businesslike, her blond hair pulled back in a neat bun, dressed in a simple navy suit. Golden-flecked blue eyes gazed solemnly at Elena. This woman was not Ryannen, the Guardian of the Celestial Court who had once tried to recruit Elena to their ranks, but she was similar enough that Elena had to look carefully to be sure. The likeness bothered Elena: Ryannen had not been kind, not at all.

Quickly, she tried to read the woman's aura, but saw nothing but white light.

After a swift all-encompassing glance at Elena the woman said levelly, "I am Mylea, one of the Principal Guardians, and I have come to administer your oath of Guardianship and assign you your first task."

Elena immediately stiffened. This was what she had been waiting for, true. But was she completely ready? "Wait a minute," she said. "I'd like to know more before I swear any oaths. Were you one of the Guardians that killed my parents?"

The Guardian frowned, a line appearing between her perfectly arched eyebrows. "I'm not here to discuss the past, Elena. You have done your best to awaken your Powers even before my approach. You have brought another human Guardian here to guide and teach you. It's clear from your actions that you are eager for the responsibilities and abilities only Guardians have. You will be given the information that you need after you take your oath."

Flustered, Elena bit her lip. Everything Mylea said was true. Elena had already accepted that she was going to be a Guardian. No matter how tragic her parents' death was, nothing Mylea said now would bring them back. Elena had to think of all the people she *could* save with her Guardian Powers in full effect.

Mylea shrugged and continued. "Your life was always fated thus," she said calmly. "I could not stop it any more than I could stop the leaves from changing in the autumn." A glimpse of humor flashed suddenly across her face, making it infinitely more human. "Which means, perhaps I could stop it, but it would be difficult and in the end would cause great harm to both you and your world. What will be will be." Then the touch of humor faded, and she stared at Elena, businesslike once more. "Time is short," she said. "Answer yes or no: Are you prepared to give your oath and receive your task?"

"Yes," Elena said, and shivered. Her agreement was irrevocable. There was no changing her mind now, she knew. But she was about to be given the Power she needed to fight Klaus.

"Come, then," Mylea said. She led Elena around the corner of the dorm and into a walled alcove where an oak tree grew. Closing her eyes for a second, she nodded, and then opened them again. "No one will bother us here. Kneel and hold out your hand."

Hesitantly, Elena got to her knees on the cold grass beneath the tree and held her right hand out before her. Mylea firmly turned Elena's hand over so that it was extended palm up, and pulled a small silver, blue-jeweled dagger from her pocket. Before Elena could react, Mylea had quickly drawn the dagger across Elena's palm in a curved pattern, blood springing up in its wake. Elena hissed at the pain and automatically tried to pull back her hand, but Mylea's grip was strong.

"Repeat after me," she said. "I, Elena Gilbert, pledge to use my Powers for the betterment of the human race. I will gladly accept the tasks given me and see them to completion. I will shelter the weak and guide the strong. I acknowledge that my tasks are for the greater good and, should I fail to fulfill them, I may be subject to losing my Powers and being reassigned to the Celestial Court." Elena hesitated—*reassigned to the Celestial Court?*—but Mylea's eyes were steady and she could feel the pull of Power all around her. Blood ran down her wrist as she repeated Mylea's words, Mylea prompting her when she hesitated. The blood dripped from her hand onto the roots of the oak tree and soaked into the earth. As Elena spoke the last words, the cut across her hand healed, leaving a pale figure eight of scar tissue across her palm.

"The symbol of infinity and of the Celestial Court," Mylea said, giving Elena a small smile. She helped Elena to her feet and kissed her ceremoniously on both cheeks. "Welcome, sister," she said.

"What does it mean by 'lose my place on Earth and be reassigned to the Celestial Court'?" Elena asked.

"I'm a human—I belong here."

Mylea frowned, tilting her head to one side to study Elena. "You are no longer a human," she said. "That is the price we have to pay."

Elena gaped at her, horrified, and Mylea waved a hand dismissively and went on. "But you will remain on Earth as long as you perform your duties properly. And now for your first task. An old vampire has come to your campus, one who has caused much damage across the world. He is strong and clever, but you have confronted him before and escaped unscathed. The history you share will give you the ability to defeat him now that your Power is blossoming. At one time, he was no longer a threat."

Elena nodded, thinking of the year Klaus had been dead. "But now he has begun to kill and brought himself to our attention once again. His fate is sealed," Mylea continued. "You must kill the vampire Damon Salvatore."

Elena gasped. *No*, she thought dazedly. *Klaus, she's supposed to say Klaus.*

In the split second in which Elena was reeling, Mylea turned neatly away, pulling an elaborate golden key from her pocket, and twisted the key in midair.

"No!" Elena said, finding her voice. But she was too late. The empty air rippled, and Mylea was gone.

tefan had a very strong sense of déjà vu. Here he was again, heavyhearted outside the dark wood door of Damon's apartment, ready to plead with his brother but knowing already that his words would be pointless. He could hear Damon moving quietly inside the apartment, the pages of a book flicking, his brother's shallow breaths, and he knew that Damon could hear him, too, hesitating in the hall.

He knocked. This time, when Damon opened the door, he didn't immediately snarl at Stefan but instead gazed at him patiently, waiting for Stefan to speak.

"I know you don't want to see me," Stefan said. "But I thought I should tell you what's going on."

Damon stepped back and waved Stefan in. "Whatever you like, little brother," he said airily. "I'm afraid I can't ask you to stay long, though. I've got a date with a delicious little undergraduate." His smile broadened as Stefan winced.

Deciding not to respond to that, Stefan sank down into one of sleek chrome-and-pale-green chairs in Damon's ultramodern living room. Damon was looking better than he had the last time Stefan had been here. His clothes and hair were perfectly, stylishly arranged, and his pale skin had a slight flush, a sure sign that Damon had been feeding freely. Stefan grimaced a little at the thought, and Damon arched one eyebrow at him.

"So, there is *something going on?*" he prompted. His voice took on a mocking tone with the last few words.

"Katherine's back," Stefan said flatly, and had the pleasure of seeing the smile fall off Damon's face. "Klaus raised her from the dead somehow."

Damon blinked slowly, his long black lashes veiling his eyes for a moment, and then he flashed his cruel smile again. "The dynamic duo together again, hmm?" he asked. "That should be quite a handful for you and your humans."

"Damon." Stefan heard the catch in his own voice. Damon had constructed a wall around himself, but the real Damon was still in there, wasn't he? He couldn't have stopped caring about Elena, stopped caring about Stefan himself, so absolutely in such a short time, could he? If Stefan's plan against Klaus was to work, he would need

Damon to care. "Klaus is determined to find out the truth about Elena," he said quickly. "They're bound to use Katherine as a weapon against you. They'll see how you've separated yourself from the rest of us. I'm begging you, please don't tell them anything. If you don't give a damn about any of us anymore, at least remember how much you hate Katherine and Klaus."

Tilting his head to one side, Damon narrowed his eyes speculatively at Stefan. "I've never been the weakest link, brother," he said. "But, as a matter of simple curiosity, tell me, *what* truth about Elena?"

The floor swung dizzyingly under Stefan's feet and he closed his eyes for a moment. He was such a fool. He hadn't asked for the details of Elena's and Damon's midnight meeting in the woods, and he'd just assumed Elena had told him she was a Guardian. He could have kept his mouth shut, and Damon would have been no danger to them, at least not on this count.

But no, Damon had known that Elena was a potential Guardian, that they had once planned for her to join them. She had told him that the Guardians had killed her parents, trying to get to her. And he knew that Elena had Power now, that she could see auras. If he had let those facts slip to Katherine or Klaus, it would have been dangerous enough. Better that Damon be warned off with a partial truth. Right? Stefan shook his head slightly. It was impossible to know what Damon might do.

Damon was still watching him, his eyes bright and cru- elly amused, and Stefan had the uncomfortable feeling that his indecision was playing out boldly across his fea- tures, plainly evident to someone who had known him as long as Damon had.

"The truth that Elena is connected to the Guardians," he said at last. "Klaus would use it against her if he could. *Please*, Damon. You say you don't care, but you can't want Klaus to kill Elena. Klaus nearly destroyed you." He could hear the begging note in his own voice. *Please, my brother,* he thought, unsure about whether Damon was reading his thoughts. *Please. Don't abandon us. There's nothing but pain that way, for all of us.*

Damon smiled briefly and flicked his fingers dismis- sively at Stefan before turning away. "No one hurts me, little brother," he said over his shoulder. "Not for long. But don't worry, I'm sure I can handle Katherine if she comes to me."

Stefan shifted closer to his brother, moving to meet Damon's eyes again. "If something happens to me," he said somberly, "tell me you'll look out for Elena. You loved her once. She could love you, if . . . if things were differ- ent." No matter what happened, Elena couldn't be left unprotected.

For a moment, Damon's mask of indifference seemed

to lift, his mouth going taut and his midnight-dark eyes narrowing. "What do you mean, if something happens to you?" he said sharply.

Stefan shook his head. "Nothing," he said. "It's a dangerous time, is all."

Damon stared at him for a moment longer, and then the mask slammed back into place. "All times are dangerous," he said, smiling faintly. "Now, if you'll excuse me . . ." He wandered off in the direction of the kitchen, and after a few minutes, Stefan realized he wasn't coming back.

Stefan pushed himself to his feet and hesitated only briefly before turning toward the door. The meeting had gone as well as he could have reasonably expected: Damon hadn't guaranteed his own silence, but he hadn't threatened them either, and he'd seemed scornful of any suggestion that he might help Katherine and Klaus. As far as protecting Elena was concerned, all Stefan could do was say his piece. He knew that if it really came down to it, his brother would do the right thing.

Stefan called a farewell, which went unanswered, and headed out the door. For all he knew, Damon had left through a window and was already winging his way across campus as a crow.

His heart sank at the thought of leaving his brother now without a good-bye, but he kept going. If they both survived, he and Damon would connect again as brothers.

He couldn't let go of that hope. But he didn't know when or how it would happen. Maybe he'd lost his brother for another century or two. The thought made him feel bleakly, unutterably alone.

att's feet dragged as he walked slowly toward the boathouse doors. In his hand, the sack he carried thrashed violently, the rabbit inside kicking and squirming. Chloe would be able to calm it with a touch of her Power.

Matt didn't like catching animals for her to feed on. He couldn't help feeling sorry for the poor things, so wide-eyed with terror. But he was responsible for Chloe. And she needed lots of blood to keep control; Stefan had warned them of that. It didn't help that seeing Klaus's army of vampires had terrified her. They were so much more powerful than she was, and she knew they would show no mercy to a vampire who fought against them. Worse, the excitement of the battle had stirred her urge to drink human blood. She didn't trust herself around the others, so she'd been sequestering herself in the boathouse ever since.

She would never hurt Matt, though; she assured him of that every night, holding him tightly, her cold body against his warmer one, her head pillowed on his shoulder in the darkness.

A board creaked under Matt's feet and he glanced down at the water lapping against the pilings beneath him. The dock creaked again, this time in the distance, as if someone else was walking across it.

Matt hesitated. There shouldn't be anyone else here. He stepped forward again, cautiously, and heard the echoing sound of another board creaking in the distance, just a second after his own footstep.

"Hello?" he called into the darkness, and then felt like an idiot. If his enemies were out there, the last thing he wanted to do was draw their attention.

He took a few steps closer to the entrance to the boathouse. The creaking didn't come again; instead, a small splash rose from the shallow lake. Maybe the noises had been an animal.

He broke into a run anyway, slamming through the boathouse doors. What if something had gotten to Chloe? Matt's eyes flew to the tableau in the center of the boathouse.

Klaus stood triumphantly in front of him, his skin lit silver by the moonlight coming through the holes in the roof.

A battered raincoat covered his broad figure, and slumped in his arms was a bleeding girl, a stranger.

God. She was young, maybe a small freshman, maybe a high-school girl from the town, and her long, dark hair was matted with the blood streaming from the side of her neck. She wasn't struggling, but she gazed at Matt with a terrified look that reminded him nauseatingly of the rabbit's expression when he'd lifted it out of the trap.

He automatically dropped the sack, hearing it thud behind him, the rabbit scrabbling out and bolting for the door. He had to help the girl. Klaus flicked his eyes toward him for a split second and Matt froze, his muscles tensed helplessly against the force holding him in place.

"Hello, boy," Klaus said, flashing his mad smile. "Come to join the party? Your girlfriend and I have been waiting for you."

Matt followed Klaus's gaze to Chloe, who was huddled in a corner as far from Klaus and the girl as possible, her knees pulled up to her chest. There was a bite mark on her neck, as if Klaus had already drunk from her, too, and she was extraordinarily pale. *She needs to feed*, Matt thought, as if he could just hand her the rabbit he'd had a moment ago. Chloe was clearly frightened, but there was something else showing in her face. Matt's stomach rolled unhappily as he identified it: *hunger.*

"Now, where were we?" Klaus turned back to Chloe.

"Ah, yes. If you just let go, everything will be so easy." His voice was soft and soothing. "Tell me everything. Tell me the secret these *humans* are hiding. How have the witches protected Elena from me? If you do, I'll let you join me. You won't be alone. You won't have to be afraid, or feel guilt, or anything anymore." His face twisted with scorn as he said the word *humans*, and he went on, his voice dropping into a lower register. "Taste the girl," he said. "You can have her. I know you can smell the rich sweetness of her blood. This is no way for you to live, hidden away, ashamed, feeding on vermin. Come to me, Chloe," he said, commanding now.

Chloe uncurled slowly, climbing to her feet. Her eyes were fixed on Klaus and on the girl, who was sobbing quietly now in Klaus's arms. From the shift in Chloe's jaw, Matt could see that her canine teeth had lengthened. Klaus beckoned, and Chloe took one stumbling step forward.

Struggling to cry out, to stop Chloe somehow, Matt realized that his tongue was as frozen as the rest of him, held still by Klaus's Power. The best he could do was let out a small, stifled moan.

Chloe heard it, though. She licked her lips, then slowly dragged her eyes from the girl's throat and focused on Matt. She stared at him for a long moment, and then stepped back, pressing herself flat against the wall. The bones of her face looked sharp and the drying blood on her own throat cracked and flaked as she shook her head.

"No," she said in a tiny voice.

Klaus smiled again and held the girl out toward her. "Come on now," he urged. His victim whimpered and closed her eyes, her face crumpling in misery. Chloe stood still against the wall, seemingly riveted by the long stream of blood running down from the girl's throat to pool on the floor at her feet.

Klaus reached for Chloe and took her by the hand. "Tell me what I want to know, and you can have her. She tastes so *good*." He tugged Chloe toward him. She gasped sharply, her nostrils flaring as she got closer to the scent of blood, and let herself be drawn closer and closer. Klaus let go of Chloe's hand and stroked her cheek. "There," he said, as if he were talking to a small child. "There we go." Cupping his hand behind her head, he pushed her firmly down, brought her toward the throat of the girl he held.

Matt tried to struggle but he couldn't move, couldn't cry out to Chloe again. Her tongue flickered out quickly across her lips.

Then Chloe pushed away from Klaus, ducking out from under his hand. "No!" she repeated, louder this time.

Klaus snarled, a maddened sound, and with one quick twist, snapped the bleeding girl's neck, dropping her in a heap on the floor.

"Tell your friends they'll all be hearing from me soon,"

Klaus said, his voice level and cold. He sounded *less* insane than usual, and for some reason, that made Matt's heart clench with fear. "I will find the truth. I'll take them apart, one by one, until I get what I want."

As he strode out the door, Klaus looked up, reaching one hand toward the sky, and with a crash of thunder, a bolt of lightning struck from the clear, cloudless sky, sparking the boathouse into flames.

Flipping over a page in her psychology textbook, Bonnie firmly pushed the thought of Zander away. She missed him—of course she did—but she would be *fine.*

Without looking up, Bonnie checked in on the other occupants of their dorm room. The gentle scritching sound of a pen came from Elena's bed, where she was writing in her journal. And on the floor, Meredith and Alaric murmured softly to each other, their hands entwined, for once not sharpening weapons or examining spell books, but just enjoying each other.

Except for the constant empty ache in Bonnie's heart, everything was fine.

Somebody pounded violently on the door, and they all looked up, tensing, ready to slip into fight mode. Meredith jumped to her feet and grabbed a knife from her desk, holding it out of sight as she cracked the door open.

Matt and Chloe, streaked with blood and covered in

ash, tumbled through the door.

Meredith was the first to react, grabbing Chloe and turning her under the light to examine the bite on her neck. It looked raw and gruesome, and Chloe nearly collapsed in Meredith's arms before Alaric steered the young vampire into Bonnie's desk chair.

"What happened?" Bonnie exclaimed.

"Klaus," Matt gasped. "Klaus was in the boathouse. There's—oh, God—he left a body in there. And set the place on fire. She was dead, though. I'm sure she was already dead before she burned."

Elena's fingers flew over her phone as she sent a quick text, and a moment later, Stefan was there, taking in the situation at a glance. He knelt in front of Chloe, examining her wound with careful fingers.

"Animal blood isn't enough to heal her right now," he said to Matt, who was watching with a tense, hunted expression, his lips tight and pale. "And a taste of human might send her over the edge." He bit his own wrist and held it to Chloe's lips. "This isn't ideal, but it's the best of some bad options."

Matt nodded tightly, and Stefan held Chloe's hand as the vampire girl gulped hungrily at his arm. "It's all right," he told her. "You're doing well."

Once Chloe had drunk enough to begin healing from Klaus's bite, she and Matt explained what had happened.

"Klaus offered me the girl if I'd tell him what I knew about Elena and why he couldn't kill her with his dagger," she said. Her eyes dropped to the floor. "It was . . ." She paused. "I wanted to say yes."

"She didn't, though," Matt told them. "Chloe did really well. She broke through Klaus's compulsion."

"But he said he would come after us one by one until he got what he wanted?" Bonnie asked faintly. "This is bad. This is really very bad." Her heart was pounding hard, drumming against her chest.

Elena sighed, tucking her hair behind her ears. "We knew that he would be coming after us," she pointed out.

"Yes," Bonnie said, her voice shaking, "but, Elena, he can get into my *dreams*. He did before, when he told us he was coming." She hugged herself tightly and took a deep breath, trying to keep her voice steady. "I don't know if I can stop him from seeing things in my dreams."

There was a nasty pause in the conversation. "I hadn't thought of that," Meredith admitted.

"I'm sorry, you guys," Elena said, her voice break-ing. "He's coming after you because of *me*. I wish I could defend you. I need to get stronger."

"You will," Meredith said firmly.

"And it's really not your fault," Bonnie said support-ively, pushing her own panic down. "If the alternative was you dying, I'd rather he was coming after us."

Elena smiled wanly. "I know, Bonnie," she said. "But even if I get more Power, I don't know how we can protect you in your dreams."

"Are there ways she can protect her dreams herself?" Stefan asked, turning to Alaric, their research expert. "Conscious dreaming and that kind of thing?"

Alaric nodded thoughtfully. "It's a good idea," he said. "I'll look it up right away." He smiled reassuringly at Bonnie. "We'll find something. We always do."

"And we all will stick together," Stefan said, looking around, his leaf-green eyes confident. "Klaus can't break us."

There was a murmur of agreement, and Bonnie automatically reached out, taking Meredith's and Matt's hands in hers. Soon, they were all holding hands, and Bonnie felt a thrum of Power, maybe from Elena, maybe from Stefan, maybe from herself, run around the circle. Perhaps it was from all of them.

But that sense of Power wasn't the only thing she felt. Everyone was nervous; everyone was scared. Klaus could come after any one of them next, and it was impossible to know what he might do.

tefan and Elena were alone in Elena's dorm room at last, taking advantage of the small moment they had together. Bonnie, Meredith, and Alaric were in the library studying up on dream control, while Stefan had offered Matt and Chloe his room for the night now that their boathouse hideaway had been destroyed.

Stefan cupped Elena's cheek gently. "What's wrong?" he said, concerned by whatever it was he saw in her eyes. Elena had thought she was hiding her fear pretty well, but Stefan had always been able to see through her masks. She was glad they were finally alone. She didn't want the others to know, not yet. They weren't determined to protect Damon, not like she and Stefan were.

"A Principal Guardian came to me today and made me

take the Guardian oath," she told him. "She gave me my first task."

For a moment, Stefan's face lightened. "But that's wonderful news," he said. "Now you'll be able to access more Power to fight Klaus, won't you?"

Elena shook her head. "My task isn't to kill Klaus," she told him simply. "They want me to kill Damon."

Stefan, eyes wide with shock, stepped back, his hand dropping from Elena's cheek.

"I'm *not* going to do it," she said. "You know that. But we have to figure out how to get around this. If I just refuse to do it, they'll"—her mouth went dry—"banish me to the Celestial Court. I won't be on Earth anymore."

"No." Stefan's arms were around her again, holding her close. "Never."

Elena pressed her face against his neck. "I can't do it," she whispered. "The Guardian told me that Damon was killing again, and I *still* can't bring myself to hurt him."

She felt Stefan stiffen at the news, but when she looked up his eyes were steady. "Elena, I love my brother. But if Damon's murdering innocent people, we have to stop him. No matter what the cost."

"I can't kill Damon," Elena said again. "The Guardians already took away two people I love, and I won't let them take away any more. We have to find another way."

"What if Damon changes?" Stefan asked. "If he's not a

threat to humans, will the Guardians change their minds?"

Elena shook her head. "I don't know," she said. "But Damon won't listen to us; he's completely shut down. Maybe if we tell him that the Guardians want him dead?"

Stefan's lip quirked into a rueful almost-smile, just for a moment. "Maybe," he said. "Or maybe he'll double his attacks just to defy them. Damon would laugh at the devil if he felt like it."

Elena nodded. It was true, and she knew Stefan was sharing both the affection and the despair Damon inspired in her.

"Maybe Andrés will have an idea," Stefan suggested. "He knows a lot more about Guardian business than we do. But are you sure we can trust him?"

"Of course we can," Elena said automatically. Andrés was *good*—she knew that without question. And he had fought beside them against Klaus.

Gripping Elena's shoulder tightly, Stefan looked into her eyes again, his face grim. "I know we can trust Andrés to do what's right," he said. "But can we trust him to save a vampire—a violent vampire? *I* don't even know if that's the right thing."

Elena swallowed. "I think I can trust Andrés to back me up," she said carefully, "even against the Guardians. He believes in me." She hoped desperately that this was true.

Stefan gave her a sad smile. "Then tomorrow we talk

to Andrés," he said. He pulled her into an embrace and stroked a hand through her hair. "Tonight, though, let's take some time and be together, you and me," he said, his voice rough. There was a long silence as Elena just let Stefan hold her.

"I want Damon to live," Stefan finally said. "I want him to change. But if it comes down to a choice between him and you, I have to choose you. There's no world for me without you, Elena. I'm not going to let you sacrifice yourself this time."

Elena didn't answer, refused to make any promises she might not be able to keep. She hoped the love flowing between them would be enough, for now.

The next morning, Elena and Stefan sat with James and Andrés in James's small, sunny kitchen. All four of them had cups of coffee and bagels in front of them, and Stefan stirred his coffee without sipping it, just to keep his hands busy. He didn't eat or drink much, but it made people more comfortable if they thought he did. It was a cheerful morning scene, except for the look of complete confusion on James's face.

"I don't understand," he said, looking from Elena to Stefan in bewilderment. "Why are you trying to save a *vampire?*"

Elena opened her mouth, then closed it and thought

for a moment. "He's Stefan's brother," she said flatly after a moment. "And we love him."

James shot Stefan a scandalized look, and Stefan tried to remember if James had any idea that Stefan was also a vampire. He didn't think so, actually.

Elena went on. "Damon's fought at our side and saved a lot of people," she said. "We need to give him a chance to get better. We can't just forget all the good he's done."

Andrés nodded. "You're reluctant to kill him when there might be some other way to control his missteps."

James shook his head. "I'm not sure I'd call eating people 'missteps,'" he said. "I'm sorry, Elena. I don't think I can help you." Stefan tensed, feeling the coffee spoon bend in his hand.

"We'll fix him," Elena said. Her chin was out determinedly. "He won't be a danger to anyone."

Andrés sighed and laid his hands flat on the table, all traces of humor gone from his face. "You took an oath," he said quietly. "The Guardians believe in rules, and, as you've agreed to their rules, you must fulfill your task or suffer the consequences. Even if you accept your removal to the Celestial Court, the task will simply pass to another Earthly Guardian." He grimaced, and Stefan's heart sank. Andrés was telling them that he might be the next one assigned to kill Damon. If Elena somehow got out of the job, they'd be fighting Andrés.

Elena's eyes were bright with tears. "There must be some way to fix this," she said. "How do I summon the Principal Guardian back? Maybe I can reason with her. Klaus is much more dangerous than Damon is. Even if you don't agree with me about saving Damon, you have to see that Klaus is the one we need to focus on."

"You can't call her," Andrés said sadly. "They only appear to assign a task, or when the task is completed." He slowly shook his head. "Elena, there's no gray area here. You're already feeling the drive to fulfill your mission, aren't you? That's only going to get worse."

Elena put her head in her hands, resting her elbows on the table. Stefan touched her shoulder, and she leaned into him as he channeled silent support to her. After a moment, she lifted her head, her mouth firm with resolve. "Okay," she said. "Then I'll try something else. I'm not giving up."

"I will help you if I can," Andrés told her. "But if your task passes to me, I won't have a choice."

Elena nodded and stood up briskly. Stefan started to follow her, but she put a hand on his shoulder and gently pressed him back down. "This one I have to do by myself," she said apologetically. She kissed him lightly, her lips warm, and Stefan tried to send all the love and trust he could to her.

I have something I have to take care of, too, he thought. He didn't know when he'd back. This might, he realized with a flare of breathless panic, be the last time they saw each other. His arms tightened around her, holding on to her for as long as he could. *Please, Elena, be careful.*

Finding Damon was easy. When Elena opened herself to the nagging ache that had been inside her all day, barely touching on her Power, the path to Damon appeared ahead of her and all she had to do was follow the vivid black and red.

This time, it led to a seedy-looking building with a sign out front that read EDDIE'S BILLIARDS. It was open, but there were only a couple of cars in the parking lot. It looked more like a nighttime place. Frankly, it didn't look like Elena's kind of place at all, and she felt a little nervous walking up to the doors. *I've been to the Dark Dimension*, she reminded herself. *I'm a Guardian. There's nothing here that can scare me.* She pushed through the doors and boldly stepped inside.

The bartender made eye contact with her for a moment and then turned back to his chore, polishing glasses. Two men sat at a small round table in the corner, smoking and talking quietly. They didn't even glance up at her. All but one of the pool tables were empty.

There, in the middle of the room, Damon leaned over the pool table, lining up his cue to take a shot. He looked tough in his leather jacket, Elena thought, rougher and somehow less elegant than he usually did. A shorter, fairer man hovered behind him. As he made the shot, Damon flicked his eyes up toward Elena, cool and black and giving nothing away.

"Game's over," he said briefly to his companion, despite the colored balls still littering the table. Damon picked up the wad of bills on the corner of the table and stuffed them into his pocket. The sandy-haired guy seemed about to speak at this, but then bit his lip and stared at the floor, remaining silent.

"You don't give up, do you?" Damon said, crossing the room toward Elena in a few quick steps. He seemed to be weighing her up with his dark, considering gaze. "I told you, I won't be any help to you anymore, princess."

Elena felt her cheeks heat up. Damon always called her *princess*, but this time the nickname lacked the affection she was used to. Now it sounded dismissive, as if he couldn't be bothered to use her real name. She stiffened, using the flash of anger to help her start talking.

"You're in trouble, Damon," she said brusquely. "The Principal Guardians want you dead. They've assigned me to kill you." For a moment, she thought Damon looked startled, and she pushed forward. "I don't want to do it, Damon," she said, letting a pleading note creep into her voice. "I *can't*. But maybe it's not too late. If you change what you're doing . . ."

Damon shrugged. "Do what you have to do, princess,"

he said lightly. "The Guardians couldn't keep me dead before—I'm not too worried now." He started to turn away, and Elena sidestepped to block his path.

"You have to take this seriously, Damon," she said. "They will *kill* you."

Damon sighed. "Frankly," he said, "I think they're overreacting. So I killed someone. It was one girl, in a world of millions of girls." He glanced over her shoulder, back at the pool table. "Jimmy? Rack them up."

Feeling like she'd been punched in the stomach, Elena gaped breathlessly, then followed him back to the table. Jimmy arranged the balls and Damon broke, carefully angling his cue. "What do you mean, you killed some-one?" she said at last in a tiny voice.

Something she couldn't quite identify flickered over Damon's face, but then it was gone. "I'm afraid I got car-ried away," he said lightly. "Happens to the best of us, I suppose." He knocked a ball into a pocket and circled the table to take another shot.

Elena's mind was turning over what she'd seen: the girl she and Stefan had found unconscious in the woods, the girl Damon had been feeding on near the athletic fields. They'd been fine in the end, hadn't they? She and Stefan had made sure they got home safely. Dread coiled inside her as she finally realized what he was saying. Damon had killed someone else, someone they hadn't found. She'd been holding out hope for him, but he was murdering again, and she hadn't even known.

She made an effort now to see Damon's aura, and it became visible almost immediately. Elena winced in dismay at the sight. It was so dark, all the color almost swallowed up in blackness now, cut with repulsive winding strains of dried-blood red. Surely there was still something else there? She saw a wisp of greenish-blue close to Damon's body, but just as quickly as it appeared, it was covered again in darkness.

Still, that glimpse of color gave her a bit of hope. Damon wasn't lost yet. He couldn't be.

Impulsively, she followed Damon to the other side of the table and laid a hand on his arm. His muscles twitched once, as if about to pull away, then grew still. "Please, Damon," she said. "I know this isn't you. You're not a killer, not anymore. I love you. Please."

Damon placed his cue carefully on the table and glared at her, his body tense and strained. "You *love* me?" he asked in a low, dangerous voice. "You don't even know me, princess. I'm not your lapdog—I'm a vampire. Do you know what that means?" Elena involuntarily stepped back, alarmed by the anger in Damon's eyes, and his lips tipped up in a tiny smirk. "Jimmy," he called over his shoulder, and the guy he'd been playing pool with came over to them, still holding his cue.

"Yeah?" he said hesitantly, and Elena heard it in his tone: he was afraid of Damon. Glancing around, she could see the bartender hurriedly averting his eyes from them, as if he, too, was afraid. The two men from the table in the corner had slipped out while she was talking to Damon.

"Give me your cue," Damon said, and Jimmy handed it to him. Damon snapped it in two as easily as Elena herself would have torn a piece of paper and looked speculatively at the pieces in his hands. From one half extended long, jagged splinters of wood, and Damon handed that half back to Jimmy.

"Now take this and stab yourself with it," he said calmly. "Keep going until I tell you to stop."

"Damon, no! Don't do it," she told Jimmy. "Fight it."

Jimmy, staring at the cue, hesitated, and Elena felt the sudden *snap* of Power as Jimmy's face went distant and dreamy, and he raised the pool cue and jabbed it hard at his own stomach. As the cue made contact, he gave a harsh exhalation of breath, but his face remained unconcerned, his mind disconnected from what his body was doing. Jimmy pulled the cue back again, and Elena could see a long bloody streak where one of the splinters had gone into his side.

"Stop it!" Elena shouted.

"Harder," Damon ordered, "and faster." Jimmy obeyed, the cue snapping back and forth roughly. Blood was running down his shirt now. Damon watched with a small smile, his eyes bright. "Being a vampire," he said to Elena, "means that I like being in control. I like blood, too. And I don't have to care about human pain, any more than you do about the pain of the insect you tread on as you walk down the street."

"Please stop it," Elena said, horrified. "Don't hurt him any more."

Damon's smile widened, and he looked away from Jimmy, turning his whole attention to Elena. Jimmy's arms kept jerking back and forth, though, thrusting the pool cue into himself even without Damon's focus on him. "I'll only stop if you leave right now, princess," Damon said.

Elena blinked away tears. She was stronger than he thought. She would prove it. "Fine," she said. "I'll go. But Damon"—and here she dared to touch his arm again, a quick soft touch—"what you said when I came in is true. I *never* give up." Something seemed to shift in Damon when Elena touched him, the slightest softening of the grim lines of his face, and Elena almost felt like she'd gotten through to him. But a second later he was as cold and distant as ever.

Elena wheeled quickly and walked away, head high. Behind her, she heard Damon speak sharply and Jimmy's grunts of pain cease.

Had she imagined the momentary change in Damon's

expression? *Please, please let that have been real,* Elena pleaded silently. Surely there was something left in that angry stranger behind her, something of the Damon she loved. She couldn't lose him. But as she felt a wrenching in her chest, she wondered if she already had.

he late afternoon sky was deep blue and golden with sunlight, and Stefan was grateful for the shade of the trees. *What kind of vampire provokes a confrontation in the daylight?* he could imagine Damon asking wryly before answering the question himself: *a very stupid one, Stefan.*

The sun was making him slightly weary like it always did, his consciousness of its light a constant low, dull throbbing like a headache, despite the ring that protected him. Klaus was older than Stefan, and stronger. The sun wouldn't bother him as much.

But Stefan didn't want to face Klaus in the darkness. The hair on the back of his neck prickled uneasily at the very idea: after so long as a vampire, now Stefan himself was afraid of a monster in the dark.

He stopped when he reached the clearing in the woods where they'd fought Klaus's family. Blood was the best way to attract any vampire's attention. Stefan let his canines lengthen, then, wincing, bit sharply into his own wrist.

"Klaus!" he shouted, turning in a semicircle, his arm extended so that the blood spattered the ground around him. *"Klaus!"*

Stefan stopped and listened to the noises of the woods: the light crackle of an animal moving through the undergrowth, the creak of tree branches in the wind. A long way away, nearer to campus, he could hear a couple hiking through the woods, laughing. No sign of Klaus. Taking a deep breath, Stefan slumped back against a tree trunk, cradling his bleeding arm protectively to his chest. He thought of Elena's warmth, of her gentle kiss. He had to save her.

From behind him came a deep, amused voice: "Hello, Salvatore."

Stefan spun around, stumbling in alarm. How had he not heard the older vampire arrive?

Klaus's threadbare raincoat was dirty, but he wore it as if it were a royal robe. Every time he saw Klaus, Stefan was struck by how tall he was, how clear and sharp his eyes were. Klaus smiled and closed the distance between them again, standing too close. He smelled nauseatingly of blood and smoke and something subtly rotting.

"You called me, Salvatore?" Klaus asked him. He laid a hand on Stefan's shoulder companionably.

"I wanted to talk," Stefan said, keeping himself from flinching under Klaus's hand. "I have an offer for you."

"Let me guess." Klaus's smile widened. "You think we should settle our differences like gentlemen?" He sounded delighted. His fingers tightened on Stefan's shoulder like a vise, and Stefan's knees buckled. Klaus was so strong, even stronger than Stefan had remembered. "While I appreciate the blood you and your brother gave to bring me back, I hold all the cards in this game, Salvatore. I don't need to play by your rules."

"Not all the cards. You can't kill Elena," Stefan blurted, and Klaus cocked his head to one side, considering.

"Are you going to tell me how?" he asked. "Tired of your lady fair already? I did wonder why she's still human after all this time. You're leaving an out from eternal love, aren't you? Clever."

"I mean, she can't be killed," Stefan said doggedly. He lifted his head proudly, trying to project confidence. Klaus had to believe him. "Kill me instead. I'm the one you hate most."

Klaus laughed, his sharp canines showing. "Oh, not clever after all," he said. "Noble and dreary instead. So Elena's the one with the out, then. She'd rather grow old and die than live forever in your arms? Your great romance must not be as strong as you thought."

"I was the one you blamed for Katherine's death," Stefan went on steadily. "I tried to kill you back in Fell's Church. You can do anything you want with me: kill me, have me join your army of followers. I won't fight you. Just leave Elena alone. You won't be able to kill her, so just let her go."

Klaus chuckled again. Suddenly, he yanked Stefan closely against him and sniffed deeply, pressing his nose against the other vampire's throat. His own scent was overwhelming, the sweet, rotting stench turning Stefan's stomach. Just as quickly, Klaus shoved Stefan away again. "You stink of lies and fear," he said. "Elena can be killed, and I'll be the one to do it. You know it, and that's why you're afraid."

Stefan made himself look Klaus squarely in the eyes. "No. She's untouchable," he stated as firmly as he could. "Kill me instead."

Klaus struck him almost languidly with one hand and Stefan felt himself flying through the air. With a loud crack, he slammed into a tree and slid to the ground, gasping for breath.

"Oh, Salvatore," Klaus said chidingly, towering above Stefan. "I do hate you. But I don't want to kill you, not anymore."

From where he lay on the ground, Stefan managed to

raise his head and grunt inquiringly. *What, then?*

"Better to kill Elena and let you live, I think," the older vampire said, his white teeth gleaming in the sunlight. "I'll kill her right in front of you, and make sure the image of her death haunts you forever, anywhere you go." His smile widened. "That'll be your fate."

Klaus turned deliberately and sauntered out of the clearing, purposely not using his vampiric speed. Just before passing out of Stefan's sight, he looked back and gave a little two-fingered salute. "I'll be seeing you soon," he said. "You and your lady love."

Stefan let his head flop back down onto the forest floor. His spine was still cracked from where Klaus had thrown him into the tree. He had failed. Klaus was convinced that there was some way to kill Elena, and he wasn't going to give up until he found it.

As soon as he could, Stefan would return to Elena and the others, give them their best chance of fighting Klaus. But a cold, dark misery was blossoming inside him and, just for the moment, Stefan let himself sink into that darkness.

onnie was padding across campus in bare feet, her ice-cream-cone pajama bottoms flapping around her ankles. *Oh, great,* she thought dismally. *I forgot to get dressed again.*

"Are you ready for the test?" Meredith said brightly next to her. Bonnie stopped and stared at her suspiciously.

"What test?" she asked. "We don't have any classes together, do we?"

"Oh, *Bonnie*," Meredith said, sighing. "Don't you even read your email? There was some kind of mix-up, it turns out, and we all have to pass a big high-school Spanish exam we missed, or we won't really have graduated."

Bonnie stared at her, frozen in horror. "But I took French," she said.

"Well, yeah," Meredith said. "That's why you should

have been studying all this time. Come on, we're going to be late." She broke into a swift-footed run, and Bonnie stumbled after her, tripping over the laces of her Converse high-tops.

Wait a second, she thought. *Wasn't I barefoot a minute ago?*

"Hang on, Meredith," she said, drawing to a halt to catch her breath. "I think this is a dream." Meredith ran on, though, straight and sure down the path, her long, dark hair flying out in the wind as she left Bonnie behind.

Definitely a dream, Bonnie thought. *In fact, I'm pretty sure I've had this dream before.* "I hate this dream," she muttered.

She tried to remember the conscious-dreaming techniques she'd been talking about with Alaric. *This is a dream*, she told herself fiercely. *Nothing is real and I can change whatever I want.* Glancing down at herself, she made her sneakers tie themselves and changed her pajamas into skinny blue jeans and a black top. "Better," she said. "Okay, forget the exam. I think I want . . ." Possibilities were flying through her mind, but then she forgot them all, because suddenly in front of her was Zander. Wonderful, darling Zander, who she missed with all her heart. And Shay.

"I hate my subconscious so much," Bonnie mumbled to herself.

Zander was gazing down at Shay with a small smile, giving her that adoring look that was supposed to be reserved for Bonnie alone. As Bonnie watched, he ran his hand gently over Shay's cheek, tipping her face toward him. *Change it!* Bonnie inwardly screamed at herself as Shay's and Zander's lips met in a soft, lingering kiss.

Before she could focus, though, everything went black for one second, and she felt a powerful, painful *yank* as she was torn from the dream. When her eyes opened, she was somewhere new, a breeze ruffling her curls. And watching her, standing alarmingly close, his face alight with laughter, was Klaus.

"Hello, little redbird," he said. "Isn't that what Damon used to call you?"

"How do you know that?" Bonnie said suspiciously. "And where am I, anyway?" The wind rose, blowing strands of hair across her face, and she shoved them back.

"I've been having a good rummage around in your mind, redbird," Klaus said. "I can't get to everything yet, but I can pick up bits and pieces." He smiled widely and engagingly. He'd be quite handsome, really, Bonnie thought wildly, if he weren't so obviously insane. Klaus went on. "That's why I picked this place to have our chat."

Bonnie's head cleared a little, and she looked around. They were outdoors, on a tiny platform sheltered by an arched cupola. In every direction, a blue expanse spread out, and far below, a touch of green. Oh, jeez. They were somewhere really high.

Bonnie *hated* heights. Forcing herself to look away from the long drop on every side, she stayed still, in the middle of the platform, as far as possible from the sides, and glared up at Klaus. "Oh, yeah?" she said. It wasn't the best line, but it was the best she could manage under the circumstances.

Klaus smiled cheerfully. "One of the pieces I came across was your memory of the orientation tour of campus. They offered to take you up in the bell tower, didn't they? But *you* said"—and suddenly an eerie echo of Bonnie's voice rose up all around them, joking, but with a touch of actual fear—*"No way, Jose, if I go up that high I'll have screaming nightmares for a week!"* As the memory of Bonnie's voice died away, Klaus grinned. "And so I thought this might be a good place for our heart-to-heart."

Bonnie remembered the incident on the tour vividly. The bell tower, the highest spot on campus, was a popular place, but Bonnie couldn't look at it without her stomach clenching up. Zander and his friends liked to party on the rooftops of buildings, but rooftops tended to be a lot bigger than the bell tower, and there Bonnie could stay away from the edges. Plus, at those parties, she'd had big, reassuring, protective Zander with her, which made all the difference.

Still, she wasn't going to let Klaus see he was getting to

her. Crossing her arms defiantly, she carefully looked only at Klaus. "I was kidding on the tour," she lied. "I just didn't want to climb all those stairs."

"Interesting," Klaus said, his smile widening, and then he raised his hands. He didn't touch Bonnie, but she found herself suddenly skidding back away from him, as if he was pushing her very hard. Her back collided at last with the railing at the edge of the platform, and she let out a helpless little *whoof* of air.

"Don't lie to me, redbird," Klaus said softly, walking toward her. "I can smell your fear."

Bonnie clenched her teeth and said nothing. She did not look behind her.

"Tell me Elena's secret, little bird," Klaus said, his voice still soft and coaxing. "You're her witch, so you must know. Why couldn't I kill her in the battle? Did you do something?"

"No idea. Maybe your knife was dull," Bonnie quipped.

She squeaked involuntarily as her feet suddenly left the ground. She was—oh, God—dangling in midair like a puppet suspended by invisible strings. Then those strings yanked her backward, her ankles banging painfully against the top of the railing as she was swept powerlessly out to hang in empty space. Bonnie caught one terrifying glimpse of the campus far below her before she slammed her eyes shut. *Don't let me fall*, she prayed. *Please, please.* Her heart was pounding so hard she couldn't breathe.

"You know, they say that if you die in your dreams, you really die in your bed," Klaus said softly, sounding like he was right next to her. "And I can tell you from personal experience that the saying's quite true." He let out a low, sickeningly excited laugh. "If I drop you, they'll be picking pieces of you out of your bedroom walls for weeks," he said. "But it doesn't have to come to that. Just tell me the truth and I'll let you down gently. I promise."

Bonnie clenched her eyes and her jaw shut tighter. Even if she were willing to betray Elena—which she *wasn't*, she never would, no matter what, she told herself firmly—she didn't believe Klaus would keep his promise. She remembered dazedly how Vickie Bennett had died, though, at Klaus's hands. She'd been torn to shreds, her blood spattered like a kid had swung around a can of red paint in her pink room. Maybe Klaus had killed Vickie in her dreams.

Klaus chuckled, and the air around Bonnie shifted again.

"What's going on?" a confused, frightened, and oh-so-familiar voice asked. Bonnie's eyes snapped open.

Next to her in midair dangled Zander. All the color was bleached out of his face, so that his wide, terrified eyes looked even more impossibly blue than usual. He was grasping at empty air with both hands, struggling to find something to hold on to.

"Bonnie?" he croaked. "Please, what's going on?"

"Your girlfriend, or ex-girlfriend, is refusing to tell me something I want to know," Klaus told him. Klaus was seated on the railing of the bell tower, his own legs dangling off the side. He smiled at Zander. "I thought if I brought you in, you might provide some incentive for her."

Zander looked at Bonnie pleadingly. "Please tell him, Bonnie," he begged. "I need this to stop. Let me down."

Bonnie gulped, panicking. "Zander," she said. "Zander, oh, no. Don't hurt him."

"Whatever happens to Zander now is your fault, red-bird," Klaus reminded her.

And then something clicked together. *Hang on*, a voice said inside Bonnie's head. The voice, cool and cynical, sounded sort of like Meredith. *Zander's not scared of heights. He loves them.*

"Stop it," she said to Klaus. "That's not Zander. That's just something you made up. If you're finding stuff inside my head, you're doing a terrible job. Zander's *nothing* like that."

Klaus gave a sharp growl of irritation, and the Zander he'd created went limp in the air beside her, his head flopping to one side. He looked disturbingly dead like that, and even though Bonnie knew it wasn't real, she had to look away.

She'd known all along this was a dream, of course. But

she'd forgotten the central thing about controlling dreams: *they weren't real.*

"This is a dream," she murmured to herself. "Nothing is real and I can change whatever I want." She looked at the false Zander and blipped him back out of existence.

"Clever, aren't you?" Klaus commented, and then, as easily as opening his hand, he let her fall.

Bonnie sucked in one frightened breath, and then remembered to make a floor under her feet. She stumbled as she landed, her ankle turning under her, but she wasn't hurt.

"It's not over yet, redbird," Klaus said, climbing down from the railing and walking toward her across the air as if it were solid, his dirty raincoat flapping in the breeze. He was still chuckling, and there was something about the sound that frightened Bonnie. Without even thinking about it, she flexed her mind and *threw* him as far as she could.

Klaus's body flew backward, as floppy as a rag doll, and Bonnie had just a second to see his startled expression turn to rage before he was only a falling black speck on the horizon. As Bonnie watched, the speck stopped falling, turned, and rose, coming back toward her. It moved alarmingly fast, and soon she could make out the outline of some great predatory bird, a hawk perhaps, swooping toward her.

Time to wake up, she thought. "It's just a dream," she

said. Nothing happened. Klaus was getting closer, much closer.

"It's only a dream," she repeated, "and I can wake up anytime I want. I want to wake up *now*."

And then she really did wake, warm under her comforter in her own cozy bed.

After one gasp of pure relief, Bonnie began to cry— great, ugly, choking sobs. She reached onto her desk, feeling for her cell phone. The images of Zander, his face intent, kissing Shay, hanging powerlessly in the air, stuck with her. They hadn't been the real Zander; Bonnie knew that intellectually. But she needed to hear his voice anyway. Just as she was about to push the button to dial, she hesitated.

It wasn't fair to call him, was it? She was the one who had said they should take some time apart, so Zander could think about what would be right for him, not just as a person, but as the Alpha of a Pack. It wouldn't be fair to call him to make herself feel better, just because Klaus had used his image in Bonnie's dream.

She turned the phone off and shoved it back onto the desk, sobbing harder.

"Bonnie?" The bed dipped as Meredith crossed the space from her own bed and sat on the edge of Bonnie's. "Are you okay?"

In the morning, Bonnie would tell Meredith and the

others everything. It was important that they know that Klaus had gotten into her dreams again, and that the techniques Alaric had researched had let Bonnie fight him off this time. But she couldn't talk about it right now, not in the dark.

"Bad dream," she said instead. "Stay here for a minute, okay?"

"Okay," Meredith said, and Bonnie felt her friend's thin, strong arm wrap around her shoulders. "It'll be all right, Bonnie," Meredith said, patting her on the back.

"I don't think so," Bonnie said, and buried her head on Meredith's shoulder and wept.

29

Meredith stuffed her econ notes into her bag as she walked across the quad. For the first time in a while, it felt almost like a normal college campus: groups of students sitting on the grass, couples holding hands and strolling the paths. A jogger brushed by Meredith as he passed, and she stepped aside. With the death of the last of the Vitale vampires, the attacks on campus had pretty much stopped, and the fear that had kept everyone inside was receding. They didn't realize that a much more dire enemy was now lurking in the shadows.

Klaus's army must be hunting, but they were keeping a much lower profile. Which was good, of course, but it meant that Meredith's class, after three cancelled sessions, had started again. And they had a lot of material to make up before midterms.

Meredith would have to find a way to fit in studying, working out, and patrolling, and she was also determined not to miss any time with Alaric while he was at Dalcrest. An irrepressible smile broke out on Meredith's face just at the thought of him: Alaric's freckles, Alaric's sharp mind, Alaric's kisses. She was supposed to be meeting him for dinner in town in just a few minutes, she realized, glancing at her watch.

When she looked up again, she saw Cristian, sitting quietly on a bench a little farther down the path, raising his eyes to meet hers.

Meredith reached inside her bag for the small knife that she carried with her. She couldn't carry her stave to class, and she really hadn't expected trouble in the middle of campus in broad daylight. She could have kicked herself: she'd been an idiot and let her guard down.

Cristian got to his feet and came toward her, hands held up unthreateningly. "Meredith?" he said quietly. "I didn't come here to fight."

Meredith gripped her knife tighter, keeping it concealed inside her bag. There were too many people around for him to attack without endangering innocent bystanders. "It didn't seem that way in the woods," she reminded him. "Don't pretend you're not working for Klaus."

Cristian shrugged. "I fought you," he said, "but I wasn't trying to hurt you." Meredith flashed back to facing off against Cristian in the battle with Klaus's vampires. They'd been so evenly matched that it had been clear they'd trained with the same parents: each blow he'd thrown she'd blocked automatically; each time she'd struck at him, he'd seemed to anticipate it. "Think about it," Cristian said. "Klaus turned me just a couple of weeks ago, but I remember everything from before. We used to spar all the time, but I'm a vampire *and* a hunter now. I should be much stronger and faster than you. If I'd wanted to kill you, I would have."

It was true. Meredith hesitated, and Cristian moved to the side of the path, sitting down on the bench again. After a moment, Meredith joined him. She didn't let go of the knife, but she couldn't help her curiosity about Cristian— her brother, her *twin*. He was taller than she was, and broader, but his hair was exactly the same shade of brown. He had her mother's mouth, with a subtle dimple on its left, and his nose was shaped like her father's.

When she met Cristian's eyes at last, his gaze was sad. "You really don't remember me, do you?" he asked.

"No," Meredith said. "What do *you* remember?" she asked.

In the reality she knew, Klaus had stolen Cristian away when he was a baby, raised him as his own. But in the Guardian-altered world, her twin brother would have grown up with her until he was sent away to boarding school for high school. Most of the supernatural-touched people in this world—Tyler, for instance—had a dual set of memories, two different sequences of events overlaying each other. Now that Klaus had made Cristian a vampire once more, would he remember both childhoods?

But Cristian was shaking his head. "I remember growing up with you, Meredith," he said. "You're my twin. We—" He laughed a sad little disbelieving laugh, just a puff of breath, really, and shook his head. "Remember how Dad made us learn Morse code? Just in case, he said? And we used to tap out messages on the wall between our bedrooms when we were supposed to be sleeping?" He looked at her hopefully, but Meredith shook her head.

"Dad made me learn Morse code," she said, "but I didn't have anyone to tap messages to."

"Klaus told me that in your reality, he took me away from home and made me a vampire when we were really little. But it's still weird for me that you don't remember me at all. We are—we were close," Cristian told her. "We used to, um, go to the beach every summer when I was home from school. Up until last summer, when I enlisted. We used to find little creatures and keep them in the tide pools, like our own tiny aquariums." His gray eyes, rimmed with heavy black lashes, were wide and sad. They were similar to Meredith's own eyes, perhaps a shade lighter, but right now they reminded her more forcibly of her mother's.

With a jolt, she realized that the army must have told her parents Cristian was missing by now.

"I'm sorry," she told him, and she did feel sorry. "I don't remember ever going to the beach as a kid. I think my parents—our parents—lost their taste for family vacations after you were gone."

Cristian sighed and put his head in his hands. "I wish you had gotten a chance to meet me when I was human," he said. "One minute I'm lying in the barracks surrounded by a bunch of other guys, wondering what ever possessed me to enlist right out of high school anyway, and the next this vampire takes me and tells me all this crazy stuff about how I've always been his, how he's putting things right." He gave another sad huff of laughter. "All my training, and the first vampire I meet takes me out immediately. Dad's going to be so mad."

"It's not your fault," Meredith told him, and winced as she realized that, yeah, their dad would be kind of mad. More sad, of course, and sickened, but he would definitely feel that Cristian should have put up a better fight.

Cristian cocked a cynical eyebrow at her and they both laughed. It was weird, Meredith realized: for a moment there, sharing the feeling of exactly what it meant to be 'Nando Sulez's child, she really had felt like Cristian was her brother.

"I wish I had come to meet you when you were still

human," she told him. "I just thought there would be more time."

Would she have been a different person if she'd grown up with a brother? she wondered. Klaus's attacks on her family had changed her parents: the ones in this reality, who hadn't lost a child, were less guarded, more open with their affections. If she had grown up with those parents and with Cristian next to her, someone to compete with, someone to help bear the weight of her parents' expectations, someone who knew all the secrets of their family, what would she be like? She'd felt less alone in the brief time she'd known Samantha: another hunter like her, her age. A brother would have changed everything, Meredith thought wistfully.

"I'm not interested in Klaus's endgame," Cristian told her. "I'm a vampire now, and that's tough for me to deal with. It's hard to fight the way I feel when I'm near Klaus. But I'm still your brother. I'm still a Sulez. I don't want to lose that. Maybe we could spend some time together? You could get to know me now." He looked at her sadly.

Meredith swallowed. "Okay," she said, and let her fingers loosen on the hilt of her knife. "Let's try it."

Dear Diary,
I have to prepare. If the Guardians won't change
my task, my Powers will be concentrated on

finding and destroying Damon, not Klaus. I need to be able to defeat Klaus on my own, by discovering my Power for myself.

For an hour today, Andrés and I tried to unlock more of my Power.

It was a complete failure.

Andrés had decided that learning to move things with my mind could be useful, so he folded pieces of paper all over James's house and encouraged me to imagine protecting my friends from evil by flinging them around. It was sickening to imagine Stefan or Bonnie or Meredith at Klaus's mercy, and I wanted to save them. I knew that if I could swing a stake at the right time, I might change things in a fight. But I couldn't even stir a page.

I'm going to be as ready as I can be, though. If I can't use my Guardian Powers to defeat Klaus, I'll fight him face-to-face. If I can't be killed by the supernatural, I have a huge advantage. Meredith and Stefan have been teaching me how to fight, how to use weapons.

Klaus is so much worse than Damon could ever be: when I think back, I can remember so many times that Damon saved innocents instead of killing them—Bonnie, the humans of the Dark

Dimension, half our high school. Me. I owe him my life. Time after time, even when he's wavered, he's turned away from the easy darkness and come down on the right side, the side that saved the helpless. I know he's strayed again—

Elena paused. She couldn't bear to think of it: Damon killing again. But she took a deep breath and faced the truth.

—but maybe it is our fault, mine and Stefan's, for not showing him we care. It was just that once I got Stefan back, all I could think of was clutching him to me so tight that he'd never slip away again. Damon needs us, though he'll never admit it, but we'll fight through the darkness that shrouds him. We will save him. If I can just remind the Guardians of all Damon's done for us in the past, they'll see that he isn't evil. They can be rational, even if they are cold and distant.

I used to hate the idea of being a Guardian, of becoming less human. But now I know that it's a gift, a sacred trust to protect the world. As a Guardian, I can stop some of the deaths, some of the suffering. Once I fully come into my Power, I can use it to defeat the right target. I can still be the one to kill Klaus.

"I called Alaric and told him I'd meet him in an hour," Meredith said. "I had to talk to you guys first." She stirred a spoonful of sugar into her tea with such careful, precise movements that Elena was sure Meredith was keeping a firm control on herself to avoid slipping into hysteria.

It was the same reason, Elena knew, that Meredith had called just the three of them to meet her at the coffeehouse: Elena, Bonnie, and Matt, Meredith's oldest friends, the tight group that had withstood so much together. Meredith loved Alaric and trusted him with all her heart, just as Elena did Stefan, but sometimes you wanted your best friends with you.

"Cristian says he wants to be my family," Meredith said. "He isn't interested in fighting on Klaus's side. But how can I believe him? I asked Zander what he could sense about Cristian, but he wasn't sure. He says that sometimes, if the person has a lot going on emotionally, his Power doesn't work on them." She glanced at Bonnie sympathetically. "Zander misses you," she said, and Bonnie stared down at her lap.

"I know," she said softly. "But I can't be the person he needs." Elena squeezed her hand beneath the table.

Matt rubbed the back of his neck. "Maybe Cristian is telling the truth," he offered. "Chloe left Ethan and stopped drinking blood. There are good vampires—we know that. Look at Stefan."

"Where is Chloe, anyway?" Bonnie asked. "You've been spending all your time with her."

"Stefan took her hunting in the woods," Matt told her. "She's afraid to go by herself since Klaus attacked her, but Stefan says if she's going to survive, she can't hide forever. And I have a game later, so Stefan can keep her company, help her stave off the blood lust."

"At least it sounds like Cristian wants to try," Elena told Meredith. "I'm scared I've lost Damon. He was so violent. It was like he wanted me to give up on him." She hadn't told Meredith and the others that Damon had confessed so casually to killing someone, but she'd told them about the brutal, frightening scene at the billiards hall.

Meredith stared down at the surface of her tea for a moment, then raised her eyes to meet Elena's. "Maybe you should," she said quietly.

Elena shook her head in immediate denial, but Meredith pushed on. "You know what he's capable of, Elena," she said. "If he really wants to be *bad* again, he's strong enough and clever enough to be really bad. The Guardians might be right. Maybe he's even a bigger threat than Klaus."

Elena clenched her fists. "I can't, Meredith," she said, her voice cracking. "I *can't*. And I can't let anyone else, either. It's *Damon*." Her eyes met Meredith's. "Cristian's your family—that's why you can't kill him without giving him a chance. Well, Damon's become my family, too."

Bonnie looked back and forth between them, wide-eyed. "What can we do?" she asked.

"Listen," Matt said suddenly. "Meredith was a hunter when she met Stefan and Damon, even though the rest of us didn't know it. She *hated* vampires, right?" They all nodded. "So"—he turned to Meredith—"how did you get past it?"

Meredith blinked. "Well," she said slowly, "I knew Stefan wasn't a killer. He loved Elena so much, and he tried to protect people. Damon . . ." She hesitated. "For a long time, I thought I probably would have to kill Damon. It was my duty. But he changed. He fought on the right side."

She looked back down at the table, her face grim. "Duty is important, Elena," she said. "A hunter or a Guardian, we are the ones responsible for saving innocent people from evil. You can't ignore that." Elena's eyes filled with tears.

"Exactly," Matt said. "So, what if Damon changes again? If we could get him to act differently—well, if you guys could, anyway; he won't ever listen to me—then we could show the Guardians he's not a threat."

"There's a reason the Guardians aren't worried about Stefan," Bonnie added.

"Maybe," Elena said. She felt her shoulders drooping and automatically stiffened her spine. She wasn't going to give up, no matter how hopeless the idea of getting Damon to change his behavior seemed. "Maybe I can get him back on track. It didn't work the first time, but that doesn't mean I can't try another approach," she said, willing a little more positivity into her voice. She would just have to keep going, think of a way to get Damon on the side of good again.

"Or we could try locking him up until he changes," Matt suggested half jokingly. "Maybe Bonnie and Alaric can come up with some kind of calming spell. We'll figure something out."

"That's the ticket," Meredith said. Elena looked up at her and Meredith gave her a small, rueful smile. "Maybe Damon will change in time to save himself," Meredith said. "And maybe Cristian is telling the truth. If we're lucky enough, neither of them will have to die." She reached across the table and squeezed Elena's hand. "We'll try," she said, and Elena nodded, squeezing back.

"At least we have each other," Elena said, looking around to meet Bonnie's and Matt's sympathetic gazes. "No matter what happens, it'll never be the worst thing, not as long as you guys are by my side."

30

Unlike his brother, who had gone so far as to join the Robert E. Lee High School football team in Fell's Church, Damon did not enjoy playing football. He had never liked team sports, even when he was young and alive. The feeling of being an anonymous part of an a group, just one cog in a great machine designed to get a ball from one end of a field to another, felt like an affront to his dignity. It didn't help that Matt—*Mutt*, Damon now had to remind himself to say—loved the sport. He was the star here on the Dalcrest field; Damon had to give him some credit for that.

But now, some five hundred years after he had stopped breathing, he certainly didn't bother to waste his time watching humans try to get a ball from one side of a field to another.

The crowd, on the other hand . . . he'd found that he liked the crowd at a football game.

Full of energy, they all focused on the same thing and their blood pounded under their skin, flushing their cheeks. He liked the smells of the stadium: sweat and beer and hot dogs and enthusiasm. He liked the cheer-leaders' colorful uniforms and the possibility of a fight breaking out in the stands as passions ran high. He liked the brightness of the lights on the fields during a night game, and the darkness in the corners of the stands. He liked . . .

Damon lost his train of thought as his eyes caught on a girl with pale gold hair, her back to him, sitting alone in the bleachers. Every line of that figure was etched in his memory forever: he'd watched her with passion and devotion, and finally with hatred. Unlike everyone else, he'd never confused her for Elena.

"Katherine," he breathed, cutting through the crowd toward her.

No human would have heard him in the crowd, but Katherine turned her head and smiled, such a sweet smile that Damon's first instinct to attack her was swept away by a rush of memory. The shy little German girl who had come to his father's palazzo, so many years ago, back when Damon was a human and Katherine was almost as inno-cent as one, had smiled at him like that.

So instead of fighting, he slipped onto the seat beside Katherine and just looked at her, keeping his face neutral.

"Damon!" Katherine said, the smile taking on a tinge of malice. "I've missed you!"

"Considering that the last time we saw each other you tore my throat out, I can't say the same," Damon told her dryly.

Katherine made a little face of wry regret. "Oh, you never could let bygones be bygones," she said, pouting. "Come, I'll apologize. It's all water under the bridge now, isn't it? We live, we die, we suffer, we heal. And here we are." She laid a hand on his arm, watching him with sharp, bright eyes.

Damon pointedly moved her hand away. "What are you doing here, Katherine?" he asked.

"I can't visit my favorite pair of brothers?" Katherine said, mock-hurt. "You never forget your first love, you know."

Damon met her eyes, keeping his own face carefully blank. "I know," he said, and Katherine froze, seeming uncertain for the first time.

"I . . ." she said, and then her hesitation was gone and she smiled again. "Of course, I owe Klaus something as well," she said carelessly. "After all, he brought me back to life, and thank goodness for that. Death was terrible."

She quirked an eyebrow at Damon. "I hear you'd know all about that."

Damon did, and yes, death had been terrible, and for him at least, those first moments coming back had been worse. But he pushed that aside. "How do you intend to repay Klaus?" he asked, keeping his tone light and almost idle. "Tell me what's going on in that scheming little head of yours, Fraulein."

Katherine's laugh was still as silvery and bubbly as the mountain stream Damon had compared it to in a sonnet, back when he was young. Back when he was an *idiot*, he thought fiercely. "A lady has to have her secrets," she said. "But I'll tell you what I told Stefan, my darling Damon. I'm not angry with your Elena anymore. She's safe from me."

"I don't really care, to be honest," Damon said coolly, but he felt a tight knot of worry loosen inside his chest.

"Of course you don't, dear heart," Katherine said comfortingly, and when she put her hand on Damon's arm this time, he let it stay. "Now," she said, patting him. "Shall we have a little fun?" She tilted her head toward the football field, toward the cheerleaders shaking their pompoms on the sidelines. Damon felt a soft pulse of Power go out of her, and as he watched, the girl on the far end of the line dropped her pompoms and her smile. With a dreamy, distant expression on her face, she began to move, her body tracing out what Damon recognized as the slow and stately steps of a *bassadanza*, a dance he hadn't seen for hundreds of years.

"Remember?" Katherine said softly beside him. They had danced this together, Damon couldn't forget, in the great hall of his father's house, the night that he had come home from university in disgrace and first laid eyes on her. He took control of another cheerleader, moved her into the still-familiar steps of the male partner in the dance. *Step forward on the ball of one foot, step forward on the other, incline your body toward your partner, feet together, hand to the side, and the lady follows you.* He could almost hear the music, coming down the centuries.

The crowd around them stirred uneasily, their attention distracted from the players on the field. The formality of the dance and the blank distance on the faces of the cheerleaders were confusing them. A vague sense of something *not quite right* permeated the stadium.

Letting out another low, silvery laugh, Katherine kept the beat with her hand as all the cheerleaders paired off, moving in time, the elegance of their steps at odds with their bright, short costumes. On the field, the football players played on, oblivious.

Katherine smiled at Damon, her eyes gleaming with what looked almost like affection. "We could have fun together, you know," she said. "You don't have to hunt alone."

Damon considered this. He didn't trust her; he'd have to be a fool to trust her after all that Katherine had done. But, still . . . "Perhaps it won't be so bad having you back after all," he told her. "Perhaps."

31

ell phone clamped to her ear, Elena hit the button to replay the message. James couldn't possibly have said what she'd thought she'd heard.

But the message was exactly the same. "Elena, my dear," James said, a thread of excitement running through his voice. "I think I've got it. I think there's a way we can kill Klaus." He paused, as if he was thinking hard, and when he spoke again, his voice was more cautious. "We have to plan carefully, though. Come to my house as soon as you get this and we'll talk. This method . . . it'll take some preparation." The message ended, and Elena frowned at her phone in exasperation. Honestly, it was just like James to be cryptic rather than leave some useful information.

But, if he really had found something . . . A bubble of

joyous excitement rose in Elena's chest. The knowledge that Klaus was out there, and that her Guardian Powers were focused on Damon instead, had been like a heavy weight on her shoulders. She didn't know when, but she had the constant nagging feeling that disaster could come at any moment. If James had a new idea, perhaps there would be an end in sight.

As she hurried across the sun-drenched campus toward James's house, Elena quickly texted Stefan to meet her there. He'd taken command of their anti-Klaus army, making the decisions and organizing the patrols while she tried to expand her Guardian Powers, and she wanted him there if James had found a solution.

She hadn't heard back from Stefan yet when she reached James's front door. He was probably in class; he'd told her that his philosophy seminar had started up again, now that it had been more than a week since the body of a student had appeared on campus. Oh, well, they could fill him in as soon as he arrived.

Elena rang the doorbell and waited impatiently. After a minute, she tried again, then knocked on the door. No one came. Andrés, she remembered, had planned to spend the afternoon at the library, and then go out to dinner.

James had probably had a quick errand. Pulling out her phone again, Elena dialed his number. It rang, and rang again. Elena cocked her head. She was pretty sure she could hear James's ringtone coming from inside the house.

So he had gone out and forgotten his phone, Elena thought nervously, shifting from one foot to the other. That didn't mean anything was wrong.

Should she just sit on the porch and wait for James? Stefan would probably be here soon, too. She looked at her watch. It was five o'clock. She was pretty sure Stefan's class let out around five thirty. It would be dark soon, though. She didn't really want to wait here alone after dark. Not with Klaus's army out there somewhere.

And what if something *was* wrong? Why would James have left, when he'd asked Elena to come over? If he was in there, and he wasn't answering . . . Elena's heart was pounding hard. She tried to look in the window over the porch, but the shades were drawn and she only saw her own worried reflection.

Making up her mind, Elena reached out and twisted the doorknob. It turned easily in her hand, and the door opened. Elena stepped inside. It wasn't the way she had been raised—Aunt Judith would be horrified to know Elena was walking into someone's house uninvited—but she was sure James would understand.

Elena had already closed the door behind her when she noticed the streak of blood. It was wide and still wet, a long stripe of blood just at hand-level, as if someone with bloody hands had strode down the hall, carelessly wiping the blood on the walls as he went.

Elena froze, and then, her mind blank, walked forward. Something in her was screaming *stop stop*, but her feet just kept going as if they weren't even under her control anymore, down the hall and into the usually neat and cheerful kitchen.

The kitchen was still flooded with sunlight through its western-facing windows. The copper pots hanging from the ceiling reflected the light back, illuminating all the corners.

And everywhere, on all the shining surfaces, were great dark splashes of blood.

James's body was slumped over the kitchen table. Elena knew at a glance that he was dead. He must be dead—no one could live with their insides spilled across the floor like that—but she went to him anyway. She still felt numb, but she realized she had clapped one hand over her own mouth, holding back the whimpering noise that wanted to come out. She made an effort and pulled the hand away from her mouth, swallowed hard. *Oh, God.*

"James," she said, and pressed her fingers against his neck, trying to find a pulse. His skin was still warm and sticky with blood, but there was no heartbeat at all. "Oh, James, oh, no," she whispered again, horrified and so, so sorry for him.

He had been half in love with her mother when he was

a student, she remembered; he'd been her father's best friend. He could be stuffy and wasn't always brave, but he had helped her. And he had been funny and smart, and he really hadn't deserved to die this way just because he had helped Elena. There was no question in her mind that this was because of her: Klaus had come after James because he was on Elena's side.

She reached for her Guardian Powers, tried to sense his aura, to see if there was anything she could do, but there was no aura left around him. James's body was here, but everything that made him a person was gone.

Hot tears were running down her face and Elena wiped furiously at them. Her hand was sticky with James's blood, and, sickened, she wiped it on one of the kitchen towels before pulling out her phone again. She needed Stefan. Stefan could help.

No answer. Elena left a brief, tense message and tucked the phone away. She had to get out of here. It would be unbearable to stay any longer in this room with its slaughterhouse smell and James's sad, accusing shell at the table. She could wait for Stefan outside.

As she was about to leave, something caught her eye. On the kitchen table, the only thing not spattered with blood, sat a single pristine sheet of expensive-looking stationery. Elena hesitated. There was something familiar about it.

Almost against her will, she walked slowly back toward the table, where she picked up the paper and turned it over. It was just as blank and clean on the other side.

Last time, she remembered, *there were dirty fingerprints.* Perhaps Klaus had washed his hands after wiping them on the walls. A deep, warming anger was building inside her. It felt like such a violation that, after . . . doing *that* to poor James, Klaus might wash his hands in the porcelain sink James had kept clean, dried his fingers on James's carefully arranged towels.

She knew what to expect from Klaus's message, but she still stiffened, hissing involuntarily through her teeth as black letters began to appear on the paper, written with long jagged downstrokes as if slashed with an invisible knife. She read them with a growing sense of dread.

Elena—
I told you I'd find out the truth. He had plenty to say by the time I let him die.
Until next time,
Klaus

Elena doubled over as if she had been punched in the stomach. *No*, she thought. *Please, no.* After everything they'd been through, Klaus had found out her secret. He'd find a way to kill her now—she was sure of it.

She had to pull herself together. She had to keep going. Elena shuddered once, her body jerking, and then took a deep breath. Carefully, she folded the paper and put it in her pocket. Stefan and the others ought to see it.

She was still operating on automatic as she walked outside, shutting James's front door firmly behind her. There was a spot of blood on her jeans and she rubbed at it absently for a moment, then raised her hand and stared at the red streaks. Without warning, she convulsed, retching into the bushes by the door.

He knew. Oh, God, Klaus knew.

32

"Thanks for meeting me," Cristian said. He grinned up at Meredith from his seat on the weight bench. "I know you don't remember," he added, "but we used to work out together a lot."

"Really?" Meredith said, interested. She could believe it, easily: anyone raised by her father would try hard to excel physically. "Which one of us was better?"

Cristian's smile widened. "That was pretty hotly disputed, as a matter of fact," he said. "You were a little faster than me, and better with the stave and martial arts, but I was stronger and better with knives and bows."

"Huh." Meredith was good with knives, she thought. Of course, in her reality—the real reality, she reminded herself—she'd had a lot more actual battle experience than Cristian. "Maybe we should see if that's still true," she said challengingly. "You know, I've gotten pretty strong."

Cristian chuckled. "Meredith," he said. "I'm a vampire now. I'm pretty sure I've gotten stronger, too."

As soon as the words were out of his mouth, his face fell. "A vampire," he repeated, rubbing one hand across his mouth. "It's hard to believe, you know?" He shook his head. "I've become the thing I'm supposed to hate." He raised his eyes to meet Meredith's, and his face was bleak.

A pang of pity swamped Meredith. She could remember how she'd felt, before the Guardians changed everything, when she'd learned that Klaus had left her wrong, a living girl with kitten vampire teeth and a need for blood.

It had gone away. But now Cristian was changed, and desolate.

"There are good vampires, you know," she told him. "My friends Stefan and Chloe, they fought with us against Klaus. Stefan's saved a lot of people." Cristian nodded, acknowledging her words, but didn't speak.

"Okay," Meredith said, mimicking her father's time-to-train, no-nonsense tone as best she could. It wouldn't help Cristian to dwell on his misery. "Enough flapping of the lips. Show me what you've got."

Cristian grinned, welcoming the change of mood, and stretched back on the weight bench, his hands on the racked barbell overhead. "Load me up," he said. "I want to see how strong I am now."

Part of this achingly reminded her of Samantha, Meredith thought, of how they'd trained together, goading each other to fight harder, longer, better. Maybe, Meredith thought as she added weight plates to the bar above Cristian, he'd want to try sparring later.

Meredith started Cristian at about two hundred pounds, which he pressed easily, his mouth giving a wry twist. "Come on," he said. "I could press this when I was alive."

There was no one else in the weight room, and so Meredith didn't have to be subtle about loading on the weights. Cristian handled as much as she could give him, his muscled but thin arms moving up and down like pistons.

"I'm so strong," he said giddily, smiling up at her.

Meredith recognized his smile. It was the smile she'd seen in the mirror on her own face when she was suddenly, startlingly happy. When she'd gotten her black belt. The night after Alaric had kissed her for the first time.

Maybe they could get past all this, become a team. Meredith let herself picture hunting with Cristian, fighting beside him. He was a vampire—a good vampire, she told herself fiercely, like Stefan—but he was a hunter, too. A Sulez.

"Your turn," Cristian said, clunking the bar back up into its support. It was so heavily loaded with weight plates now that the bar itself was bending.

Meredith laughed. "You know I can't lift that much. You win, okay?"

"Aw, come on," Cristian said. "I'll cut you some slack since you're human. And, you know, a girl." Meredith looked up to snap at him that being a girl had very little to do with how much she'd be able to press, and caught a teasing glint in his eye. Right then, she could believe he was her brother. Cristian started taking the plates off and putting them back in their racks.

"All right," Meredith said, and fastidiously, showily wiped off the bench, although it wasn't actually sweaty: apparently sweating was one of those things vampires didn't do.

Cristian started her off at a hundred and fifty pounds, heavy but manageable, and watched as Meredith began a set of reps.

"So," she said, keeping her voice casual and focusing on raising and lowering the bar. "What's it like?"

"What's what like?" Cristian asked absently. She could just glimpse him out of the corner of her eye, examining the weights, picking what to put on next.

"Being a vampire."

"Oh." Cristian moved across the room, just out of Meredith's sight, but his voice was clear and thoughtful, a little dreamy. "It's a rush, really," he said. "I can hear everything and smell everything. All my senses are heightened, like, a million percent. They say I'll get more Power, I'll be able to turn into animals and birds, make people do whatever I want."

He sounded excited at the prospect, his tone losing the bitterness it had held when he talked about becoming something he hated, and Meredith wished she could see his face.

"More?" he said brightly when he was right above her, extra weight plates in hand. His smile was bland, giving nothing away.

"Okay," she said, and instead of helping her get the bar back onto its support, he simply steadied it with one hand and slid more weight onto each side. Meredith grunted as he let go: it was heavier than she usually made it now, but still manageable. Almost too much, but she didn't want to let Cristian know that. In a funny way they were still competing despite his vampire strength, and she was going to take as much as she could.

Cristian was still really close, spotting her as she lifted, and Meredith's arms shook and strained after a couple of reps.

"The details are sharper, you know?" Cristian said suddenly. "I can even hear the blood rushing through your veins from here."

Meredith went cold and breathless. There had been

something almost hungry about the way he spoke about her blood. "Take the bar," she ordered. "This is too much." She needed to get up.

Cristian reached for the bar, but instead of guiding it back into its support, he carefully added still more weight to each side.

"Stop it," Meredith croaked. It was far too heavy now, and Cristian must know that. She was in trouble here, real trouble, but she needed to stay calm, needed Cristian not to realize that she was scared.

"You forgot something about vampires," Cristian said, and smiled down at her, that same teasing, brotherly smile. "Dad would be so disappointed." He let go of the bar and it crashed down toward Meredith's chest; she was unable to support its weight.

She grunted as it fell, managing to slow it enough to keep it from cracking her rib cage, but with no breath or energy to focus on anything except protecting her chest from the dead weight of the bar. She couldn't breathe, couldn't speak, and she turned her head to look at him, her heart beating hard, and made a muffled, breathless moan. No one would hear her. She could die right here, at the hands of her brother.

Cristian went on. "A vampire, as you should know from our training, Meredith, is completely focused on his or her sire when they're first turned."

Maybe she could shift it, this weight pressing down on her, driving all the breath from her lungs. She couldn't breathe. Black spots swam in front of her eyes.

"All that matters to me is Klaus, what Klaus wants," Cristian told her. "If you were a good hunter, you would have remembered that bond trumps everything else. I don't know how you could have imagined my human family"—his voice curdled on the word, like there was something disgusting in it—"would matter to me more than that."

Meredith pushed at the bar helplessly, dizzy now with pain. She tried to signal Cristian with her eyes, desperately: fine, whatever, be Klaus's if you must, but don't kill me like this. Let me up so we can fight as we've been trained.

Cristian was kneeling beside her now, his face so close to hers. "Klaus wants you dead," he whispered, "you and all your friends. And I'll do whatever I can to make him happy." His gray eyes, just like her mother's eyes, held hers as he took hold of the bar she was clutching and pushed it down onto her chest.

Everything went black for a moment. Red flowers bloomed and burst in the darkness, and Meredith realized muzzily that it was her brain sending out random signals as it began to shut down from lack of oxygen.

She was beginning to float, as if she was suspended in a black sea. It would be good to rest. She was so tired.

Then a voice snapped through the darkness in

Meredith's mind, her father's voice. *Meredith!* it said. It was impatient, firm but not unkind, the exact tone that had gotten her out of bed to run laps before school, encouraged her to practice a tae kwon do form when all she wanted to do was go out with her friends. *You're a Sulez*, the voice said. *You must fight!*

With a nearly superhuman effort, Meredith opened her eyes. Everything was blurry and she felt so slow, as if she was trying to move underwater.

Cristian's hand had relaxed on the bar. He must have thought all the fight in her was gone.

Meredith took every bit of strength she had gathered and pushed the bar up and away from her, tumbling her unwary vampire brother over with the bar on top of him. She had one glimpse of Cristian's startled, infuriated face before she ran as fast as she could, legs weak, heart pounding, gasping for breath, straight out of the weight room, out of the gym, and onto the paths of campus.

She had to slow as she approached her dorm, her legs sore and her lungs burning now that that original surge of adrenaline had worn off. Meredith tried to push herself onward, but she was stumbling now. At any moment, Cristian might grab her. He could have caught her by now, of course.

Just outside the dorm, she gathered her courage and spun around. No one was there. He had intended to kill her alone and in secret, and he would no doubt try again. Meredith unlocked the door and staggered in, flopping down to sit on the bottom step of the staircase.

She was still gasping for breath, and she choked on a sob. Meredith had wanted to know her brother, but he was already gone; he was Klaus's family now.

As she rubbed at her strained muscles, Meredith realized dully what she was going to have to do. She was going to have to kill Cristian.

33

Damon licked a trace of blood carefully from the back of his hand and smiled at Katherine. They'd come across a couple walking through the woods just after dawn and fed together, and now it was midmorning, sunlight streaming down through the trees and casting black and golden shadows on the path. Damon felt full and content, ready to go home and sleep away the brightest of the daylight hours. A slight unease crossed his mind as he remembered the expression of panic on his victim's face, and he pushed it away: he was a vampire; this was what he was supposed to do.

Dabbing delicately at the corners of her mouth, Katherine cocked her head at him, as dainty and quizzical as a little songbird. "Why didn't you kill yours?" she asked.

Shrugging defensively, Damon slipped his sunglasses

out of his pocket and over his eyes. He wasn't, to be completely honest, sure why he hadn't killed the girl this morning, or why he hadn't killed any of his victims since the blond jogger he'd hunted down more than a week before. He could remember how good the kill had felt, the rush as her life passed into him, but he wasn't eager to repeat the experience, not when the lingering aftertaste was guilt. He didn't want to feel anything for them; he wanted to take the blood and go. If that meant letting them live, that was fine with Damon.

Shielded behind the sunglasses, he said none of this, but merely smirked at Katherine and asked, "Why didn't you?"

"Oh, we're all keeping a low profile. Too many deaths and this campus will panic again. Klaus wants to keep the humans happy and easy to hunt while he finishes off your girl and her friends." Katherine eyed Damon as she smoothed her long golden hair, and he kept his expression carefully blank. Whatever Katherine wanted from him, she wasn't going to get it by bringing up Elena.

"Of course," Damon said, and added, "You know, you came back from death much saner and more practical, my dear." Katherine dimpled at him, and mock-curtsied gracefully.

They walked peacefully together, listening to the chirps and calls of sparrows, finches, and robins overhead.

The quick rattle of a woodpecker drilling a tree sounded a little way away, and Damon could hear the rustle and patter of small, furry creatures in the undergrowth. He stretched luxuriously, thinking of his bed.

"So," Katherine said, breaking the comfortable silence between them. "Elena." She said it again, stretching the syllables of the word out as if she was tasting them: "E-ley-na."

"What about her?" Damon asked. His voice was careless, but he felt an uncomfortable heat at the back of his neck.

Katherine fixed him knowingly with her jewel-blue gaze, and Damon frowned at her behind his sunglasses.

"Tell me about her," she said softly, her expression coaxing. "I want to know."

Damon stopped walking and pulled Katherine to face him. "I thought you weren't angry at Elena anymore," he said, deflecting the question. "You're supposed to leave her alone, Katherine."

Katherine shrugged gracefully. "I'm not angry at her," she said. "But Klaus is." Her eyes glittered. "I thought you didn't care about Elena anymore. You were quite clear about it, you know. Why won't you tell me anything?"

"I . . ." Damon's heart fluttered in his chest, quicker than its usual vampire-slow beat. "I just don't want to," he said finally.

Katherine laughed quietly, her beautiful bell-like laugh. "Oh, Damon," she said, and shook her head mockingly. "You might be wicked in theory, but your heart is so pure. What happened?"

Grimacing, Damon turned away from her, letting go of her hand. "My heart is not pure," he said pettishly.

"You've gotten soft," Katherine said. "You don't like hurting people anymore."

Damon shoved his sunglasses farther up his nose and shrugged. "It'll pass."

Cool hands touched his cheeks and then Katherine gently pulled off Damon's sunglasses, gazing into his eyes. "Love changes you," she said. "And it never fades, no matter how much you might want it to." Rising onto her tiptoes, she kissed him lightly on the cheek. "Don't make the mistakes I've made, Damon," she said sadly. "Don't fight love, whatever form it takes."

Damon brought his hand up to touch the spot where Katherine's lips had kissed him. He felt stunned and lost.

Handing him his sunglasses, Katherine sighed. "I don't really owe you any favors, Damon," she told him, "but I'm feeling sentimental. Your Elena's in class right now. Rhodes Hall. I don't know exactly what Klaus is going to do, but he's planning something. You might want to get over there and stop it."

Gripping the sunglasses, Damon stared at her in

confusion. "What?" he asked.

There was something soft and wistful in Katherine's eyes, but her voice was firm. "Better hurry," she said, raising an eyebrow.

Damon felt as if a living creature was clawing its way through his chest, something huge and painful. Was this what love felt like, after all?

"Thank you," he said absently. He walked away from Katherine a few paces, then sped into a run. He gathered his Power and began transforming, feeling his body twist as he changed into a crow. A moment later, he was aloft, stretching his wings to catch the airstream as he flapped his way quickly toward campus.

lena trailed out of her freshman English section near the end of the crowd, still stuffing her notebook into her bag. Zipping it closed, she looked up to see Andrés waiting patiently in the hall directly outside her classroom.

"Hey," she said. "What's going on?"

"Stefan and I think it's not a great idea for you to be on your own right now," he said, falling into step beside her. "He and Meredith both have class, so I'll walk you wherever you're going."

"I have Powers of my own, you know," Elena said, a little haughtily. "Even if they're not really fighting ones yet, I'm not a damsel in distress."

Andrés nodded, a slow, solemn dip of his head. "Forgive me," he said formally. "I don't think any of us should be alone now. James's death proves that."

"I'm sorry," Elena said. "I know it's been hard for you, especially since you were living at James's house."

Andrés nodded. "It has," he said, and then made a visible effort to be more cheerful, throwing back his shoulders and pasting on a smile. "But I must take advantage of the chance that allows me more time with my charming and beautiful friend."

"Oh, in that case," Elena said, following his lead, and took Andrés's proffered arm. As they moved down the hall, she examined him carefully out of the corner of her eye. Despite his courtliness, Andrés looked haggard and worn, the lines at the corners of his eyes more pronounced. He looked older than twenty now.

James's death had hit them all hard. It felt more real, somehow, than Chad's death. It had happened in James's house, not on a battlefield, and so proved that death could come for them anywhere. When Elena had looked in the mirror the last few mornings, the face gazing back at her was grimmer, her eyes rimmed with gray circles.

Still, they had to keep going, for one another. Whistling in the dark, people called it, when you kept your own spirits up by finding any happiness you could.

Squeezing Andrés's arm affectionately, Elena asked, "How are you settling into Matt's room?" The police had sealed James's house, so Matt had offered up his own empty room to their visitor. Matt himself was back to camping out in the half-burned boathouse with Chloe.

"Ah," Andrés said, his face relaxing into a smile as they stepped onto the elevator and pushed the button for the ground floor. "The dormitory life is very strange to me. There is always something happening."

Elena was laughing at Andrés's tale of a drunken freshman wandering into his room at three in the morning, and Andrés's own polite and befuddled attempts to steer the intruder back to his own dormitory, when the elevator jerked violently to a stop.

"What's happening?" Elena said warily.

"Maybe it's an electrical problem," Andrés said, but his voice was doubtful.

Elena pushed the button for the ground floor again, and the elevator gave a deep groan and then began to shake. They both gasped and steadied themselves, hands against the walls.

"I'll try the emergency button," Elena said. She pushed it, but nothing happened.

"Weird," she said, and flinched at the uncertain note in her own voice. "It seems disconnected, too." She hesitated. "Do you have a weapon?" she asked. Andrés shook his head, his face pale.

The elevator rattled again, and then the lights went out, leaving them in the dark. Elena found Andrés's warm hand and clutched it.

"Is this . . . do you think this could just be a coincidence?" she whispered. Andrés squeezed her hand
reassuringly.

"I don't know," he said, his voice troubled. "Can you
see anything?"

Of course not, Elena was about to say. The elevator was
pitch-black. She couldn't even see Andrés despite the fact
that he was holding her protectively close to him. Then she
realized what he meant, and closed her eyes for a moment
to reach deep inside herself, calling on her Power.

When she opened her eyes again, she could see the
warm, living green of Andrés's aura, lighting up the darkness. But at the edges of her consciousness was something
else.

There was an even thicker blackness moving closer. It
hurt to look at it as it seemed to breathe through the cracks
in the elevator doors, as amorphous as fog. Elena instinctively shut her eyes and turned her head away, burying it
in Andrés's shoulder.

"Elena!" he said, alarmed. "What is it?"

For a long time nothing happened. There was a
moment when she relaxed despite herself—*nothing's here*,
she thought, caught in a wave of relief, *nothing's here*.

"It's okay," she said, with half an embarrassed laugh
behind her words. "I just—"

Then a tile from the elevator roof was kicked in, and the blackness was all around her. Flinching, Elena looked up, straining to see something.

"Hello, my pretty one." Klaus's voice came from above. "You've been waiting for me, haven't you?" His voice was as casual as if he'd just come by to chat.

"Hello, Klaus," Elena said, trying to keep her voice steady. She pressed herself against Andrés. She felt like she was falling.

"I know what you are," Klaus said smugly, his voice a singsong. A loud bang came against the side of the elevator, and Elena and Andrés both jumped, sucking in their breath. "I know what your secret is." *Bang.* "I can't kill you with anything magic." *Bang.* "And I can't kill you with my vampires." *Bang.* He was banging his big black boots against the side of the elevator, Elena realized. He must be sitting on the edge of the service access hatch in the roof, his legs dangling down. His boots banged once more and then Klaus said gaily, "But you know what? If I cut the cable here at the top of the elevator, you won't survive."

Elena cringed. She rode in elevators every day and it had never before occurred to her how vulnerable they were. Her English class was on the ninth floor. They were dangling above a long, long drop, and the cables were the only thing keeping them from falling straight through to the basement.

Andrés sucked in a quiet breath next to her, and Elena saw the life-green aura around him begin to grow. He was trying to form a protective shield to shelter them with, she realized, as he had done in the battle against Klaus and his vampires.

"Stop that," Klaus snapped from above them, and a bolt of blackness flew from him and hit Andrés's growing shield of green, which snapped and deflated like a popped balloon. Andrés cried out in pain.

Elena wrapped her arms around Andrés protectively, but she could feel him tensing to try again. His breath sounded rough and panicky. "My power comes from the earth, Elena," he whispered. "Dangling so far above it, I'm not sure if I can help. But I will try."

Above them in the darkness, Klaus laughed jeeringly. "Might be too late there, boy," he said, and a strange scraping noise came once and then again, a screech of metal on metal.

"He's cutting through the cable," Andrés breathed in her ear. There was a faint green light around him again as he tried to expand his aura, but it wasn't going to grow fast enough to protect them, Elena knew.

This is it, Elena thought, and took Andrés's hand. She had never been afraid of falling before, but now she was terrified.

Then a thud came from above, and another, and a

series of shuffling, thumping noises, and suddenly a body plummeted past them and landed heavily on the floor. Two bodies, Elena realized, thrashing and growling at their feet. She tried to concentrate, breathing hard, and after a moment, saw Klaus's aura again, darker than dark, and clashing with it, bloodred and sulky gray and flaring blue all tangled together.

"Damon," she whispered.

Shadowed, the barely-visible Damon managed to push off Klaus and scramble to his feet. "Elena," he gasped, and then a surge of Power from Klaus slammed him against the wall. He let out a pained grunt. Elena reached forward and tried to pull him toward her, but he was crushed tightly, his body jammed against the wall. Klaus chuckled darkly.

There was a flash of green.

Suddenly, all at once, Damon came loose. He fell back from the wall into Elena, and she staggered, holding him up in the second it took for him to regain his balance.

"Get her out of here!" Andrés shouted. "I can't hold it!"

Klaus, face twisted with rage, was trapped by the glowing green barrier of Andrés's protective aura, the eerie green lighting his face. As Elena stared openmouthed, Klaus forced a hand through the green. Damon grabbed her in his arms and leaped straight up into the elevator shaft.

Elena barely had time to take a breath before Damon was kicking his way through a door at the top of the shaft, and she found herself slumped on the tiles outside the elevator door on the top floor of the building. There were no classrooms here, just offices, and the hall was quiet.

Damon lay beside her, still clutching her, and panting harshly. Blood was trickling from his nose and he unwrapped one of his arms from around her to wipe at it with his sleeve.

"We have to go back," she told him, as soon as she could speak.

Damon stared at her. "Are you kidding me?" he gasped. "We barely got away as it is."

Elena shook her head stubbornly. "We can't abandon Andrés," she said.

Damon's stare sharpened to a glare. "Your friend from the elevator made his choice," he said coldly. "He wanted me to save you. Do you think he'll thank me if I drop right back down there instead of getting you out of here?"

A crash came from inside the elevator shaft, rattling the building. Elena pulled herself to her feet, steadying herself against the walls. She felt fragile, but determined, as if she was made of glass and steel.

"We're both going back," she said. "I don't care what Andrés would choose. I'm not leaving here without him. Take me down."

Damon clenched his jaw and glared harder. Elena simply stood and waited, immovable.

Finally, Damon swore to himself and climbed to his feet. "Let the record show," he said, grabbing her by the arms again and pulling her close to him, "that I tried to save you, and that you are the most infuriatingly stubborn person I've ever known."

"I missed you, too, Damon," Elena said, closing her eyes and pressing her face against his chest.

On the way up the shaft, Elena realized, Damon must have wrapped her in some stray edge of his Power, because the trip had been smooth and almost momentary. On the way down, apparently he wasn't bothering to protect her. Her hair flew upward and the skin on her face stung with the passing wind. *He's got me*, she told herself, but her body screamed that she was plummeting.

They landed on the top of the elevator amid a plume of dust, and Elena choked and coughed for several minutes, wiping at the tears on her face.

"We have to get in there," she said frantically, feeling around in the dark, as soon as she could speak again. The elevator must have collapsed when it hit the bottom of the shaft. Instead of a neat box of metal, she could feel the sharp edges and long, broken pieces of shattered beams and the remains of walls. "Andrés could still be alive," she told Damon. She knelt and began to feel along what had been the elevator's top. The space Klaus and Damon had come through must still be here somewhere.

Damon grabbed her hands. "No," he said. "You say you can see auras now? Use your Power. There's no one in there."

He was right. As soon as Elena really looked, she could see that there was no trace of Andrés's green or that terrible chilling blackness that Klaus carried with him.

"Do you think they're dead?" she whispered.

Damon let out a short, bitter laugh. "Hardly," he said. "It would take more than a fall down an elevator shaft to kill Klaus. And if your human pal with the shield was dead in there, I'd be able to smell his blood." He shook his head. "No, Klaus escaped again. And he took your Andrés with him."

"We have to save him," Elena said, and, when Damon didn't reply immediately, she yanked on his leather jacket, pulling him closer so she could stare demandingly into his unfathomable black eyes. Damon was going to help her whether he wanted to or not. She wasn't letting him get away again. "We have to save Andrés."

lena moved fast. She couldn't stop, couldn't think about what might be happening to Andrés, or that they might be too late. She had to stay cool, stay focused. She pulled out her phone and called the others, filling them in on the situation and telling them to prepare for a fight and meet her in a clearing in the woods just on the edge of campus.

"We're taking the battle to Klaus," she told Damon, shoving her phone briskly back into her bag. "This time, we're going to win."

They stopped by Elena's room to drop off her school-bag and, by the time they reached the clearing, the others had already gathered. Bonnie and Alaric were looking through a spell book together, while Stefan, Meredith, Zander, and Shay talked tactics on the other side of the clearing. Zander's eyes, Elena noticed, glanced in Bonnie's direction, but she was focused on her book. Everyone else was busily sharpening stakes or organizing weapons.

Silence fell over the clearing when Elena entered with Damon. Meredith's hand tightened on her stave, and Matt drew Chloe a little closer to him, protectively.

Elena was looking at Stefan, who stepped forward, his mouth grim.

"Damon saved me from Klaus," she announced, loud enough so everyone could hear. "He's fighting for us now."

Stefan and Damon stared at each other from opposite sides of the clearing. After a moment, Stefan nodded awkwardly. "Thank you," he said.

Damon shrugged. "I tried to stay away," he said, "but I guess you can't manage without me." Stefan's mouth tugged up into a reluctant half smile, and then the brothers turned away from each other, Damon wandering over toward Bonnie and Alaric while Stefan came to Elena.

"Are you sure you're all right?" he asked her, running his hands lightly over her shoulders as if to reassure himself that she wasn't obviously injured.

"I'm fine," Elena answered, and kissed him. Stefan pulled her closer and she leaned into his embrace, taking comfort in the strength of his arms around her. "Andrés held Klaus off, Stefan. He was so brave, and he told Damon to get me away. They saved me." She swallowed back a sob. *"We can't let Klaus kill him."*

"We won't," Stefan promised, his mouth against her hair. "We'll get there in time."

Elena sniffed back her tears. "You can't know that."

"We'll do our best," Stefan told her. "It will have to be good enough."

The sun was low in the sky, and afternoon sunlight spread across the grass between the trees. Elena spent the next few minutes sharpening stakes. They didn't have wood from the blessed tree, but ordinary white ash would at least hurt Klaus. And any wood would kill his vampire descendants.

"All right," Stefan said at last, calling everyone together. "I think we're as ready as we're going to be." Elena looked around at the gathered group: Meredith and Alaric, hand in hand, looking strong and ready for anything. Bonnie, her cheeks flushed and her curls going in every direction, but sticking her chin out defiantly. Matt and Chloe, pale but determined. Zander, still human-form for now, shooting wistful, confused glances at Bonnie, flanked by Shay and the other werewolves, an empty space among them.

Damon stood alone on the other side of the circle, watching Elena. When Stefan cleared his throat, preparing to speak, Damon shifted his eyes to watch his brother instead. He looked, Elena thought, resigned. Not happy, but not angry anymore.

Stefan smiled softly at Elena beside him and looked around at rest of the group. "We'll find Andrés," he said. "Today we're going to rescue him, and we're going to kill Klaus and his vampires. We're a team now, all of us. No one—none of us here, and no one else on this campus or in this town—will be safe as long as Klaus and his followers are alive. We've already seen what they are capable of. They killed James, who was kind and knowledgeable. They killed Chad, who was smart and loyal." The werewolves shifted angrily, and Stefan went on. "They've attacked innocent people across this campus and across this town in the last few weeks, and before that, the vampires in Klaus's army slaughtered the innocent all over the world. We have to do what we can. We're the only ones who can fend off the darkness, because we're the only ones here who know the truth." His eyes caught on Damon's and they held each other's gaze for a long moment until Damon finally glanced away, fiddling with the cuff of his jacket. "It's time for us to take a stand," Stefan said.

There was a murmur of agreement, and everyone was turning to one another, picking up their weapons and gathering themselves, ready to fight. Elena grabbed Stefan in a tight, hard hug, her heart bursting with love. He tried so hard to take care of everyone.

"Are you ready, Elena?" Stefan asked her, and she let him go and nodded, wiping a hand quickly across her eyes.

Breathing deeply, she reached deep inside herself, thinking protection, thinking evil, trying to trigger her Power in the way Andrés had taught her.

When she opened her eyes, she felt a strong, almost undeniable pull, jerking her toward Damon. Unable to stop herself, she stepped forward before she felt Stefan's hand on her arm, restraining her.

"No," he breathed. "You must find Klaus."

Elena nodded, avoiding Damon's startled eyes. The pull to Damon was intense: she tried to ignore it, but she knew it was her Guardian task calling to her. Closing her eyes again, she breathed and concentrated on Klaus. Images flew in rapid succession across her mind: his cold, brutal kiss, his laughter as he kicked his feet at the top of the elevator, the way he had thrown Chad's poor wrecked body across the clearing.

This time, when she opened her eyes, the dark tug inside her was leading out of the clearing, away from Damon, and she felt like she could almost taste the thick, black, noxious fog of Klaus's aura.

Elena headed where her Power led her, and her friends followed, walking close together. As they went, Zander and Shay and the other werewolves who could change without the moon transformed, loping along beside the humans with their ears cocked for any sounds of attack, their mouths open to catch the scents the wind carried.

They skirted around the edge of campus, sticking to the trees and trying to stay out of sight. Elena expected her Power to lead them farther into the woods, toward where they had fought Klaus before, but instead it tugged her back onto the campus.

At the back of the campus lay the old stables. As they approached, the miasma of darkness seemed to be pulling her along toward the building, and an equal darkness was gathering overhead. Black clouds were hovering over the stables, low and threatening. Zander cocked his ears forward, his tail stiffening, and one of the human-form werewolves—Marcus, Elena thought—tilted his head as if he were listening.

"Zander says that's not a natural storm brewing," Marcus said apprehensively.

"No," Elena said. "Klaus can handle lightning." The werewolves stared at her in alarm for a moment, their shaggy heads going up, ears erect, then refocused their attention on the door to the stables, looking even warier than before.

"He knows we're coming," Stefan said tensely. "That's what the storm clouds are showing. He's ready for us. Bonnie, Alaric, to the sides. Stay clear of the fighting, but keep casting as many spells as you can. Damon, Meredith, Chloe, I want you with me in the first wave. Zander, whatever you think best for the Pack. Matt and Elena, take weapons but hang back."

Elena nodded. Part of her wanted to rebel against being kept in the rear while her friends were in battle, but it made sense. She and Matt were strong, but not as strong as vampires or werewolves, and not as well able to protect themselves and others as the magic-users. If she was supposed to kill Damon, she assumed some magic fighting Powers would show up eventually, but she didn't know how handy aura-reading and tracking would be now that they'd found Klaus.

As they reached the door, there was a beat of hesitation.

"For God's sake," Damon said scornfully. "They already know we're out here." Slamming one elegant Italian-made boot into the center of the stable doors, he kicked them wide open.

It was only because of the speed of his vampiric reflexes that Damon survived at all. As soon as the doors opened, a heavy pointed beam that had been carefully rigged on top of them slammed down. Damon was able to twitch automatically aside just enough so that the blow caught him in the shoulder, propelling him backward and out the door, rather than through the chest. Clutching his shoulder, he folded over and fell into the dirt.

Automatically, Elena ran forward, only half-aware of Matt keeping pace beside her. The others, the fighters, were streaming through the doors: Meredith with her stave swinging, Stefan's face twisted with fury, werewolves leaping into the fray.

With Matt's help, Elena pulled Damon out of the way and felt at his chest, checking his injury. The beam had pierced his shoulder, leaving a gaping wound that both Elena's fists could have fit inside. The ground below him was already black and swampy with blood.

"It looks pretty bad," Matt said.

"Won't kill me," Damon gasped, clutching at the wound with one hand as if he could pull its edges back together. "Get back to the fight, you idiots."

"It could kill you if anyone passes by with a stake," Elena snapped. "You can't defend yourself like this." The pull of her Power toward Damon was making her itch again. *He's defenseless*, something inside her said. *Finish him.*

She felt a presence behind her and turned hurriedly as Stefan, back out of the fight, knelt in the bloody mud beside his brother, running his eyes over him clinically. They exchanged a long glance, and Elena knew they were communicating silently.

"Here," Stefan said. He bit neatly at his own wrist and held it to his brother's mouth. Damon eyed him, then drank deeply, his throat working.

"Thanks," he said at last. "Save me some vampires. I'll be there in a second." He lay back, breathing deeply. Elena could see that the wound was already knitting itself together, new flesh and muscle raw beneath the torn skin.

Stefan whirled and ran back to the stable, Matt behind him. Elena bent over Damon in the mud and waited until he pushed himself wearily up on his elbows, then to his feet.

"Ugh," he said. "I'm not at my best now, princess. But they've ruined my jacket, and that gives me a reason to fight." He shot her a pale echo of his usual brilliant smile.

"Well, since you've come all this way," Elena answered, keeping her voice light with difficulty. She resisted the urge to support him toward the stables, and by the time they reached the doors, he was walking strongly.

Inside, it looked like hell. Damon swore and slipped past her, throwing himself into the battle.

Her friends were fighting hard; she could see that at a glance. Meredith was engaged in a near-dance of thrust and parry with an olive-skinned, quick-footed vampire who could only be her twin brother. Bonnie and Alaric stood at opposite corners of the stable, their arms raised above their heads, chanting loudly, raising some sort of protective spell over their allies. Andrés was here, too, she saw, tied and slung carelessly beside one wall, but he was pressing his bound hands into the earth and raising a green swell of protective Power as well.

Werewolves wove throughout the crowd, fighting together, human-form and wolf-form, as a Pack. Damon, Stefan, and even Chloe grappled with vampires, while

Matt quickly staked Chloe's opponent from behind.

Suddenly, Elena's mind cleared. She'd been hanging back as Stefan had ordered, used to being the fragile one, less of a fighter than the others. But she couldn't be killed by the supernatural now.

Clutching her stake tightly, Elena threw herself into the battle, exhilarated. Her Power tugged at her, and she looked to see Damon wrestling with one of Klaus's vampires, his teeth bared and bloody. Her Power urged her to attack him, and she clamped down on her emotions. *Not Damon*, she told herself sternly.

A dark-skinned vampire swung her around by the shoulder, his face gleeful, and tried to sink his fangs into her neck. With a stroke of luck and speed, Elena shoved the stake into his chest.

At her first push, it didn't go deep enough to reach the vampire's heart. For a second, both Elena and the vampire stared down at the stake halfway into his chest, and then Elena gathered her strength and slammed it home. The vampire crumpled to the ground, looking pale and somehow smaller. Elena, savagely triumphant, looked around for her next opponent.

But there were so many vampires. And, in the center of everything, his face alight with glee, was Klaus. A few feet away from him, Stefan staked his opponent and charged toward Klaus, fangs bared.

Klaus raised his hands above his head to an opening in the ruined roof and, with a crash of thunder, lightning struck. Klaus laughed and aimed it toward Stefan, but Bonnie, fast as lightning herself, threw up her hands and shouted in Latin. The bolt changed direction in midair, hitting one of the old stalls and blowing its door off. The stall began to burn merrily. Klaus shouted, a high screech of rage, and shoved his hands up, blasting Stefan off his feet.

Elena screamed and tried to run to Stefan, but there was too much in the way, too many struggling fighters. Why couldn't she release more of her Powers? She could feel them there, beneath those locked doors in her mind, and she knew she'd be stronger if she could just reach them.

Her Power itched at her, and Elena involuntarily glanced away from where Stefan had fallen, to see Damon rip the throat out of his opponent.

In a flash, Elena understood. "Damon!" she called, and he was instantly at her side, wiping blood from his mouth on the back of his sleeve.

"Are you all right?" he asked.

"Fight me," Elena said, and he stared at her, bewildered. "Fight me!" she said again. "That is how I unlock my Power."

Damon frowned. Then he nodded, and hit her in the arm. It wasn't a hard hit, certainly not by Damon's standards, but it hurt and jolted her backward.

Something inside Elena broke wide open, and Power rushed into her. Suddenly, she knew how to do this. She was full of Power now, ready to unleash, and it was all focused on Damon. *Not him,* she told her Power again. *Not Damon.* With what felt like a huge physical effort, she tore her attention away from him, back toward Klaus and Stefan.

She waved a hand and one of the beams from the hayloft came free, and she slammed it toward Klaus, knocking him backward as Stefan scrambled up.

There was a thin squeal, barely audible over the now louder crackle of the flames, and Elena wheeled to see Bonnie in the grasp of one of Klaus's vampires, kicking furiously at him as she struggled. His hand was clamped over her mouth to prevent her from casting any spells.

With a pulse of fury, Elena shoved a jagged board through the vampire's chest and watched him fall lifeless to the ground.

Klaus was on his feet again now. Stefan had been tackled by another of Klaus's descendants, and nearer to her, Damon struggled with a huge, red-haired, brutal-looking vampire. *A Viking,* thought Elena. Klaus was calling lightning all around him, and the air was thick with dark, choking smoke.

No, Elena thought, and walked toward Klaus, pushing the fire ahead of her. She had to keep it away from her friends, keep it tight around Klaus himself.

The flames were all around her now. Looking back,

though, she could see the air was clearer where her friends fought, and it looked like they might be winning. As she watched, Meredith pressed her stave against her brother's heart, and he said something to her. They were too far away and the flames were too loud for Elena to hear his words, but Meredith's face twisted into the saddest smile as she rammed the stave through his heart.

Elena coughed and coughed again. It was hard to catch her breath amid all this smoke, and her eyes were stinging. She used her mind to shove the flames closer to Klaus. It was so tiring, though, this new Power of hers, and she was so dizzy. She could feel the Power draining out of her now that it was no longer focused on Damon, and she tried to cling to it. Elena hacked and wheezed again. Klaus was glaring at her, reaching for her, and his filthy hands, splattered with ash and mud and blood, brushed her arm.

She gathered the last of her energy and poured her strength into her new Power, forcing the flames higher between her friends and Klaus's vampires, forcing them apart, forcing her friends backward, away from the end of the stable where she faced Klaus. Around Klaus and Elena, the fire roared.

"Elena! Elena!" She could hear their voices shouting, and she caught sight of Stefan's agonized face just before the walls collapsed on top of her and Klaus, bringing them down.

36

Stefan clenched his fists together, the bite of his nails against his palms helping to stave off the fog of misery that was enfolding him. Elena wasn't dead. He wouldn't believe that.

Full dark had fallen, and firefighters had finally put out the blaze that had consumed the old stables. They were carefully working through the debris, dragging out body after body.

Outside the protective barriers, screened by a stand of trees, Stefan and the others waited. Meredith and Bonnie clung to each other, Bonnie in tears. Andrés was seated, dazed and silent, on the ground, his eyes fixed on the slow movements of the firefighters.

Stefan remembered the look on Elena's face as the fiery wall had come down upon her. She had seemed so resigned, so peaceful as she looked back at him one last time, the flames she had put between them rising faster. The wall had fallen so fast—how could she possibly have escaped?

A hand landed on his shoulder, and Stefan looked up to see Damon frowning past him at the remains of the stable. "She's not in there, you know," Damon said. "Elena's got the luck of the devil. She'd never get trapped in there."

Stefan leaned into his brother's hand, just a little. He was tired and grief-stricken, and there was a comfort in Damon's familiarity. "She died twice before her high-school graduation," he told Damon bitterly. "I don't know if I'd call that lucky. And both times, it was our fault."

Damon sighed. "She came back, though," he said gently. "Not everyone gets to do that. Hardly anyone, really." His lips twitched into a half smile. "Me, of course."

Stefan twisted away, his eyes burning. "Don't joke," he said in a furious, low mutter. "How can—even you—how can you joke about this now? Do you care at all?" But he shouldn't have been surprised. Damon had spent the last few weeks showing—violently, capriciously—how little he cared, for any of them.

Damon looked at him, his dark eyes steady. "I care," he said. "You know I do. Even when I don't want to. But I know she's not dead. If you don't trust Elena's luck, think of Klaus. It would take more than a fire to kill him."

"Fire kills vampires," Stefan said stubbornly. "Even old ones."

"He played with lightning," Damon said, and shuddered. "I don't think there's much that could kill Klaus."

The firefighters had stopped their investigation, every inch of burned wood and earth turned over, and were covering the bodies with dark canvases.

I'll check it out, Damon told Stefan silently, and transformed into a crow, flapping through the night to land in a tree near the corpses.

A few moments later, he was back, becoming himself again before his feet had even hit the ground so that he stumbled a few paces, less polished and poised than usual. Stefan was vaguely aware of everyone, all their allies, gathering around, but his eyes were fixed beseechingly on Damon. He opened his mouth, but the question he needed to ask wouldn't come. *Is Elena there?* he thought desperately. *Is she?*

If Elena was gone, if she had sacrificed herself to save them, Stefan would be dead by morning. There was nothing for him without her.

"Elena's not there," Damon said shortly. "Neither is Klaus. It's all Klaus's descendants."

Bonnie gave one short, broken sob of relief and Meredith squeezed her hand hard, knuckles whitening.

"Klaus must have her," Stefan said, the world swimming

back into focus now that he had a purpose. "We have to find them before we're too late."

His eyes met Damon's, leaf-green and black holding, for once, exactly the same expression: fear and hope in equal measure. Damon nodded. Stefan's fingers relaxed where they still clutched Damon's shirt and he pulled his brother to him in a brief embrace, trying to send him all the love and gratitude he would never be able to put into words. Damon was back. And if anyone could help Stefan save Elena, it was Damon.

"Is there anything you can do?" Stefan asked Andrés. He could hear the pleading note in his own voice.

All around them, the others looked tense, waiting for the answer. Bonnie was tending to Shay's shoulder, bandaging a nasty vampire bite, and her deft fingers stiffened with anxiety until Shay gave a quiet grunt.

"I hope I can," said Andrés. "I'll try." He knelt and laid his palms flat against the ground beneath the trees. Watching him, Stefan felt the cracklings of Power in the air. Andrés held very still, brown eyes narrowed and focused. New blades of grass poked through the earth, curling around his fingers.

"This isn't as effective as Elena's tracking Power," he explained, "but sometimes I can sense people. If she's touching the Earth, I will know where she is."

Andrés sat there for what seemed like a long time, his

face peaceful and alert. As he sank his fingers deeper into the ground, digging the tips into the soil at the base of a white birch tree, the tree unfurled new leaves.

"Faster," Damon ordered, his voice low and dangerous, but Andrés did not respond with even a twitch. It was as if he had sunk so deeply into himself—or into his communion with the soil, Stefan wasn't sure which—that he couldn't hear them anymore.

Stefan's pulse was pounding faster than he could remember since before he'd become a vampire. He clenched and unclenched his fists, keeping himself from shaking Andrés. The Guardian was doing the best he could, and distracting him would not make him work faster. But Elena, oh, Elena.

Farther away, he could hear Matt searching the woods, calling, "Chloe! Chloe!" The young vampire had made it out of the stables; Stefan was sure he had seen her, blackened with ash but otherwise unhurt. Now, however, she was nowhere to be found. Stefan's heart ached in sympathy. The girl Matt loved was missing, too.

"Strange," Andrés said. It was the first word he had spoken in a while, and Stefan's attention immediately snapped back to him. Andrés tilted his head back to look up at Damon and Stefan, his forehead crinkling in confusion. "Elena's alive," he said. "I'm sure she's alive, but it feels like she's underground."

Stefan sagged in relief: alive. He looked at Damon

for confirmation. "The tunnels?" he asked, and Damon nodded. Klaus must have taken her to the tunnels that crisscrossed the ground underneath the campus, the ones the Vitale Society had used.

Meredith, sitting nearby with Alaric, jumped to her feet. "Where's the closest entrance?" she asked.

Stefan tried to picture the maze of passages Matt had sketched for him before their battle against the Vitale vampires. There were many blank areas and half-drawn entrances on his mental map, because Matt had only traveled a little way in what seemed to be a vast, twisting labyrinth underlying the campus and maybe the town. But, of what he knew . . .

"The vampires' safe house," Stefan said decisively.

37

Elena's shoulder banged against something hard, and she made a small sound of protest. All she wanted to do was sleep, but someone wouldn't let her rest. Her legs hurt.

Her head jolted against something, and Elena's perspective shifted. Someone was pulling her along by her legs, she realized, the rest of her body sliding along on the ground. Her hair caught, jerking her head before it came loose, and she groaned again. Slowly, she opened her eyes.

"Back with me, little one?" Klaus said, sounding disconcertingly jovial. He was the one dragging her, Elena realized, and although it was dark, he clearly had sensed when she awoke. He laughed, his dark, disturbing chuckle making her cringe. "I can't kill you with my teeth, or with my dagger, but an ordinary knife will work, won't it? I could tie you up and drop you in the lake to drown. What do you think?"

Elena's mouth was dry, and it took a couple of tries to get any sound out. "I think," she said at last, thickly, "that Stefan is going to save me."

Klaus laughed again. "Your precious Stefan won't be able to find you," he said. "No one can save you now."

They hadn't been to the safe house since they had left with Chloe, the night of Klaus's resurrection. When they arrived, the faint scent of vervain still lingered in the basement, and Stefan's skin itched in reaction. Meredith pried up a trapdoor in the floor, and Stefan lowered himself in first, the others following.

Everyone but Matt had come, weapons in hand, carrying flashlights and lanterns, tense and ready to fight. Matt had stayed behind to search for Chloe. Bonnie, Alaric, and Meredith stuck close together, their faces pale and strained. Shay, Zander, and the other werewolves stayed together, too, alert to every noise or scent in the darkness. And Damon, Stefan, and Andrés formed the vanguard, each one of them straining for some sign of Elena.

They seemed to walk for miles, through underground passages that narrowed as they went, changing from concrete passages to dusty tunnels carved from dirt. Andrés stopped frequently and touched the floor and walls, listening with his hands before picking a direction.

"Did you come this way when you smoked the tunnels?" Stefan asked Meredith as they waited impatiently during one of these stops, and she shook her head, wide-eyed.

"We're a lot deeper underground than I knew the tunnels went," she said. "I had no idea the Vitale Society had anything this elaborate."

"I wonder if it was the Vitale Society, actually," Bonnie interjected suddenly. "They used these tunnels, but I keep getting a sense that there's something older here. Something creepy."

Silently, Alaric raised his flashlight higher, illuminating a series of runes carved deep into the rock above them. "I can't read them," he said, "but these must predate Dalcrest by centuries."

The darkness that pressed in from all sides, now that Stefan focused on it, seemed to breathe with ageless secrets. It was as if there was something huge and sleeping, just out of sight, wrapped in itself and waiting to awaken. His chest ached with anxiety. *Elena . . .*

The steady thump of Klaus's footsteps stopped, but Elena was still sliding forward. With a shock, she realized that he was pulling her to him and she flailed desperately, trying to jerk herself away.

She was so tired, though. She'd used more of her Power than she ever had before, and she felt drained and helpless. Elena could do no more than struggle weakly as Klaus picked her up, gathering her in his arms as gently as if she was a baby.

"No," she whispered hoarsely.

She felt Klaus's hand stroking her hair back, and she shuddered with repulsion at the gentle touch in the dark. She struggled weakly, but his Power was holding her in place.

"I could have let the fire kill you," he whispered, his voice intimate and almost tender, "but what's poetic in that? My bite may not hurt you, but I want a taste of the girl that fascinates vampires so much. I've never tasted a Guardian before. Is your blood especially sweet?"

He pressed his mouth against her neck and Elena cringed. She couldn't fight anymore. His fangs pushed into her, rough and demanding, and it felt as if her throat was being split open. She tried to scream, but only a whimper came out.

He can't kill me this way, she reminded herself desperately. And yet it felt as if her life was draining away.

Andrés was standing perfectly still, one hand pressed against the rock.

"What is it?" Stefan said sharply.

Andrés opened his eyes. His face was desolate. "I've lost her," he said. "She was so close but now . . . she's not touching the Earth anymore. I don't know where she is."

"Elena! Elena!" Stefan shouted as he ran, bursting past the rest of the group. She couldn't be gone. Behind him, he could hear the pounding of Damon's boots close on his tail.

Ahead of the flashlights, they rounded the corner into complete darkness. Stefan funneled Power to his eyes so that he could see.

Just ahead of them, Klaus raised his head, blood streaming from his mouth and dripping down his chin. In his arms, Elena lay limply, her silken, golden hair tangled and dirty, hanging down over Klaus's arm. Stefan snarled and rushed forward.

Klaus licked at his lips, his pink tongue slow, and then he shuddered, a smile on his face. Slowly, still smiling, he collapsed to the ground, Elena landing with a thud in front of him. Stefan's heart plummeted even as he leaped toward her. Elena lay in the center of the path. She was motionless and very pale, her head turned to one side, eyes closed.

Blood was everywhere, staining her once-white top a deep, rich red. Her throat was covered with gore.

And beyond her, as limp as a discarded toy, lay Klaus. Although there was no mark on him other than a thin streak of blood at the corner of his mouth, Stefan had no doubt that he was dead. No one living looked like that, as if everything that had been part of him was gone, leaving a wax dummy in his place. Especially not the lightning-handler Klaus, who had shimmered with golden, filthy rage. He looked like a badly preserved corpse.

Elena, though . . .

To Stefan's wonder, Elena stirred, her eyelashes fluttering.

Stefan gathered her into his arms. She was so pale, but her heartbeat was steady. Above him, Damon hovered, his mouth twisted with anxiety.

"She'll live," Damon muttered, partly to himself, partly to Stefan.

Stefan opened his mouth to agree, but all that came out was a broken sob. He began to kiss Elena, peppering her cheeks and mouth and forehead and hands with light kisses.

"Stefan," she murmured weakly, and smiled. "My Stefan."

"What happened?" Bonnie asked as the others rounded the bend and ran forward. Only Andrés stood still just past the bend in the tunnel, staring at Elena, his face full of wonder.

"She's the One," he breathed.

"The One what?" Elena asked, still smiling dazedly. She raised her hand and stroked Stefan's cheek.

Andrés seemed to be having trouble speaking. He

swallowed, licked his lips, and swallowed again, looking a little lost. "There's a legend," he said finally, hesitantly. "A Guardian legend. It says that one day a sworn Guardian, one born of a Principal Guardian, will come to Earth. Her blood, the blood of Guardians carried through generations, will be anathema to the Oldest creatures of darkness."

"What does that mean?" Stefan asked sharply.

Andrés lifted his flashlight, lighting up Klaus's pathetic, diminished corpse. "It means," he said, his voice full of wonder, "that Elena's blood has killed Klaus. It would kill any of the Old Ones, the handful of vampires and demons that have walked the Earth since the dawn of human civilization . . . maybe before. It means," he said, "that Elena is a very valuable weapon."

"Hang on," Damon said. "That can't be right. I've drunk Elena's blood. Stefan's drunk Elena's blood."

Andrés shrugged. "Perhaps its qualities are only fatal to the Old Ones. That's all the legend tells of."

"And her blood is special," Stefan said, his voice rough. He and Damon exchanged quick, embarrassed glances. Elena's blood was rich and heady, countless times more potent than any other blood Stefan had ever tasted. He had thought the difference was because of the love they shared.

"But . . ." Bonnie said, frowning. "Your parents weren't Guardians, were they?" she asked Elena. Elena shook her head, but her eyes were clouding over and her eyelids drooping. She needed rest, and proper medical care.

"We can talk about this later," Stefan said abruptly, and stood, lifting Elena carefully and gently into his arms. "She needs to get out of here."

"Well, whether she's the One or not," Meredith said, looking at the dead monster at her feet, "Elena killed Klaus." They all straightened unconsciously, smiling. They had nothing left to fear.

38

"Chloe?" Matt called cautiously, sticking his head into one of the empty sheds that surrounded the burned-out stables. The sky was starting to lighten in the east, signifying the end of a long night. There were still a few firefighters and EMTs near the blocked-off stables, turning over the ashes, so he had to be quiet. He took a deep breath, trying to calm down. Chloe had to be somewhere, he reminded himself. He had seen her after the fight, weary but not seriously hurt. She had probably just retreated, overwhelmed by all the blood and by the adrenaline from the fight. She would turn up soon.

The shed was silent and dark. Matt raised his flashlight and shone it around the empty walls of the tiny space: nowhere here for anyone to hide. As he was about to move on, a faint scratching noise caught his attention. Not completely empty, then.

Focusing the flashlight on the ground, he caught a glimpse of bright eyes and a long tail before a mouse zipped out of sight again. Nothing else.

"Chloe!" he hissed, heading for the old barn, the last outbuilding he hadn't yet searched.

Three werewolves, the most battered and bloody of the Pack after the battle, had stayed behind after the rest had left to hunt for Klaus and Elena. But they were gone now. They'd offered to help Matt search for Chloe, but he'd waved them off: at that point, he'd still been sure that he'd find her any minute.

"I'll be fine," Matt had told Spencer. "Go take care of your injuries. I'll find her. It's probably stupid to be so worried."

Spencer had always struck Matt as being more about hair gel than brains, but he'd pinned him with a surprisingly shrewd look. "Listen, man," he'd drawled in his preppy, rich-surfer-boy accent, still managing to sound sort of laid-back despite the pain in his voice. "I'm wishing you the best here, I am, but vampires . . ."

"I know," Matt had said, wincing. He did know; he could have written the book on reasons not to date vampires, but that was when he'd been thinking of Elena, not himself, and before he had met Chloe. Now it was different. "I'll find her," he had said, absurdly touched by Spencer's concern. "Thanks, though. Really."

He'd felt wistful while he watched Spencer and his friends walk off, like he would be the last person left in the world once the werewolves were out of sight.

Where could Chloe be? They had been shoulder-to-shoulder coming out of the stable after half the roof fell in. Chloe had been shaking, her pupils dilated and her hands streaked with blood, but she had been with him.

And then, sometime during the rise of panic as they realized that Elena had been under the fiery roof when it collapsed, Chloe was just gone.

Thinking of Elena in Klaus's grasp gave him a pang of guilt. This was Elena, his friend and the girl who'd been the sun he orbited around for so long. He wanted to be searching for her with the rest of them. But he needed to find Chloe, too.

The barn was rickety, one of its broad double doors hanging crookedly by a single hinge. Matt approached it with caution—he wouldn't do Chloe any good if he was caught and pinned under a falling barn door.

The half-broken door wobbled and creaked, but did not fall as he edged his way through the gap between it and the side of the barn, shining his flashlight inside. Dust rose in the beam of light, specks floating thickly in midair.

Inside, something shifted, and Matt walked forward,

sweeping the flashlight back and forth. Far in the back, he saw something white.

As he came closer, Matt realized that it was Chloe's face staring into the flashlight's beam, wild with panic. After such a long search, it took Matt a moment to process what was going on: his first reaction was a simple swell of relief—thank God he'd found Chloe at last. Then he realized that Chloe was streaked with blood and that, quiet in her arms, lay Tristan.

Chloe blinked at Matt blankly for a moment, and then her face filled with dismayed realization. She pushed Tristan away from her, horrified. The werewolf let out a weak cry of distress as he hit the floor with a thump, then lay still.

"Oh, no," Chloe said, dropping to her knees beside him. "Oh, no. I didn't mean to."

Matt ran toward her. "Is he alive?" he asked.

Chloe had tried so hard, and he'd been there every step of the way, helped her as much as he could. Life was unfair enough. But now Chloe's head was bent over Tristan and she was patting her hand urgently over his body, trying to wake him.

Matt got down on the other side of Tristan and tried to check the werewolf's injuries. God, the poor guy was bleeding everywhere. He must have smelled like a banquet to Chloe.

"I'm so sorry, Tristan," Chloe whispered. "Please wake up."

"Tristan, can you hear me?" Matt asked, checking his pulse. The werewolf's heart was beating slowly and steadily, and he was breathing well. The Pack was tough. But the werewolf's eyes were unfocused, and he didn't respond when Matt called his name again, shaking him gently.

"I think I might have, um, calmed him down," Chloe said, stricken. "Like the rabbits."

"We should get him some help," Matt said brusquely, not looking at her.

She didn't answer. Matt looked up and saw the horror and guilt on her face, tears running over her rounded cheeks, making tracks through the blood around her mouth. She'd joked to him once that she was an ugly crier, and now she scrubbed at her running nose with the back of her sleeve. In the semidarkness, her eyes seemed like black pits of misery.

"Come on," he said, more gently. "This isn't the end of the world. We'll start over. You shouldn't have been in a battle right now. It was too hard on you to be around all that action. All that blood." Despite himself, his voice stumbled a little over the word *blood*. Matt gulped unhappily and went on, working to make his voice confident. "Everyone slips up when they're breaking an addiction. We'll get back to the boathouse, away from everyone. It's going to be fine." He sounded desperate, even to himself.

Chloe shook her head. "Matt . . ." she began.

"It was a mistake," Matt told her firmly. "Tristan's going to be all right. So will you."

Chloe shook her head again, harder this time, the ringlets Matt had always found so adorable flying around her head. "I'm not," she said miserably. "I'm not going to be all right. I love you, Matt, I do." Her voice broke in a sob, and then she took a deep breath and began again. "I love you, but I can't live like this. Stefan was right; I'm not really living at all now. I'm not strong enough. It's not getting better for me."

"You are strong enough," Matt argued. "I'll help you." Dawn was breaking outside, and he could see the ash and blood streaked on Chloe's tear-blotched skin now, the deep circles beneath her eyes.

"I'm so glad I got to stay with you for a while," she said. "You took such good care of me." She leaned forward, across Tristan's unconscious body, and kissed him. Her lips were soft and tasted of copper and salt. Her hand found his, and she pressed something small and hard into his palm.

Pulling back from the kiss at last, she said, her voice thin, "I hope someday you'll find someone who deserves you, Matt," and got to her feet.

"Don't . . ." Matt said, panicking, and reached out for her. "I need you, Chloe."

Chloe looked down at him, her face calm and sure now. She even smiled a little. "This is the right thing," she told him.

In a few steps, she'd crossed the barn and was slipping out through the gap between the doors. The sunrise was well underway now, and her body was dark against the pink-and-golden light.

Then there was a burst of fire, and Chloe crumpled into a heap of ash.

Matt looked down at the small hard object she had pressed into his palm. It was a little pin in the shape of a *V*, made of blue stone. He had one, too: the Vitale badge Ethan had given all of them, back when he and Chloe and the other pledges were all human, all innocent. The lapis lazuli charm that defended Chloe from the daylight.

He closed his fist tightly around it, ignoring the pain as its sharp edges pressed into his palm, and gave a dry, heaving sob.

He would have to get up in a minute. Tristan needed his help. But for a moment, Matt bent his head and let the tears come.

tefan and Elena couldn't stop touching each other. Little touches, hands entwining, a light kiss, or a stroke to the cheek.

"You're alive," Stefan said to her, his eyes wide. "I thought I'd lost you."

"Never," said Elena, reaching up from her bed to tug him closer until he was sitting on the bed, his side against hers. "I'm not going anywhere without you."

Klaus was dead. And Elena had *survived*. The sheer amazement of it had her buzzing with joy.

But Stefan stroked her hair back from her face, and the look in his eyes—loving, but somehow still laced with concern—made her effervescence flatten.

"What is it?" she asked, suddenly apprehensive.

Stefan shook his head. "The task isn't gone," he said.

"The Guardians still might take you away."

Elena had been avoiding that thought with everything she had, but at Stefan's words, she stilled and let the knowledge flood over her: the Guardians still expected her to kill Damon. And the punishment for not doing so would be leaving Earth. Losing Stefan.

"I will love you whatever happens," Stefan said. His brows were drawn tight, and Elena knew the terrors that warred in him: the fear of losing Elena after all, and the fear of losing Damon. "Whatever you decide, Elena, I trust you." He raised his head, and his gaze was steady and true, his eyes shining.

Elena reached up and ran her fingers over Stefan's forehead, trying to erase the lines of his frown. "I think . . ." she said slowly, "I think I can see a way that we can save both me and Damon. I hope."

Just then, Andrés tapped gently on the half-open door to Elena's room and she greeted him with a smile.

"How are you feeling?" he asked seriously. "I can come back later if you're resting."

"No, don't," she said, patting the chair by her bedside. "I want you to fill me in on everything that's going on."

"If you want to talk Guardian business, I could leave you two here, maybe get Elena something to eat," Stefan said. "I didn't want to leave her alone."

Stefan kissed Elena once more and she tried to pour all

the love and reassurance she felt into their embrace. When he finally pulled back, the lines of his face were softer, more relaxed. Whatever Elena was planning, his gaze assured her, he would be with her. As he left, Andrés took the chair by her bed. "Stefan's been looking after you?" he asked.

"Oh, yes," Elena said, stretching luxuriously, and trying to turn off her serious thoughts for a moment. She'd almost died—she had the right to be babied and indulged for one day, surely. "He tried to make me something called a hot milk posset earlier today. Supposedly, I am at a delicate stage in my recovery." She started to laugh, but the laugh abruptly cut off when she caught the look in Andrés's eyes. "What's the matter?" she said in a different, sharper tone, sitting up. "What's happened?"

Andrés waved a hand dismissively. "Nothing has happened," he said. "Only, perhaps we should talk after you've had more time to recover. What I have to say is not bad news, I don't think, but it is . . ." He hesitated. "Surprising," he concluded at last.

"Now you have to tell me," Elena said. "Or I'll worry myself into a coma." Seeing the flicker of concern on Andrés's face, she hurriedly added: "I'm joking."

"All right, then," Andrés said. "You know how we found you in the tunnels, correct?"

Elena nodded. "Klaus was dead," she said. "You said

that there was a legend that the blood of a Guardian born of a Principal Guardian would kill Old Ones." She shook her head. "That's the first thing I don't understand. How could I have that kind of family history without knowing it?"

"I'm having trouble understanding, too," Andrés said. "Celestial Guardians don't have children, not that I'd ever heard. They're not"—he frowned—"people, not exactly. That is what I've believed, at least. I think we both have a lot to learn." He reached inside his jacket and withdrew a small leather-bound book. "I have brought you something that I hope will illuminate some of your questions," he told her. "I began to read it, and then I realized that it was intended for your eyes, not mine. The police finally let me return to James's house, and I found this there. I believe this is what he called you about, when he said he had found a way to kill Klaus, and that he hid it before Klaus killed him. It must have been sent to him after your parents died."

"My parents? What is it?" Elena asked, reaching out and taking the book. It felt oddly comfortable in her hand, as if it naturally belonged to her.

Andrés hesitated for a long moment before he answered. "I think it's better that you find that out for yourself," he said at last. He stood and touched Elena on the shoulder briefly. "I'll let myself out."

Elena nodded and watched him go. Andrés shot her a small smile as he closed the door behind him. Then, wonderingly, she turned her attention to the book. It was quite plain, without any patterns or words embossed on the outside, and was covered in a very soft pale-brown leather. Opening it, she saw that it was a journal, handwritten in a large, looping, dashing script, as if the writer had been in a hurry to get a million thoughts and feelings out onto the page.

I will not let them have Elena, she read, the words halfway down the first page, and gasped. Glancing down the page, names popped up at her: Thomas, her father, Margaret, her sister. Was this her mother's journal? Her chest felt tight suddenly, and she had to blink hard. Her beautiful, poised mother, the one who had been so clever with her hands and with her heart, who Elena had loved and admired so much—finding this was almost like hearing her speak once more.

After a moment, she composed herself and began to read again.

> *Elena turned twelve yesterday. I was getting down the birthday candles from the cabinet when the eternity mark on my palm began to itch and burn. It had almost faded into invisibility after so many years, but when I looked at my hand, it was*

suddenly as clear as the day I was first initiated into my duties.

I knew my sisters were calling for me, reminding me of what they think I owe them.

But I will not let them have Elena.

Not now, and maybe not ever.

I will not repeat the mistakes I have made, so disastrously, in the past.

Thomas understands. Despite what he agreed to when we were young, when Elena was just the idea of a child to him instead of her own funny, determined, sharp-witted self, he knows that we can't just let her go. And Margaret, sweet baby Margaret, the Guardians will want her, too, eventually, because of who I used to be.

The Powers my darling girls will have are almost unimaginable.

And so the Celestial Guardians, once my sisters and brothers, want to get their hands on them as early as possible, want to bring them up to be weapons instead of children, clear-eyed warriors with no trace of humanity about them.

Once, I would have let them. I stepped away from Katherine when she was only an infant, pretended that I had died, so that she could fulfill the destiny I believed was inevitable and right for her.

Elena stopped reading. Her mother had once had another child? The name must be a coincidence, though: the Katherine she knew, Damon's and Stefan's Katherine, was hundreds of years older than her. And about as far from being a Guardian as possible.

There were plenty of Guardians who looked rather like Elena, though. She reviewed in her mind's eye the faces that she'd seen in the Celestial Court: businesslike, blue-eyed blondes, crisp and cool. Could one of them have been her elder sister? Still, though, she couldn't shake off her unease: Katherine, her mirror image. She read on.

But Katherine was a sickly child, and the Guardians turned their backs on her, rejected the great power she could have been. She would not come into her Power for years, and they did not think she would survive long enough to see that day. A human child who probably wouldn't live to grow up wasn't worth their time, they thought.

My heart ached for her. I had abandoned my daughter for nothing. From a careful distance, I watched her grow: pretty and lively despite her illnesses, brave even in the shadow of the pain she suffered, adored by her father, loved by the household. She did not need the mother she had never known. Perhaps this was better, I thought. She could live a happy, human life, even if it was a short one.

Then, disaster struck. A servant, thinking it would save her, offered Katherine up to a vampire to be transformed. My sweet daughter, a creature of joy and light, was dragged unceremoniously into the darkness. And the creature who performed the deed was one of the worst of his kind: Klaus, an Old One. If Katherine had come into her Power, if the Guardians had made her one of them, Katherine's blood would have killed him. But without that protection, it merely bound them together, tying him to her with a fascination neither of them understood.

My darling girl was lost, all her charm and intelligence subverted into what, before long, seemed to be merely a vicious, broken doll, Klaus's plaything. I don't know if the real Katherine is still there underneath that shadowed life she must live now.

Elena gasped, a harsh sound to her own ears in the room's silence. There was no denying the truth now. Katherine's illness, Klaus's cruel gift, all the details Stefan had told her were here. Katherine, who had hated her and tried to kill her, who had loved Stefan and Damon centuries before

Elena herself did, who had destroyed Stefan and Damon, was her *half sister.*

Part of her wanted to slam the book shut, to shove it to the back of her closet and never, never think about it again. But she couldn't stop herself from reading on.

> *I wandered for many years, mourning my daughter, turning my back on the Guardians who had once been my family. But, after centuries of loneliness, I met my sweet, honest, blindingly intelligent Thomas, and fell deeply, hopelessly, madly in love. We were so happy for a while.*
>
> *And then the Guardians found us.*
>
> *They came to us and told us that the Old Ones were gaining in Power. They were too strong, too cruel. They would destroy humanity if they could, would enslave the world in darkness and evil.*
>
> *The Guardians begged me to have another child. Only an Earthly Guardian with the blood of a Principal Guardian could kill an Old One so that the Old One could never be resurrected. My peculiar situation—a Principal Guardian who had abandoned her post to live a human life, who had fallen in love—made me their only chance.*
>
> *Thomas knew everything about my past. He trusted me to make the right choice, and I chose*

to say yes, under certain conditions. I would bear a child who could destroy the Old Ones, but she would not be taken from me. She would not be raised as a weapon but as a human girl. And, when she was old enough, she would be given a free choice: to come into her Power or not.

And they agreed. Elena's blood, Margaret's blood, was so precious that they would agree to anything.

But now they want to break that agreement. They want to take my darling Elena now, even though she is only twelve years old.

I will save Elena and Margaret, as I couldn't save Katherine. I will.

Elena is fiercely protective already of her friends and of her younger sister. I think she will choose to become a Guardian when she's given the choice, will decide to protect the larger world in the best way that she can. But it must be her decision, not theirs. Margaret is too young for me to tell yet whether she will have the makings of a Guardian. Perhaps she will choose another path. But no matter what I think they'll want in the end, they must have time to grow up before they have to make that decision.

I am afraid. The Guardians are ruthless, and

they will not be pleased when I refuse to turn Elena over to them.

If anything should happen to me, and to Thomas, before the girls are grown, I have made arrangements to shield my daughters from the Guardians. Judith, my closest friend, will pretend to be my sister and raise Elena and Margaret to adulthood. I have already cast certain charms: as long as the girls are in her custody, the Guardians will not be able to locate them.

I would die, happily, to protect their innocence. The Guardians will never find them, not until they are grown women and can choose for themselves.

I cannot see the future. I do not know what will happen to any of my daughters any more than any parent does, but I have done my best to protect Elena and Margaret, as I was not wise enough to protect Katherine. I pray that this will be enough. And I pray that someday, somehow, Katherine, too, will find her way back into the light. That all three of my girls will be safe from harm.

Tears ran down Elena's cheeks. She felt as if a burden she'd been carrying for weeks had suddenly flown off her shoulders. Her parents *hadn't* planned to turn her over to the Guardians, hadn't had a child just to discard her. Her mother had loved her as much as Elena had always thought.

She had to think carefully now. Eyes narrowing, she shoved her pillows against the wall and sat up. Margaret was safe with Aunt Judith for the moment, and that was good. She couldn't consider all the ramifications of *Katherine* being her sister, not now.

But the fact that she, Elena, was special to the Guardians, *precious* to them, that her blood had unique Powers the Guardians were desperate to have on their side? The confirmation in her mother's journal might be the last piece she needed to put her plan to save Damon in motion.

40

Ice cubes clinked lightly in his glass as Damon raised it in a toast to Katherine. "Here's to you, darling," he said. "The last survivor of Klaus's army. Lucky that you missed the battle, isn't it?"

With a sly smile, Katherine fluttered her eyelashes expressively, taking a sip of her own drink, and patted the sofa cushion next to her, inviting Damon to sit.

"Thank you for warning me," she said. "I may have been indebted to Klaus for bringing me back, but I didn't think I owed him another death. I never had any intention of fighting you and your precious princess again. I may be older and stronger than you, but there's always been too much luck on your side."

"Not *my* precious princess," Damon said with a grimace.

"Stefan's. She was never really mine."

"Oh, well," Katherine said lightly, "I think it's always been a little more complicated than that, hasn't it?"

Damon narrowed his eyes. "You knew about Elena being a Guardian, didn't you?" he demanded. "And you never told Klaus. Why?"

A small, slightly smug smile crossed Katherine's face. "You should have learned by now that you can never ask a girl to give up all her secrets. And I'm full of secrets. Always." Damon frowned. He had never been able to get Katherine to tell him anything she didn't want to.

A knock on the door interrupted them, and Damon rose and opened the door to find Elena herself outside. Her face was pale and strained, and her jewel-blue eyes seemed huge as they stared at each other. Damon cocked an eyebrow and threw her his most brilliant smile, refusing to acknowledge the tremor of nervousness that ran through him.

She cared for him—he knew that. He'd tried to throw that fact back in her face, to deny it, and it hadn't worked. But there was also something in her that was driving her toward *killing* him, her Guardian's task pushing for fulfillment. Ever since he had saved her in the elevator, he had been able to feel that Elena was holding herself back. And he still loved her, would probably always love her. Part of him wanted to bow his head before her, take the punishment she was duty-bound to give him.

And whatever happened to him, he would probably deserve it.

Elena looked past him at Katherine and paled even further, although he wouldn't have thought that was possible. Damon turned and found that Katherine was standing absolutely still just a few feet away, looking back at Elena with a faint, secretive smile.

"So now you know," Katherine said to Elena. "And you're smart enough to use it."

"Did you know? Back when we first met?" Elena asked her abruptly, as if the words had been jerked out of her against her will.

Katherine shook her head. "You learn a lot when you're dead sometimes," she said, the faint smile spreading.

"Know what?" Damon said, looking back and forth between them.

Katherine came closer, trailing her fingers lightly across Damon's arm. "Like I said," she told him, "a girl has to have her secrets." She winked at Elena. "I'm going to leave town for a little while. I think it's better if I keep out of your way from now on."

Elena nodded. "You're probably right. Good-bye, Katherine," she said. "And thank you."

A flash of humor crossed Katherine's face. "Right back at you," she said, and for a moment, the resemblance between them struck Damon more strongly than it ever had before.

Then Elena, all business now, turned to Damon. "It's time for us to face the Guardians. Are you ready?" she asked him.

Damon downed the rest of his drink quickly, then slammed the glass down on his polished steel coffee table, and inwardly cursed his vampiric tolerance for alcohol. It might have been easier, he thought, to face what was coming if he had been a little bit drunk. "Ready as I'll ever be," he drawled.

Bonnie sniffed at the rich and varied scents as she turned over her store of herbs.

"Where does this one go?" Matt asked her, holding up a bag of purple petals.

"That's aconite. It's used for protection," Bonnie replied. "Put it over there with the dogwood and agrimony."

"Got it," Matt said, placing the aconite in a neat pile amidst the other herbs, as if it was the most normal task.

For their lives, it was pretty much as close to normal as it got. She was low on a bunch of herbs, unsurprisingly, after all the spells for protection and strength she had been performing in the past few weeks. She would have to drive down to Fell's Church soon and ask Mrs. Flowers to help her restock her supplies, now that things were quiet.

She wriggled with pleasure at the thought of a nice, normal visit home. It was so *good* to feel safe; it had been such a long time since she had.

Meredith and Elena were both out, and Bonnie had taken advantage of the room and the time without them to spread out piles of dried and fresh herbs all across the floor. Her best friends were both total neat freaks and would doubtless complain about the fragrant dust and crumbled bits of leaves this would leave behind. It was just *amazing* to worry about something as ordinary as what Meredith would say when she stepped in the remains of a pile of celandine (which was useful for happiness and aided in escaping entrapments).

Almost amazing. There was a steady ache inside her these days, a reminder of what she had lost, one that couldn't be cured by any herb. But she wasn't the only one who was in pain.

"I think you're really brave, Matt," Bonnie said. Matt looked up at her, startled by the abrupt shift in the conversation.

"When life hands you lemons . . ." Matt drifted off, not even able to complete the halfhearted joke. She knew he was devastated by losing Chloe, but he never let it change him. Bonnie admired that.

Before she could tell him as much, there was a knock at the door, and she tensed. An unexpected tap at the door usually meant disaster.

Nevertheless, she got up and opened the door, managing at the last minute to stop herself from kicking a little pile of chinaberry seeds (for luck and change) into Elena's slippers.

Slouched against her door frame, his hands tucked into his jeans pockets, was Zander. He smiled at her tentatively. "Can I come in?" he asked.

He smelled so *good*, she thought. He looked gorgeous, too, and Bonnie just wanted to wrap her arms around him and hold on. She had missed him so much lately.

But she'd lost the right to grab on to Zander whenever she felt like it; she'd been the one to walk away. So instead of leaping into his arms, Bonnie just stepped back to let him in, feeling some kind of powdery leaves crumble under her bare heel.

"Oh, hey, Matt," Zander said as he stepped into the room, and then pulled up short, his eyes widening as he took in the little heaps of herbs on every available surface.

"Hey, Zander," Matt said. "I was just heading out, actually. Football practice."

Matt gave Bonnie a pointed look that said, *Don't screw up a second chance.* Bonnie smiled at her friend as he slipped out the door.

"Jeez," Zander said, impressed as he explored more of the room. Bonnie followed him. "Meredith is going to *murder* you. Do you want help cleaning this up?"

"Um." Bonnie looked around. Now that she saw the room through Zander's eyes, it looked much worse than she'd realized. "Wow. Maybe, yeah. But I know that's not why you're here. What's up?"

Zander took Bonnie's hand and together they carefully navigated their way through the room without knocking over any piles. When they finally arrived at her bed, which was probably the clearest surface in the room—she didn't like the smell of mixed herbs all over her sheets—they sat down and he took her hands in his big, warm ones.

"Listen, Bonnie," he said. "I've been thinking about what you said, that being Alpha to the Pack is such an important responsibility, and that I need another werewolf by my side who really understands that, to be my partner and help me. And you're right. Shay's perfect for that."

"Oh," Bonnie said, her voice tiny. Something was crumbling inside her, as fragile as a dead leaf. She tried to gently pull her hands away from Zander's, but he tightened his grip.

"No," he said, distressed. "I'm saying this wrong. Let me start over. Bonnie, look at me." She looked up, her vision clouded with tears, and met Zander's sea-blue eyes. "You, Bonnie," he said softly. "I love *you*. When we were fighting Klaus's army, I saw you casting spells to protect everyone, with this fierce kind of light in your face. You were so strong, and so powerful, and you could have been *killed*. Or I could have been killed, and we wouldn't have been together at the end. It made me realize what I should have known all along: you're the only one I want."

The crumbling thing in Bonnie's chest stopped its dry disintegration and began to melt instead, filling her with warmth. But she couldn't let Zander sacrifice the good of his Pack for her. "But nothing's changed," she said at last. "I love you, too, but what if loving me destroys everything else that matters to you?"

Zander pulled her closer. "It won't," he said. "The wolves on the Council can't choose who I love. I don't love Shay. I love *you*. Shay and I can lead the Pack together, but if it ever came down to it, I would rather lose that than lose you." He raised Bonnie's hand to his lips and kissed it softly, his eyes shining. "I can choose my own destiny," he said. "And I choose *you*. If you'll have me."

"If I'll have you?" Bonnie choked on her tears, wiped at her eyes, and then punched Zander softly in the shoulder. "You dork," she said lovingly, and kissed him.

41

"Are you sure this will do what we need?" Elena asked Bonnie. They'd chosen Stefan's spacious, uncluttered single to summon the Principal Guardian. When Elena had called Bonnie, she'd come right up, her hand held tightly in Zander's. She looked so happy, but when she handed Damon the potion she'd made for him, her small face creased with anxiety.

"I think so," she said. "The valerian will slow his heart rate even more than usual, and the aconite ought to make his breathing really shallow. It will probably feel pretty weird," she told Damon, "but I don't think it'll hurt you."

Damon looked down at the thick green mixture in the cup. "Of course it won't," he said reassuringly. "You can't poison a vampire."

"I put honey in to make it taste better," Bonnie said.

"Thank you, redbird," Damon said, and kissed her lightly on the cheek. "Whether this plan works or not, I'm grateful." Bonnie grinned, a little flustered, and he added, "You and your wolf had better go. We wouldn't want the Guardians to think you were involved." Zander and Damon nodded to each other and Zander took Bonnie's hand again.

When they left, it was just the three of them: Elena, Damon, and Andrés. Stefan had wanted to come, to stand by his brother's side in what might be Damon's last moments, but Damon hadn't let him. *An angry Guardian is dangerous,* he'd said. And, at best, Mylea would be very angry.

Damon drank Bonnie's potion in one long swallow and grimaced. "The honey doesn't help that much," he commented. Elena hugged him and he gently rubbed her back. "Whatever happens, it's not your fault," he said. Then he shuddered and leaned back against the wall, pressing one hand against his chest. "Ugh," he said faintly. "I don't feel . . ." His eyes rolled back in his head and he slid down the wall, landing in a crumpled heap on the floor.

"Damon!" she cried, and then caught herself. This was *supposed* to happen. He looked vulnerable like that, she thought, and smaller, and she dragged her eyes away from him. This would be easier if she didn't look at Damon.

"Are you ready to call the Guardian?" Elena asked Andrés, and he nodded, holding tightly to her hand. His mouth was tense, and there was none of the usual warmth and humor in his eyes.

Elena concentrated on the link between herself and Andrés, energy flowing back and forth between them, moving as steadily and rhythmically as the tide. As that energy found a balance and began to grow, she forced open the doors of Power inside herself.

OH. As soon as her Power was unleashed, everything in her swung to attention, snapping toward Damon. She wanted to . . . she didn't want to hurt him, exactly; it wasn't anger the Power was nursing inside her, but something cold and clean that wanted to destroy him. Not vengeance, not passion, but a cool, urgent instruction: *This needs to be eliminated.*

This must be what it was to have an unfulfilled task. It would be so easy to give in to that cold urgency, to do what she was expected to do. What she *wanted* to do.

No. She couldn't do it. Or, at least, she *wouldn't.*

With a physical effort, she turned her attention back to Andrés. With the doors inside her mind wide open, she could see his expansive aura, shimmering green around him, filling half the room. Using immense concentration, she tried to move her own aura, blending her gold into Andrés's green. Slowly, the colors slid together and mixed, filling the room. Power sang through Elena's veins, and everything she could see was touched with light. She met

Andrés's eyes, and his face was filled with wonder. They were stronger like this, more than twice as strong, and she felt the summoning go out with the Power of a shout.

"Guardians," Elena said, holding on to Andrés's hand. "Mylea. I call on you. My task is complete."

Nothing happened.

For a long moment, they stood like that, hand-in-hand, eyes on each other, auras expanded to fill the room with Power, and felt nothing change.

Finally, something shifted infinitesimally, just a small adjustment in the universe. There was no physical change, but Elena knew that someone was listening at last, as if they'd flicked the call-waiting button on a phone.

"Mylea," she said. "I have killed Damon Salvatore. Now that my task is complete, come and release me from my compulsion."

There was still no answer. And then Andrés slowly stiffened. His eyes rolled back and his aura faded, changing from green to a clear wash of white. His fingers trembled in Elena's.

"Andrés!" she called, alarmed.

His eyes, unseeing, fixed on hers. The eerie white aura around him throbbed.

"I am coming, Elena." Mylea's voice came through Andrés's mouth, sounding crisply businesslike. Elena could imagine her ticking Elena's name off a clipboard before stepping onto some kind of interdimensional escalator.

Released, Andrés gasped and staggered. Making a face as if there was a strange taste in his mouth, he said, "That was . . . weird."

Elena couldn't stop herself from looking at Damon. His bones stood out distinctly, as if his pale skin had grown a size tighter, and his straight black hair was tousled. She could snap his neck with her mind, she thought, and she bit the inside of her cheek hard, looking away again, shaking.

Mylea stepped through nothingness and into the room. Her eyes went immediately to Damon. "He's not dead yet," she said coolly.

"No." Elena took a deep breath. "And I won't let Damon die," she said. "You have to revoke the task."

The Principal Guardian sighed briefly, but her face was, Elena thought, slightly sympathetic, and when she spoke, her voice was calm. "I was concerned that a task so tied to your own life would be difficult for you as your first duty," she said. "I apologize, and I understand why you have called me here to complete the job. You will not be punished for your foolish attachment to the vampire. But Damon Salvatore must die." She reached for Damon, and Andrés and Elena moved to shield the vampire's unconscious body.

"Why?" Elena burst out. It was so unfair. "There are worse vampires than Damon," she said indignantly. "Until recently, he hadn't killed anyone for"—she wasn't sure, she realized, and this wasn't her strongest argument, anyway—"a long time," she finished lamely. "Why send me after Damon when truly evil vampires like Klaus and his descendants were around?" She could hear what she was almost saying: *He's only a vicious killer some of the time. Let him go.*

"It is not your job to question the decisions of the Celestial Court," Mylea told her sternly. "Time and again, Damon Salvatore has proven himself unable to control his emotions. He has no concept of right and wrong. We feel that he may grow to be as great a danger to humanity as any of the Old Ones."

"May," Elena said. "You mean you think he could just as easily go the other way. There's as great a chance that he will never kill again."

"It's not a chance we're prepared to take," Mylea said flatly. "Damon Salvatore is a murderer and so has forfeited his right to any consideration on our parts. Now *step aside.*"

It was time to gamble. Elena took a deep breath.

"You need me," she said, and the Guardian frowned at her. "I am the daughter of a Principal Guardian. I killed Klaus, and I can destroy the most dangerous Old Ones, the ones you haven't found another way of getting rid of. I won't help you if you kill Damon."

She glanced at Andrés, just the tiniest flick of her eyelashes, and he nodded. They had agreed that the most difficult part of their plan was making the Guardian believe that Elena wouldn't fight the Old Ones, would let innocent people suffer if she didn't get her way. Apparently Andrés, at least, thought she sounded convincing enough for Mylea to believe her.

Mylea tilted her head to one side and stared at Elena, as if she was examining an interesting new specimen under some kind of special Guardian microscope. "The vampire is so important to you that you would risk punishment, risk being taken from your home and assigned to the Celestial Court?"

Elena nodded, her jaw clenched.

"The vampire should be conscious for this," Mylea said. Before Andrés and Elena had a chance to block her again, she knelt beside Damon and pressed two fingers to his forehead. He blinked and stirred, and Mylea rose and left him without a glance, turning her gaze back to Elena.

"Would you risk your life for Damon Salvatore?" Mylea asked her.

"*Yes,*" Elena said immediately. There didn't seem to be anything else to add.

"And what about you, vampire?" Mylea asked, looking over Elena's shoulder to address Damon. "Do you care so much for Elena that you would change your life for her?"

Damon pulled himself up to sit with his back against the wall. "Yes," he said steadily.

Mylea gave a slightly unpleasant smile. "I suppose we will see," she said, and reached for them both. She pressed their hands together, and Elena clasped her hand with Damon's and gave him a small smile. He squeezed her fingers reassuringly.

"There," Mylea said after a moment. "It is done."

That pull toward Damon, that cold feeling that he was a problem that needed to be eliminated, was completely gone. It was as if that connection had just suddenly snapped. But it had been replaced. She still felt *connected*. There was a great sense of *Damon* permeating through her, as if the air she breathed was made of him. His eyes widened, and she realized she could feel his heart beating in time with her own. Amazement was coming from Damon, running through the connection between them, and the lightest touch of fear. Concentrating, she tried to see Damon's aura.

A braided rope of light seemed to lead from her chest to Damon's, her aura's gold and the peacock-blue-and-black of Damon's aura twisted together.

"Now you are connected," Mylea said matter-of-factly. "If Damon kills, Elena will die. If Damon feeds on a human without their knowing, aware permission—no use of Power or illusion, but true agreement—Elena will suffer. In the event that Elena dies, the bond—the curse—will pass to a member of her family. If the bond is somehow broken, Damon will return to our attention and be eliminated immediately."

Damon's eyes widened. Through the bond between them, Elena felt a throb of dismay. "I'll starve," he said.

Mylea smiled. "You won't starve," she said. "Perhaps your brother will teach you his more humane methods of feeding. Or perhaps you will find willing humans, if you can honestly gain their trust."

The bond was vibrating now with a curious mixture of disgust and relief, but Damon's face was as closed off as Elena had ever seen it. She rubbed reflexively at her chest, pushing the intense emotions away.

"The bond will lose some of its intensity over time," Mylea said, almost sympathetically. "You feel each other's emotions strongly because it is so new." She looked between them. "It will connect you forever, and it may be deadly to one or both of you in the end."

"I understand," Elena told her and then, ignoring Mylea, she turned to Damon. "I trust you," she told him. "You'll do whatever you have to do to save me. As I've done for you."

Damon stared at her for a long moment, his dark eyes unfathomable, and Elena felt the connection between them flood with a sorrowful affection. "I will, princess," he promised.

His lips curved into a smile Elena had never seen on Damon's face before: neither his quick bitter smirk nor his brief and brilliant smile, but something warmer and gentler. And then the connection between them filled with love.

eredith ran across campus, her feet pounding in a steady rhythm, her breath coming in harsh, painful gasps. Her legs were aching. She'd been running for a long time, looping across the campus paths again and again. Stinging sweat trickled into her eyes, making them blink and water.

The harder she ran, the longer she could keep herself from thinking about anything except the slap of her running shoes against the ground or the sound of her own breath.

The day was starting to edge into evening as she took the curve past the history building again and started up the hill toward the dining hall. When she crested the hill, Alaric was waiting at the top.

"Hi," Meredith said, coming to a stop as she drew even with him. "Are you waiting for me?" She pulled up one foot to stretch out her quadriceps; she didn't want to cramp up.

"I wanted to make sure that you were okay," Alaric said.

"I'm fine," Meredith said dully. She let her foot drop and instead laced her hands behind her and folded forward, so that her head was almost touching her knees. She could feel her spine lengthening, and she had also begun to feel the ache from running for so long.

"Meredith?" Alaric knelt down beside her so that he could look up into her face. Meredith concentrated on the golden freckles scattered across his nose and the tops of his cheekbones, because she didn't want to meet his worried brown eyes. Their color was like honey against his tanned skin.

"Meredith?" Alaric said again. "Could you unpretzel yourself and talk to me for a minute? Please?"

Meredith unfolded, but didn't meet Alaric's eyes. Instead, she twisted from side to side, pulling her shoulders forward in turn. "I have to stretch or my muscles will get sore," she muttered.

Alaric stood and watched her, waiting calmly.

After a while, Meredith began to feel childish for not meeting Alaric's gaze, and she straightened and looked him squarely in the eye. He was still just standing there patiently, his face soft with sympathy.

"I know," she said. "I know everything you're going to say."

"Do you?" Alaric asked. He reached out and tucked back a long piece of hair that had come out of her ponytail, his hand lingering against her cheek. "Because I don't have the faintest idea what to say. I can't imagine what it must feel like to meet your brother for the first time and then have to kill him."

"Yeah," Meredith sighed, and wiped the sweat off her face. "I don't know what to feel, either. It's almost like Cristian was never real to me. He was just a *story*, something the Guardians could change in an instant."

She drew a line with the toe of her sneaker in the dust at the side of the path. "Ultimately," she said, "I never knew him at all. He talked about . . . oh, going to the beach and stuff, and the way our dad is. I could imagine that world, the world where we were a team." She pressed the heels of her hands against her eyes. "But everything was a lie, for him and for me."

Alaric wrapped his arm around her shoulders and pulled Meredith closer to him. "It's not fair," he said seriously. "Klaus destroyed a lot of people's lives. In the end, you were a big part of bringing him down and stopping that destruction, and you should be proud of that. And that other life, the one where he grew up happy, with a sister, it wasn't a lie. There was a world where Cristian loved you, and you loved him. That's still true. You and your friends made that happen."

Burying her face against Alaric's neck, Meredith said in a muffled voice, "My parents will never get over this, losing him again."

"Maybe it's better that they knew Cristian for this long, that they got to see him grow up instead of losing him when he was three, the way things were in the world you remember," Alaric suggested gently.

"Maybe." Meredith rolled her head on Alaric's shoulder until she was leaning against his shoulder and gazing out across the campus. "Do you know what Cristian said to me, at the end? I was about to stake him, and he said in this low, sort of secretive voice, 'Dad would be so proud of you.' And you know what? He was right. Maybe part of Cristian wanted me to kill him, for me to be strong."

Alaric tightened his arms around her. "You *are* strong, Meredith. You're the bravest person I've ever known."

"You're brave, too," Meredith said, sinking into his embrace. She thought of Alaric chanting spells, trying to raise Power to protect them all during the battle, going up against a vampire army with nothing but a stake and a spell book. "I love you so much," she said. "I want you with me, always."

Alaric's lips brushed across the back of her neck. "Me too," he murmured. "It's an honor to fight beside you, Meredith Sulez. And don't you ever forget it."

43

Above Elena's and Damon's heads, the stars glittered in great long swathes across the dark night. The air was clear and chilly with the smells of autumn, and the sky seemed so deep that Elena felt like she could just fall into it, swim farther and farther among the stars forever.

"So," Damon said dryly. "You managed to avoid killing me. I suppose I should be grateful?"

The bond between them hummed with wry humor, and more than a touch of nervousness. It was strange being able to read Damon's emotions like this, seeing more than he allowed to show on his face. "Gratitude would be nice," she said cautiously, "but it's not necessary. Just try to keep returning the favor, okay?"

She felt him startle a little beside her, a shock zinging

along their bond, and then he said, breezily, "Oh, I'd almost forgotten. You're trusting me not to hurt you, then?"

Elena stopped walking and put her hand on Damon's arm, pulling him to a stop beside her. "Yes," she said, gazing steadily into his eyes, letting him see the love she carried for him. "I am. You've been a lot of things, Damon Salvatore, but you've always been a gentleman."

Damon's eyes widened, and then he gave her the lovely, sweet smile she had seen for the first time in Stefan's room. "Well," he said, "it would break all the rules of chivalry to disappoint a lady."

Elena tipped her head back and gazed at the stars for a few minutes, enjoying the cool evening breeze that brushed her hair back from her face. With Klaus and his descendants gone, with Damon calm and peaceful at her side, it was good to be able to enjoy the night.

"Does your great trust in me mean you're planning to take both Salvatore brothers for one more spin?" Damon asked, still looking up at the stars. His tone was definitely joking now, a bit rough, but Elena could hear an undercurrent of longing in it, and feel his wistfulness in the connection between them. In some ways, it would be so easy: she'd spent a long time suspended between the brothers, loving Stefan, wanting Damon. It was almost comfortable at this point to love them both. But she had grown up at least a little now, she thought, and maybe it was time to shut those doors forever, to choose her true path.

"You'll always have a part of me, Damon." She pressed her hand to her chest, where she could feel the slight tug and ebb of the bond between them. "But I want my forever to be with Stefan."

"I know," Damon said. He turned to face her and ghosted his hand lightly across her hair, down over her shoulders. "I think maybe it's time for me to move on. There's a big world out there, and there are still a few places I haven't seen. Maybe there's somewhere else I belong."

Unexpectedly, Elena found herself crying, big, fat, babyish tears running hot over her cheeks and dripping off her chin. "You don't have to go," she choked. "I don't want you to leave."

"Hey," Damon said, startled, and moved closer, running his hand gently across her back. "I won't be gone forever. I think this slightly alarming *thing* between us"— he touched his chest lightly—"means I'll never be too far away."

"Oh, *Damon*," Elena choked.

Damon looked down at her seriously for a long moment. "It's the right thing, you know," he said. "Not that I've ever been particularly interested in doing the right thing. I've got a sinking feeling I'm about to learn."

He leaned down and brushed a light kiss across her

mouth. His lips were soft and cold, and to Elena, they tasted like memories. Pulling back, he stood with her for a moment longer under the stars, his perfect pale skin shining in their light, his eyes gleaming, his velvety hair as dark as the night around them.

"Good-bye, Elena," he said. "Don't forget me."

44

Concentrating, Stefan carefully knotted his tie. He looked, he knew, sleek and elegant in his best suit, a good match for lovely, golden Elena.

He'd made reservations at the nicest restaurant in town for a welcome-back dinner from her visit to Fell's Church to see Aunt Judith and Margaret. Klaus was dead; Damon was saved. Just for once, there was time for Elena to be a college girl, have fun without doom hanging over her.

So: French food. Roses on the table. A night of forgetting their pasts and instead enjoying the present together, like any couple in love. He ran down the two flights of stairs between their rooms, feeling light with happiness.

Elena's door was ajar. He tapped on it lightly, then pushed it inward, expecting to see Meredith and Bonnie bustling around Elena, helping her get ready for their big night.

Instead, the room was lit with candles, hundreds of tiny flames reflecting from the windows and mirrors to create a dazzling, glimmering play of light. Meredith and Bonnie were nowhere in sight and even their stuff seemed to have disappeared. The air was full of sweet scents, and Stefan saw scattered flowers among the candles: orchids and gardenias, orange blossoms and asters. In the language of flowers, all symbols of love in its many forms.

In the middle of the room stood Elena, dressed in a simple white sundress with lace detailing, waiting for him. He didn't think he had ever seen her look more beautiful. Her creamy skin, touched with just the faintest wash of pink, her jewel-blue eyes, her golden hair, all caught the light of the candle flames, shining as if she were an angel. But most beautiful of all were not her features but the look of pure, open love on her face. When her gaze met Stefan's, hers was full of fierce joy.

"Stefan," she said quietly. "I finally know what our future will look like."

Stepping forward into the room, Stefan came straight to her. However Elena saw their future, he would be there beside her, without question. He had learned long ago that his happiness, his life, was intimately tied to this one human girl, this one girl in all the world. He would go anywhere she wanted him to.

Elena took his hand and clasped it. "I love you, Stefan,"

she said. "That's the most important thing. I need to make sure you know it, because I haven't always treated you as well as I should have."

Stefan's voice caught in his throat, but he smiled at her. "I love you, too," he managed to say. "Always, always, always."

"The first time I saw you—remember that? Back outside the main office in high school—you just brushed past me without even looking. Right then, I decided that I was going to have you, that you were going to fall in love with me. No boy was going to treat me like that." Elena smiled a wry, self-deprecating smile. "But then you saved me from Tyler, and you were so sad and noble and *good*. I wanted to protect you, the way you'd protected me. And when we kissed, the whole world fell away."

Stefan made a soft sound, remembering, and his hand turned in Elena's grasp, twining their fingers together.

"You've saved me so many times and in so many ways, Stefan," Elena went on, "and I've saved you. We've plotted and planned together, we've fought and defeated all our enemies. There isn't anyone who loves me the way you do, and I could never love anyone else as much as I love you. I know what I want now. I want to be with you forever."

She let go of Stefan's hand and reached for something on the desk beside her that he hadn't noticed before. It was a silver goblet, intricately worked with threads of gold and set with jewels, a precious and beautiful item. The goblet was full of what looked like pure, clear water. Except the water was glowing with a shining light. He glanced up at Elena in sudden comprehension, and she nodded.

"The water from the Fountain of Eternal Youth and Life," she said solemnly. "I've always known that the day would come when I would drink it. I don't want to live, or die, without you. There's enough left for the others, if they want it someday. They might not. I don't know if I'd want forever, if it wasn't forever with you. I can't—" Her voice broke. "I can't imagine ever leaving you behind. But I had to wait until I was ready, until I was the person I wanted to be for the rest of forever. And now I know who I am." Elena raised the goblet to Stefan. "If . . . if you'll have me, Stefan, if you'll have me forever, I want to spend it with you."

Stefan's heart was overflowing, and he felt a hot tear run down his cheek. He had spent so long in the darkness alone, so long as a monster. And then this creature of life and light had found him, and he hadn't been alone anymore.

"Yes," he said joyfully, "Elena, all I want out of forever is you."

Elena raised the goblet and drank deeply, and then turned a happy, laughing face up to meet Stefan's kiss. Her joy resonated through him as their lips connected, and he sent his own back to her. *Forever,* they both felt, *forever.*

Stefan clung to her, almost overwhelmed. After more than five hundred years lost and wandering, he realized, he finally felt he was home for good.

ear Diary,

Forever.

The prospect should feel scary, I suppose: my time on Earth has been so relatively short. A lot has happened to me, more than most people get to experience in a lifetime, but I still have so much to learn and do.

But I'm sure of Stefan, and I'm sure about forever. All I can feel is overwhelming, riotous joy.

It's not even just Stefan and me, and the prospect of eternity to learn all the little things we don't know about each other, even yet: What was the color of Stefan's mother's eyes? What will his lips taste like, on a bright spring morning two hundred years from now? Where would he go, if he could go anywhere? And we can go everywhere. We'll have time.

That's so much of my happiness, but it's not all of it.

I finally know who I am. It's ironic in a lot of ways that I should be a Guardian, when I loathed and feared them with such passion. But an Earthly Guardian is different; Andrés has taught me that: I can be compassionate and loving and human, and I can use my Guardian Powers to protect my home, to protect the people I care about, to keep evil from destroying the innocent.

There's my bond with Damon, too. Finally I know how I can care for Damon and love Stefan at the same time. There's a connection between Damon and me that'll last forever, that will keep him from being consumed by the darkness that has always threatened him. No matter where he is, I'll hold a piece of him and he'll have a piece of me.

Through everything, Stefan will be by my side.

And with us will be all my beloved friends, each of them so powerful and good, each in their own way. I love them all so much.

I'm trembling, but it's with anticipation. I'm not afraid anymore. I can't wait to see what the future holds, for all of us.

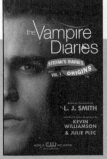
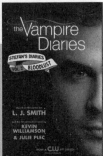
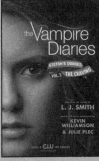
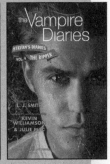
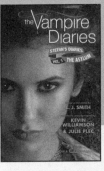
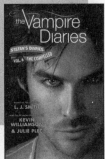

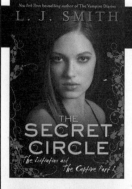
 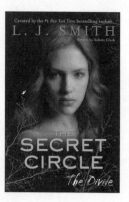